About the Author

Peter Jones started professional life as a particularly rubbish graphic designer, followed by a stint as a mediocre petrol pump attendant. After that he got embroiled in the murky world of credit card banking. Fun times.

Now, Peter spends his days – most of them, anyway – writing.

"The Truth About This Charming Man" is his *second* novel. Rumour has it that a third is just around the corner.

He is also the author of three and a half popular self-help books on the subjects of happiness, staying slim and dating. If you're overweight, lonely, or unhappy – he's your guy.

Peter doesn't own a large departmental store and probably isn't the same guy you've seen on the TV show *Dragons' Den*.

You can find out more about Peter Jones, his books, speaking engagements, and other author malarkey at: www.peterjonesauthor.com

Also by Peter Jones

FICTION

The Good Guy's Guide To Getting The Girl
soundhaven books

NON-FICTION

How To Do Everything And Be Happy
Harper Collins / Audible

How To Start Dating And Stop Waiting
soundhaven books / Audible

From Invisible To Irresistible
soundhaven books / Audible

How To Eat Loads And Stay Slim
co-authored with Della Galton
soundhaven books / Audible

The Truth About This Charming Man

Peter Jones

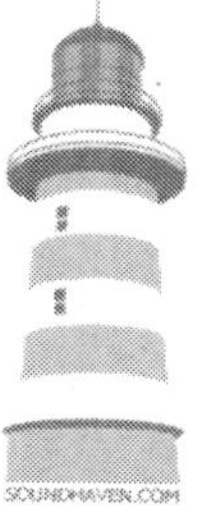

SOUNDHAVEN BOOKS

Published 2016 in Great Britain,
by soundhaven books
(soundhaven.com limited)
http://www.soundhaven.com

Please visit
www.soundhaven.com
for contact details

British Cataloguing Publication data:
A catalogue record of this book is available from the British Library

This book is also available as an ebook.
Please visit www.soundhaven.com for more details.

For Valerie,
with love

To Susie
Best wishes
x

Act I

Scene One

Zlata Ruzencova must be the worst theatrical agent in London. In five years she has only ever managed to secure me two acting jobs. A track record that's even less impressive when you realise that:

A) I'm the only actor she actually has 'on her books', and
B) that first role was playing a part she'd devised!

Still, she did find me Nathia. And though working for Nathia can be something of a challenge (the role being somewhat *unusual*) I have had quite a run. And it does pay well. I should probably be more grateful. But it's hard to be grateful when you're sitting in the back of a cab fuming over the disappearance of your watch.

"Zlata – have you got my watch? Zlata?"

"Hello. Zlata is not here at the moments. She is very busy person. Please do leave nice message after the noise. Beeeeep."

"Zlata – quit messing about. Zlata. Zlata!" But she's hung up.

Nathia's smiling when she opens the door. A big, warm, welcoming smile that promises an evening of laughter and cocktails. It's fake, of course – she's just rehearsing. In our four years together I've learnt more from Nathia than I ever learnt at drama school.

The smile falters when she sees that it's me. "You're late," she says with enough venom to poison a small army. She turns and stomps back into her apartment, and I notice she's already in full costume: slim-fit high-waist sleek-black trousers, semi-translucent shirt, killer heels – the usual Nathia attire. I glance at the ornate wall clock, which seems to glare back from inside its black wooden case. Even the pendulum is swinging back and forth in an impatient manner.

"We've got plenty of time," I shout from the hallway as I hang up my jacket and turn off my mobile phone. "They're not due for another forty minutes, and you know what they're like; Rachel's probably still herding Michael out the door."

But Nathia doesn't say anything, and as I enter her palatial kitchen she's chopping carrots in a way that suggests parts of my anatomy could be next.

Tanya's here. Of course. She doesn't say anything either. Just leans against the fridge, watching the master chef at work whilst occasionally sipping beer from a bottle. She's wearing a ripped T-shirt that seems slightly incongruent for a woman who looks every one of her forty-six years. When the slogan on the front catches my eye I fail spectacularly to hide a frown. Who'd have thought it was possible to get that many expletives into one sentence? Isn't language a wonderful thing.

She doesn't like me very much, Tanya. I'm an obstacle. I stand between her and what she wants – which, in broad terms, is an end to what she sees as a 'farce'. She turns slowly to look in my direction and I give her my biggest broadest smile, but she turns away with a shake of her head, and I'm slightly disappointed when all those piercings fail to jangle.

"Look," I say, "sorry about cutting it a bit fine. I lost track of time. Literally, actually. You remember Zlata – my agent? Well, she's been doing an evening class in – would you believe – *watch stealing*! You know, right off your wrist? I mean, who the hell thought running a class like that would be a good idea? Anyway, it turns out my agent is the star pupil!" I proffer my naked wrist as evidence. Neither woman seems the slightest bit interested.

"Are you planning on standing there all night?" asks Nathia without looking up. "Only I'd quite like you to change for dinner? If that would be all right with you?"

"Sure," I say. I know better than to question her authority, but I do so anyway. "We don't need to catch up first? Nothing that I need to know?"

"Like what?" she asks after a moment. I shrug.

"I dunno. The usual: am I still working for Amnesty International? Has my Dad had his knee operation? Have I started writing that book I'm always going on about? That sort of thing."

"Nothing's changed," says Nathia, and I swear I see Tanya wince slightly. "Just go and get ready."

"Okay," I say, and turn to leave.

"And Edwin," adds Nathia, "wear the blue shirt tonight."

My name isn't Edwin. It's William. Will to my friends. Though it could just as easily be Gary, or Roger, or Stephan – just tell me who you'd like me to be and watch me morph into someone else. It's not lying. Lying is an untruth. This is acting. It's telling a story, and stories are a good thing: they teach us. They help us to make sense of the world. They allow us to stay safe – in that way they're better than the truth.

And sometimes – in order to tell the story as best we can – actors need to forget about the person behind the mask, let go of the person we would normally be and instead allow the character we've taken on to become as real as possible. Nobody knows this better than Nathia Brockenhurst. It's how we came to meet, four years ago, in a dingy little south London pub.

"What's this?" I asked, taking the folder from the scratched, beer-stained table and leafing through the half dozen pages. It wasn't a script. That much was obvious.

"Non disclosure agreement," said Nathia. I had only the vaguest notion of what that was, something that must have been evident from the look on my face. "It's a legal document," continued Nathia. "It states that anything we discuss is strictly confidential and must go no further or there will be ... ramifications."

"Er, okay," I said. "Is that ... usual?" Other than periodically working for Zlata and giving private drama lessons to spoilt brats, my glittering theatrical career had consisted mainly of waiting tables, pulling pints, or flagging people down on the street and persuading them to part with their direct debit details. If you'd told me that *successful* actors signed legal documents and secured roles in seedy backstreet pubs, I'd have probably believed you.

"Sign it," said Nathia, producing an expensive looking pen from her handbag. "Then we can talk." I did as I was told, and once Nathia had taken back the signed document and given me a copy, she took a deep breath, and fixed me with a look of solemnity. "I'm gay," she said.

"Right," I said taking a moment to consider how this might have any bearing on the so-called 'interesting job offer' that Zlata had told me we were here to discuss. "Okay."

"And that's a problem," she continued.

"It is?" Nathia shuffled in her seat, glanced around the tired bar to see if the landlord or his other patrons might be listening, but she had nothing to worry about. Everyone else was either mesmerised by the large plasma television, throwing darts in the general direction of a dart board, or trying very hard to remain upright. Nathia put her arms on the table between us and leant forward.

"The people I work for ... well, let's just say that they're somewhat traditional." I nodded for her to continue, though I had no idea where she was going with this. "Sure," she said, "it's the twenty-first century, and they can cope with me being a woman in a man's world – *just* – but homosexuality is a step too far."

"That's ..." I said, running a hand through my hair, feeling it slide through my fingers, "... surprising." Until now I'd always thought theatre had something of a reputation for attracting your more liberal types. I'd never once heard it described as a 'man's world'. Or homophobic. "Who do you work for again?"

"A small firm of venture capitalists, William. That's all you need to know for now."

"Venture capitalists?"

"Yes."

"But I thought ... My agent said –"

"Are you going to let me finish?" snapped Nathia.

"Of course," I said. "Sorry."

"Anyway," she continued, "even though my employer and his clients expect me to spend all of my daylight hours – and a fair proportion of my night time ones – doing their evil bidding, occasionally they need to know that I'm still human. That despite my ruthless business instincts, on the inside at least, I'm just an adorable little pussycat. And a heterosexual one at that." She paused for a moment to take a sip from her orange juice; I picked up my beer and did the same. "There are functions," she continued, "and fund-raisers, and parties, and all manner of 'after work socials', and whilst it's not compulsory to turn up to these events with a partner in tow, the absence of someone I can rather quaintly refer to as 'my boyfriend' is becoming a problem."

"Right," I said, trying and failing to keep a frown from forming. "Well – can't you just invent someone?" I reached for my pint.

"Oh, believe me, I've tried," said Nathia. "Within hours of inventing a fictitious love-interest, my boss's wife called me up, and invited 'Bertram' and me to dinner."

"Bertram?!" I said, very nearly spraying her with a mouthful of beer.

"It's the first name I could think of! Anyway," she said, glaring at me, "needless to say I couldn't accept the invite. Instead I had to invent a plausible sounding explanation as to why Bertram and I wouldn't be available, and then a week or so later an even more elaborate story to explain why 'he' wasn't on the scene anymore!"

"I take it you're not very good at coming up with stories?"

"On the contrary," said Nathia, "I'm a master! Having introduced the *possibility* of a Bertram I'm now beating off advances left right and centre from any man with a drink in his hand who now sees me as your regular good time girl! After all, why else would I be foot loose and fancy free? Quite frankly, William, I've had enough!" She sat back in her chair, arms folded tightly across her chest, and fixed me with a look so intense I found myself trying not to breathe. "You look confused," she said after a moment.

"Sorry, no. I mean yes. A bit. Look – I understand that you're, well, that you have a bit of dilemma, with how much you can tell your colleagues, about 'things'. I get that. It's just ... my agent said you had a *job*! An acting job! That's what I do – I'm an actor!"

"I know," said Nathia.

"So?" I said. "Do you have a job?"

Nathia sighed irritably. "Bertram!" she said.

"Sorry?"

"I need you to play the part of Bertram." The words bounced around in my head whilst my brain made sense of them.

"Your made-up boyfriend?" I asked.

"Yes."

"You need me to *be* Bertram?"

"That's what I said."

"But –"

Nathia raised a hand to silence me, and with the other reached into her bag to pull out a second, much larger document than the first. It hit the table with a distinctive thud, before she pushed it towards me.

"You would be required," she said, adopting the tone of someone who's spent far too many hours in corporate boardrooms, "to play the part of Bertram, my doting boyfriend, at various social functions – the schedule of which will be mutually agreed between ourselves." I turned the first page and began leafing through the document. "In addition," continued Nathia, "I will require you to come to my office, say once a month, to 'take me out for lunch', and to make the occasional phone call to my PA for suitably boyfriend-sounding reasons that we can work out later. I will also provide you with a mobile phone that you will be required to answer, as Bertram, during office hours. In return I am prepared to pay you a monthly fee which I trust you'll find extremely generous, as well as reimburse you for all reasonable expenses, such as travel, phone calls, food and bar bills, and any clothes that you need to purchase in order to fulfil your 'Bertram' duties." She paused for a moment to take in what I was currently wearing. "For instance," she said, "I'm not sure Bertram would wear a coat that so obviously came from an army surplus store." I ignored her remark and continued to thumb through the contract.

"So?" she asked. "Any questions? Comments?" I scratched the stubble on my chin, then raised my eyes.

"I'm still not sure about the name Bertram," I said.

For legal reasons I can't tell you what was in that contract. Neither can I tell you my fee. I can tell you that at the end of month one I stood to earn more than I'd earned in my entire previous acting career. I picked up the pen and signed on the dotted line.

From that moment on, things got considerably easier for Ms Brockenhurst and myself. She had a boyfriend she could mention, receive flowers from, blame for all manner of things, and if necessary, point to. More than that, she now had somewhere she could conceivably be whilst *actually* being somewhere else. She was free to discover the real Nathia Brockenhurst, to be whoever she wanted, see whoever she wanted – people like Tanya. And all this behind closed doors, safe in the knowledge that someone else was contractually obliged to cover for her.

As for me – I could finally start paying back some of my more desperate debts. Enter stage left: *Edwin Clarkson.*

Much thought went into that name, and we decided early on that Nathia would always address me as Edwin to reduce the possibility of blurting out my real name.

Over the years Edwin has been introduced to most of Nathia's work colleagues – the ones that matter anyway – at various work functions or get-togethers, including regular dinner dates with Michael and Rachel Richmond, her boss and his young wife.

Once a month I follow the river round to Nathia's luxury apartment in Chelsea, don my Edwin costume, and spend a pleasant enough evening sinking bottles of Merlot whilst I entertain Michael and Rachel with torrid tales of Edwin's life working for human rights organisations – all painstakingly researched on Google, earlier that afternoon.

The door bell sounds. My cue that the evening of duplicity has begun. I open my designated drawer, take out a pair of thick framed glasses and after a final mirror check, leave the bedroom to meet my audience.

Michael roars with laughter, at the hilarity of his own wit, and slaps his palms on the table so hard I fear Nathia's antique mahogany furniture may have finally met its match. He picks up his glass, finds it empty, and then attempts to reach across the table for the bottle.

"Oh, Michael – allow me," I say, grabbing the bottle of port and refilling his glass. I throw him a smile, and not for the first time I study his face: he looks like he's been chiselled out of granite. And whilst he wears expensive shirts, in pastel colours, with floral ties, they do nothing to soften features that are almost jagged.

In many ways Michael Richmond is a man out of time. A century or two ago he'd have a bushy moustache, impressive sideburns, and a belly the size of a small country. He'd spend his evenings smoking expensive cigars and talking about his time in Africa. Roll back the centuries still further and I can imagine him dressed in animal furs, sporting a heavy copper helmet, and wielding a blade high above his head before he conquers another village, and takes his pick of the wenches available. But instead Michael goes to the gym. He watches his weight. He pops statins. And on evenings such as this, he shares stories of boring corporate deals negotiated across expensive but dull conference room tables. Is it any wonder that he drinks too much, laughs too loudly, and always looks as if he might explode at any given moment? That granite exterior is holding a lifetime of frustration in place.

I hand him his port and glance across the table at Rachel, who's watching me in that way she does.

Rachel's altogether more interesting. On the surface she's a working class girl, born and bred in the East End to a British father and Jordanian mother, destined to live a simple, honest existence. That is, until Michael booked a table at the bar and brasserie where she worked, and stole her away from a life of waitressing. But behind that shy smile, those beautiful soft cappuccino eyes, and her tall, lean, slightly Arabian veneer, is someone else. And sometimes, when she's asked me an innocent sounding question, she stays quiet after I've given my answer, like she's waiting for me to say more, waiting for me to give myself away. I'd be lying if I said it doesn't give me something of a buzz.

That's not how Nathia sees it, of course. She thinks Rachel's developed some sort of girly crush. One that might lead to all manner of complications further down the line if it's not nipped in the bud. Which is ridiculous, but explains why she wanted me to wear the plain blue shirt tonight. Rachel prefers the striped one.

"Anyway," slurs Michael, though I can't for the life of me remember what he was talking about, "Nathia said we should check the place out, so check the place out we did. Didn't we? Precious?"

"Yes," says Rachel. "We did."

"Fuck me Edwin," continues Michael with a shake of his head. "What a fucking dive. Ghastly fucking people, eating ghastly fucking food. The owner... what was his name again? Oh for fuck's sake... foreign chap. Wasn't even a proper name. Just a collection of fucking sounds..."

"Jarad," says Rachel.

"Yesss! That was it! *Jar head*! You've never met a more nervous man in your entire fucking life," says Michael, waving his glass around so much it's a wonder the walls aren't splashed with port. "Whilst his business partner – the so-called brains of the operation – couldn't even be fucking bothered to turn up! Left this mouse of a man to blunder through probably the most important meeting of his fucking life. Fucking idiot!" Michael shakes his head at the memory, before pouring half the glass down his throat, and suppressing a belch. "I mean doesn't that seem a little fucking odd to you, Edwin? I have the power to completely transform their shabby, two-bit, here-today-gone-tomorrow, two-man enterprise into whatever they fucking want it to be. I'm fucking Santa Claus! I'm their own personal fucking Jesus! No wait – *I'm fucking God*! I'm granting them a fucking audience with fucking God! And yet one of them can't make the fucking meeting – *with God* – because..." he makes air quotes with his fingers, "they're '*busy*'! I tell you Edwin, there's something fishy about the whole enterprise. And I fucking hate fish!" The belch he's been trying to contain finally makes it into the open, and it lasts a full three or four seconds before Michael waves his hand about as some sort of apology. I look down into my lap and try and hide a smirk.

"He liked you though, didn't he? Precious? That fucking... 'Jar-head' fellow. Couldn't keep his fucking eyes off you."

"I can't say I noticed," says Rachel with a smile. A false one, but convincing enough to the untrained eye. She takes a breath, and puts a hand on her husband's. "Sometimes, darling, I wish you'd remember that these are people's dreams that you're playing with."

"Oh fucking poppycock! Dreams? It's business! There's no place for dreamers in business! Don't you agree, Edwin?"

"Well..." I bluster, accompanied with some appropriately vague hand gestures. I know better than to express an actual opinion. This way Michael's imagination is filling in the gaps with whatever he'd like me to say.

"If anyone wants me to consider investing my money – or my clients' money – then I need more than fucking *dreams.* I need to see potential! Real potential! That's why Nathia suggested we invest in the fucking place! Because of their reputation for '*outstanding cuisine*'. And having had many a fine meal in these humble surroundings, lovingly prepared by her own fair hands –"

"You're very welcome," says Nathia, raising her wine glass.

"–I thought the girl knew a thing or two about food! But fuck me! Just how fucking wrong can you be?" Michael slaps both palms flat on the table and blasts us with another belly laugh.

"Well," says Nathia with a sigh, "clearly I let my initial enthusiasm run away with me. I apologise." Michael wafts away her apology.

"No need," he says with the faintest of slurs. "But the last thing this country needs is another fucking chain of ghastly restaurants serving fucking foreign muck, to the fucking ghastly masses." And with that he picks up his port glass again and drains the contents. I look across at Rachel. Her hands are in her lap, and the smile – false or otherwise – is gone. And not for the first time I have this piercing stab of regret that she's so obviously trapped inside a marriage that makes her unhappy. If things were different, if we'd met under different circumstances, ones where I'm not contractually obliged to be someone else, I think we could be good friends. Maybe more than friends. Michael belches yet again.

"Nathia darling," he says, "we need more port."

"I think, Michael," says Rachel, placing her hand on her husband's for the second time that evening, "that we should make a move."

"Already?" he slurs.

"Yes. Already," she says, her voice wobbling slightly. She gets up from the table, and flashes me and Nathia a polite smile. "Excuse me a moment," she says, and leaves the room. Nathia and I exchange looks, then she too gets up from the table and follows Rachel.

"Edwin," says Michael, his voice considerably lower than its usual bellow, "whilst the girls are out of the room, have you ever thought about getting into the investment business?"

"Me?" I blink. "Really? I'm not sure I have the constitution for it."

"Fucking nonsense!" says Michael. "You're a sharp cookie. Anyone can see that. And the thing is, a rather interesting investment opportunity came across my desk the other day which I think might be just up your street; *Vanadium Global*."

"Sounds very grand," I say.

"Doesn't it," says Michael with a nod. "Ironically though, they're too small at the moment for *Steele & Richmond* to climb into bed with. Which is a real fucking shame, because they're going places. Anyone with half a fucking brain can see that. Which is why I thought of you, Edwin. It might be a good way to get your feet wet."

I wrinkle my nose. "I don't know, Michael," I say. "I'm not really the –"

"Michael," says Rachel. She's standing in the doorway, her jacket draped over her arm. Michael gives a resigned sniff and eases himself out of his chair.

"Pop into my office next time you're in the neighbourhood," he says with a wink, "and we'll discuss it further."

"I thought I told you to wear the blue shirt," says Nathia as we close the door on our guests.

"Did you?" I say, glancing down to look at my chest as if I'm expecting to see something other than stripes.

"You know I did," she adds before walking back into the dining room.

I hate this bit. The obligatory deconstruction of the entire evening; what I said, to whom, and whether any of it might have, in some obscure way, undermined the elaborate fabric of fiction we've been weaving these past four years. All whilst we gather up dirty dishes and spent glasses and cart them through to the kitchen. If I actually worked in theatre I'd probably be in a cab right now. I take off my Edwin glasses and put them in my pocket.

"I don't really like the blue shirt," I say as I enter the dining room.

"Doesn't matter," says Nathia as she gathers up cutlery.

"I'm not sure it's *Edwin*. It's a little too conservative. In the political sense I mean. It makes me look like a... police detective... or something. Not Edwin at all." I look at the destruction and chaos on the dining room table and let out a sigh. How can four people make such a mess? I reach for the empty bottles.

"It really doesn't matter, William," says Nathia, using my real name for the first time in so long it makes the hairs on the back of my neck stand up. Something isn't right. I follow her through to the kitchen.

"Everything okay?" I ask. She turns and leans against the work surface.

"I'm tired," she says. I nod.

"It was an extraordinarily long evening. How many bottles of Merlot did we get through? Three? Four? I think Michael finished half a bottle of port by himself."

"No," says Nathia with a shake of her head; she looks as if she has great invisible weights hanging from her shoulders. "I'm tired of this. This endless – farce. This isn't me. It never was." She lifts her eyes from the floor and gives me a long weary look.

"I was going to wait a few more weeks," she says, opening the drawer where she normally keeps her collection of instruction manuals and warranty documents for the kitchen paraphernalia, but instead produces a white envelope. She passes it to me and resumes her stance against the work surface.

"What's this?" I ask, though I think I can guess. Nathia takes a deep breath.

"Formal termination notice," she says. "Effective immediately, your services are no longer required."

Scene Two

Though the pavement is hot enough to fry an egg on, and the park across the road is heaving with tourists treating it like a naturist resort in the Algarve, no amount of sunshine is going to shift the cloud over my head. It hangs there like a giant floating lump of coal, casting a shadow over my entire life. Nathia only 'dumped' me a week ago, yet it feels as if the blackness has been there forever.

"Never mind William," says Zlata, "I will find you new client. Lots of clients. Some new ladies that need nice pretend boyfriend." She smiles and picks up a small cup of coffee-scented sludge. She drinks the lot in one go, and for a moment I'm sure I get a caffeine buzz simply by sitting opposite.

"Zlata," I say after one of my heavier sighs of the morning, "I don't want to be someone's pretend boyfriend!"

"Ah! You say that now," says Zlata, "but what about when the rent is due and you don't have the moneys? Then I think you will pretend to be anyone's boyfriend. Maybe even mine! And maybe not pretend." She winks at me, then hunts around in her handbag.

"You know Zlata, once upon a time I wanted to be an actor."

"You are still actor," she says without looking up from the bag on her lap, a mass of chestnut curls obscuring her face. "What is today if not acting? Now hurry up and drink your English tea, and then we go back to work."

"I mean a *real* actor! In a theatre! Or on film! For crying out loud, I'd be understudy to one of Cinderella's coach men if it finally meant a life on stage." She doesn't reply. She's too busy lighting a cigarette. Inhaling deeply as if this might be the last pack of tobacco-related products in existence.

"You are too good to be understudy," she says eventually.

"Yeah? Says who!"

"Says me." She adds a very European shrug to emphasise the point.

"And that's very kind of you to say Zlata, but sadly it doesn't make one jot of difference what you think of my acting abilities."

"Really?" she says. "Not one jot?"

"I'm afraid not."

"Oh. I see." She takes a thoughtful drag on her cigarette and then rests it in the ash tray before leaning across the table. "Tell me William, how many womens have you loved in your life?"

"What's that got to do with anything?"

"Tell me," she says, the question hanging in the air.

"I dunno," I say after a moment. I do know. Of course I know.

"So, not that manys," says Zlata. "Five years we know each other. Five! And in all that times you have just the one girlfriend. Just one. And she left you."

"I prefer being single," I lie.

"And good for you. One time, I was almost single. It looked like the peaceful life."

"What exactly is your point?" I ask.

"Even though you have no girlfriend, I have watched you acting the romantic hero; always with the cheeky smile, and the twinkly eyes, and the wink, and the good hair. The ladies, *they want you*! And the gentlemens, *they hate you*! But also, *they want to be you.* Do they know you only have the sex with two womens in your whole life? No! They believe you to be the great Casanova! Roger the Romantic Hero! You, William, are *very* good actor." She picks up her cigarette, gives me a look that clearly says 'so there' in any language, and takes a long drag.

"You asked me how many women I've *loved*," I say, making no attempt to hide the irritation in my voice. "Nobody mentioned anything about sex."

"Pffff. Please," says Zlata. "With you is same thing. Drink your English tea."

Carol Brown was my first proper girlfriend. Statuesque. Athletic. Driven. I met her within days of starting drama school and we were pretty much inseparable from that moment on.

I was twenty five when I finally sent myself to drama school. That was almost ten years ago. And for those three years the London Academy of Music and Dramatic Art nurtured my dreams and whipped them into a frenzy of possibilities. Life looked good back then. And Carol and I were a team. A dynamic-thespian-duo; as obsessed with all things theatrical as we were with each other. Back then the two things seemed intrinsically linked. We spent long evenings discussing Shakespeare, the parts we'd like to play, and what we would bring to the role. And long days, wrapped in each other's arms, whether an exercise required it or not. We always found ways to bring our intimacy into our craft, and vice versa.

But, less than a month after we graduated, Carol landed a major part in a touring company. She changed her name, boarded a bus at Victoria Coach Station, and left me and our relationship standing in the rain. I can't say I blame her. When an opportunity like that lands in your lap you have to take it. But I've often wondered whether I'd have done the same.

Then there was Isla. We met soon after. And she was nice. Barely an inch over five foot. Curvy. Covered in freckles. She was the polar opposite of Carol and actually it felt refreshing to spend time with someone who wasn't constantly quoting lines from plays, or treating each and every moment like an impromptu performance. Although she worked as a theatre nurse at Great Ormond Street, and we used to joke about that; how we were both in 'theatre' – except that I wasn't. I was at home. Looking for work.

Having stepped back into the real world I'd joined a throng of theatre-loving hopefuls, all scouring the classified pages of *The Stage* newspaper for anything that resembled paid acting work. I remember the first time I realised just how little work there was, and how many other hopefuls were competing for it. I'd always heard it was tough making a living as a full time actor, but I'd never thought to actually check. Occasionally I'd get an audition, and I, like so many others, would wait in line for hours and hours for a shot at a part that in all likelihood had already been cast.

Eventually, after months of living on my girlfriend's charity, whilst slowly deconstructing my sanity on a daily basis, I did what all professionals do when their chosen career lets them down. I took to teaching.

Afternoons were spent filling young minds with false hope, honing whatever theatrical skills they had for a profession that's already too crowded to accommodate them, all whilst taking their parents' money. It's not dishonesty. It's the way of the world. Reality is harsh, brutal, and unforgiving. My clients paid me to provide them and their offspring with something altogether more palatable.

But despite this crushingly disappointing start to my theatrical career, things between Isla and I were pretty good. At least for a while.

Then one particularly chilly morning in March, an eccentric gum chewing woman of indeterminate years – all wild bleached blonde hair (with dark roots), pristine makeup (and plenty of it) – turned up on my doorstep.

"Hello," she said, as I opened the door. "You are Lewis, the actor. Yes?"

"If you say so," I replied. It was very early in the morning. Too early to be standing on my doorstep talking to a tall lady in a fake-fur-coat that just about covered her shoulders, and a snake-skin mini-skirt that was barely long enough to cover, well, anything.

I on the other hand was still in my dressing gown, my hair looked as if it had declared independence from the rest of my head, and the only reason I'd opened the door at all was because I was in a grumpy mood, and this would have been a perfect opportunity to tell whoever it was that I didn't want to buy whatever they were peddling, and that Jesus and I had never seen eye to eye after he'd inspired yet another lousy Lloyd Webber musical. The woman frowned.

"I am sure this is place," she said, retrieving a scrappy piece of paper from her bag. "I copy it very carefully. M. R. Lewis."

"M?" I said. "I'm not an M. I'm a W. For William. William Lewis."

"You are sure? I definitely copy down M and R. See here."

"I think you might mean 'Mister'. M R. It's short for mister. It's a title. Like Doctor. Or Sir. Or King." She gave me a look. One that a few months later I'd come to know as the *I know what I mean* look.

"But you are actor?" she asked.

"Well, that's somewhat debateable," I said, scratching my unshaven chin. The woman gave an impatient sigh.

"I look for acting teacher!"

"Right. Well, yes sadly I am that. Although normally not until much later, and definitely after I've had a shower and at least two cups of coffee."

"Good," said the woman, her face beaming. "Then I am at right place." She extended a hand. "My name is Zlata Ruzencova."

"Zlata Ruz…"

"Ruzencova. It is Czech name. I am Czech. I was born in Czech Republic. I live there my whole life."

"Er, congratulations," I said, still shaking her hand.

"And now I wish to be famous actress." I let go of her hand.

"Why?" I asked.

"I do not understand."

"Why do you want to be an actress?"

"It is like dream," said Zlata with a shrug. "And everybody want for something, yes? If only glass of water."

"Right," I said. "Well, I can definitely teach you to act, but as for the fame bit, you're on your own I'm afraid."

Zlata considered this for a moment. "That is acceptable," she said. "May I enter your house?"

I opened my mouth to say something along the lines of, *do you know what time it is? Because I don't! Which means it must be very early because generally I don't look at a clock before midday*, but then closed it again. Zlata was still smiling at me, which meant that anything I said that didn't involve inviting her in would make me look like an arse.

"Sure," I said with a sigh. "Why not."

She tottered into my flat on platform heels and I made her a coffee whilst she yabbered on about how cosy my tiny little bedsit was, how much she liked Isla's taste in clothes (the ones that were drying on the clothes horse), and how the view from my window of the neighbouring off-licence, fire station and building site was so much more interesting than anything she had. Then I dressed in the bathroom whilst she continued to yabber from the other side of the door. And eventually, when I managed to get a word in edgeways, I explained to her how – and more importantly *when* – I taught my private clients.

And so on Monday and Wednesday afternoons Zlata and I began working on obtaining her LAMDA acting exams. Two-hour sessions that usually overran, sometimes by several more hours – though by the end of each session very little acting was taking place. Instead Zlata would be perched on the window sill, blowing great plumes of smoke out of the window, whilst she drank copious amounts of coffee and shared anecdotes of how she'd left the Czech Republic in search of her fortune, and how London would be the first of many stops on her quest for world domination.

I liked her. I still do. At some point I no longer thought of her as a client; she'd entered that small select group of people I think of as friends. And evidently that was a problem. Suddenly Isla was cross all the time, and no end of '*she's just a friend*' or '*you should try and get to know her, you might like her*' conversations could save us. So far as she was concerned, aside from family members, there should only ever be room in a man's life for one female.

One Tuesday morning Isla left me. Love, she said – as she stood there and stuffed her suitcase with dirty washing and tears – is a connection that only really works when all other distractions have been eliminated. I said nothing. Just rocked back and forth on the balls of my feet, and wondered how it was possible for two people to spend so much time in each other's lives and not really know each other at all.

The truth of it is, theatre was, and always has been, the only real *love* in my life. And if anything was a *distraction*, then it was Isla. When she left I took on more classes, applied for every theatrical part I could find, and taught Zlata three times a week.

On the days that Zlata wasn't with me honing her craft as an actress, she was at the local college learning business studies. In the evenings she took classes in *Neuro Linguistic Programming* (I'm still not entirely sure what that is), *Kendo* (a martial art that involves bamboo canes), and *Close Up Table Magic*. You really can learn anything these days, and Zlata's never been one to place limits on herself. Eighteen weeks to the day after walking through my door she announced that I'd taught her everything she needed to know, and that she'd decided to become a theatrical agent.

"An ... agent?" I said.

"Yes," replied Zlata.

"Do you know anything about being ... an agent?" I asked.

"I know lots of things," said Zlata defiantly. "And you, William, will be my first client."

"Me?!" I'd always dreamt of having an agent, but I never thought it would happen like this.

"Yes."

"You can actually find me work? Proper acting work – not just handing out leaflets in Oxford Street?"

"I have already," she said, beaming from ear to ear with triumphant pride. I was gobsmacked. And suddenly extremely suspicious.

"Hang on – you mean you've got me an audition?"

"No! I know what I mean! Not audition! Work!"

"Okay, calm down! What is it then?" And once she'd told me I collapsed into an armchair, and waited for my brain to catch up with my ears.

"You want me to do what?" I said eventually.

Much to my considerable surprise the room, small though it was, was filling up with people. We might actually run out of chairs! I shook my head in disbelief.

One thing you learn pretty quickly at drama school is that finding an audience can be a *challenge*. And anyone who harbours quaint notions about concentrating on giving a stellar performance, whilst *someone else* takes on the responsibility of putting bums on seats, soon finds that that's the easiest way to ensure that there will be more people on stage than sitting in front of it. Much of my time as a drama student had been spent handing out leaflets on street corners, or putting up posters in local libraries – time that would have been better spent learning lines – but there's little point in learning lines if no one's there to hear them. Sometimes we'd dispense with all the leafleting and postering, and just hand out free tickets ... and we'd *still* struggle to fill more than the first three rows.

But not today.

Though I hadn't told Zlata, I'd fully expected to spend the morning sitting in an empty hotel conference room, commiserating with my friend over her latest failed business exploit. But instead my ears were buzzing with all the excited chatter from folks who'd come far and wide to listen to the sage advice and wisdom from two people who were, in their own special way, experts in their field.

The only potential fly in this ointment of Zlata's creation, was that those 'experts' were, in fact, Zlata and me. And the subject we were *supposed* to be experts in, was *flirting*.

NLP, Kendo, Table Magic... all those evening classes my friend was so keen on attending had taught her one thing above everything else; people will pay to learn stuff! And whilst there will always be a market for the bog standard subjects you were supposed to learn at school, what people *really* want to know are the skills you *didn't* learn in the classroom. Particularly – so Zlata reckoned – those skills that everyone's *supposed* to develop naturally, but invariably don't. Like what you're supposed to say and do when you meet someone who you quite like the look of.

Which is fine for Zlata, because she pretty much likes the look of anyone vaguely masculine, and has a complete absence of fears or doubts that might otherwise impose limitations on what she thinks she's capable of. She's spent a *lot* of time honing her seduction skills. She's the perfect person to teach 'flirting techniques'. I suppose it really isn't all that surprising that Isla felt threatened.

I, on the other hand, know nothing. At least, back then, and certainly when it came to matters of the heart. The two great romances of my life had happened largely by accident. They certainly hadn't left me with anything I could pass on in the way of wisdom.

Which is why Zlata had asked me to spend the day being *someone else*; my first real acting role since drama college. Today there was half a tub of gel in my hair. Today you'd be able to detect my cologne long before I entered the room. Today my trousers were in danger of cutting off the blood supply to my feet. Today I was 'Gary'.

"Hello? Hello? Can everyone hear me?" boomed Zlata's voice from every speaker in the room, causing about half a dozen people to slap their hands over their ears. I bounded over to my friend who was standing next to the PA control panel, and turned the volume down from ten to a more manageable six.

"Trust me," I said. "They can definitely hear you."

"Jolly good," said Zlata. "What's that, Roger? I don't need the microphone? Oo, you are the cheeky man! I will deal with you later." I frowned and then looked around for someone who might answer to the name of Roger. "What's that?" she continued. "Well you'll just have to wait and see, won't you!" said Zlata, presumably still addressing her imaginary friend, as she walked down the centre aisle, and jumped onto the small makeshift stage at the other end of the room.

"Now then," she said, placing the microphone in a stand and surveying the gathering in front of her. "Who do we haves here?"

"And so, ladies and gentlemens, now we'll split into two groups. The ladies will come with me, and the gentlemens – you will be with Roger."

Whilst the attendees moved themselves and their chairs to one end of the room or the other, I sat at the focal point of the semi circle that was forming around me, and fumed. All morning Zlata been referring to me as Roger and we'd *agreed* that my name was going to be *Gary*.

Names are hugely important when creating good characters, as important as the right costume, your accent or intonation, the way you move. And 'Gary' is the *perfect* name. He's the boy about town. A modern day Lothario. All spiky hair and *Paco Rabanne*, with a patter to match. Gary is the sort of man who can charm the birds from the trees. And by birds I'm not referring to the feathered variety. I looked up at the group of men who were sitting there, hungry for whatever pearls of wisdom I had for them. Who were they more likely to believe when it came to matters of seduction? Roger the dodger, your lodger, an old-time codger? Or *Gary*?

"Right guys," I growled, my leather bomber jacket creaking slightly as I rolled my shoulders. I ran a hand through my spikey hair and then forced a smile. "My name's Gary," I said.

"Sorry, did you just say your name was Gary?" asked a thirty-something guy, his arms folded across his chest. I tried to recall his name.

"I thought your name was Roger?" said a shorter man sitting next to him. He'd definitely introduced himself earlier as Jonathan. And he looked as if he should be playing outside on his bike, rather than sending himself on a 'flirting' course.

"Oh, *that*," I said with a smirk. "That's just Zlata's pet name for me. You can call me Gary."

"Zlata has a pet name for you?" asked the first man.

"That's right."

"And it's Roger?" asked Jonathan.

"Just her little joke," I said. "Now then –"

"But why 'Roger'?" he persisted. I took a breath and locked eyes.

"Well I guess she must *really* like the name," I said without the slightest hint of bitterness. "Now then," I continued, pushing up the sleeves on my jacket, "shall we talk about women?" The circle of men shuffled expectantly.

"Everybody wants something," I started, delivering the script that Zlata had outlined. "Even if it's just a glass of water." Puzzled looks were exchanged, but I soldiered on. "And women – well, they're romantic creatures; most of them are brought up on a steady diet of fairy tales, and regardless of who they grow up to be, a small part of every woman never really lets go of the idea that inside *they are a princess,* and that one day, a handsome prince will ride into their lives and whisk them away." I paused for effect. "So, you can imagine how bitterly disappointed they must feel most of the time!" Around me men tittered and nudged each other and exchanged crude jokes. I waited for them to settle back down again.

I leant forward, resting my elbows on my thighs. Most of the group did the same.

"You see, what a woman *doesn't* want is to meet *the man of her dreams* through 'a dating agency' or on the internet. Or even at a nightclub. She *wants* the romance. She *wants* to bump into him at the supermarket. She *wants* there to be a mix up of luggage at the airport. She *wants* to be rescued from the kerbside by a handsome RAC man in a big truck." I glanced at Jonathan. He looked confused. But most of the other men nodded sagely to each other whilst the rest scribbled notes.

"So ... we've got to wait around in supermarkets or mis-label our luggage every time we travel?" asked the defiant thirty-something guy.

"No," I said slowly. "You're missing the point."

"So what is 'the point'?"

"No woman wants to feel that a meeting is orchestrated. They want the *chance encounter.* They want the feeling that destiny brought the two of you together. That it was some-how inevitable. Inescapable." Jonathan raised his hand again.

"But haven't we got to meet a woman in the first place?" he asked.

"Listen," I said, leaning forwards again. "Guys like you always tell me that they never meet women. Well, that's just *bollocks.* Unless you never leave the house you're meeting women every single day of your life. There are about two dozen on the other side of this room, for cryin' out loud! And every time you're in the same room as a woman it's a potential 'moment', just waiting to be seized."

"So you're talking about 'chatting women up'?" asked Jonathan.

"No! I'm talking about nudging the situation a little. Creating that inevitability. Giving destiny a helping hand."

"But how do we do that?" asked Jonathan, the desperation turning his voice into a shrill whine.

"That depends on the situation," I said.

"So, I should crash into her with my shopping trolley?" asked thirty-something guy.

"It lacks elegance," I said, "but if that works for you."

"But isn't this cheating?" asked Jonathan.

"Yeah. Doesn't it, like, take the romance out of the situation?" asked another man.

"Oh, wake up gentlemen!" I said leaning back in my chair, putting my hands behind my head, and chewing on imaginary gum. "This is the twenty-first century! Do you want to wait for a girl to fall in your lap or do you want to do something about it? If you want the *fairy tale* then you need to be sitting over there with the other girls." I jerked my head in the direction of Zlata. "Over here, we're about *giving* the ladies *what they want.* We're about *creating* the fairy tale."

"So we've got to somehow generate romance out of thin air!?" said thirty-something guy. "How are we supposed to do that?"

A dozen or more faces stared back at me; a smorgasbord of dissatisfaction. Some glared at me in contempt. Some pleaded with me to rescue them from their lonely, loveless lives. Others just frowned in confusion. I was losing them.

So much for Zlata's *script* – if I'm honest, it wasn't doing much for me either. It lacked substance. It was all 'what' without any of the 'how' – and these men needed the '*how*', and I wasn't sure I could give them that.

"That's a valid point," said another guy – older than the others, quieter, somehow more solid – "generating rapport without any common ground would be quite a challenge," he mused. "Although I suppose it must be similar to how actors develop a relationship with their audience," he continued.

I blinked.

"Er, yeah," I growled, as I straightened my jacket. "That's a ... good ... analogy."

"But we still don't know *how*!" whined Jonathan. I locked eyes.

"Have you ever been hurt?" I asked.

"How do you mean?" asked Jonathan.

"I mean have you ever had your heart broken? Has a woman you've had feelings for ever cheated on you? Have you ever felt rejected? Or just completely ignored?"

Jonathan said nothing, just shuffled in his chair and looked sheepish.

"I'll take that as a yes," I said with a sanctimonious sniff.

I looked from one man to the next, at the painful memories in every pair of eyes. Now that I was off script I could feel Gary gathering momentum, as if Zlata's pre-prepared words had been holding him back.

"Most people try to do whatever they can to get rid of that pain," continued Gary. "Some people bury those feelings – pretend like it never happened. Some harden their heart, build an invisible wall around themselves. And others will spend hours in therapy, deconstructing their hurt, piece by piece. But if you do any of those things you're missing an opportunity. *Pain is power.*"

"Power?" asked thirty something guy.

"What those ladies over there *want* – more than anything else in the world – is *emotion*. They want to *feel* something. Actually, that's all anybody really wants, but for now let's assume I'm just talking about girls. If you want to get a woman's attention – I mean really *get it* – then you need to generate a *feeling*.

"Let's assume, gentlemen, that you've finally plucked up the courage to leave that squalid bedsit you call home, and you find yourself in the same room as a walking, talking, female – an amazing, magical, breath-taking goddess of a woman, one that you would not mind giving up one side of the bed for and every shelf in your bathroom. Regardless of whether you find yourself in the supermarket, or at the airport, or on the hard shoulder of the M25, you are, in that moment, *an actor*, on a stage, and *she* is your audience. And it's your job to give the audience what she's come for – you need to make her *feel something*.

"So, here's what you do – you reach inside yourself, and you dredge up that pain you've been hauling around all this time; you find an emotion so deep and so raw that it feels like you're ripping out a very part of your soul. And then, you mould that into whatever you need it to be. Maybe you pretty it up with some nice words: 'Hello. How are you? Lovely day isn't it? I can't help but notice that you seem to have broken down by the side of this here motorway...' Whatever! It doesn't matter what you actually say. The only thing that matters is that *underneath* is all that emotion, all that *feeling*. You take those feelings, and you throw 'em at your audience, through your words, and your actions – and you keep on doing it until you *make them feel it too*. And if you can make them laugh, and make them cry, and then make them laugh again, well, you have finally *seized the moment*."

The group remained quiet. Wide eyed and awe struck. Their minds and imaginations processing advice that they'd never heard before. And though I could see glimmers of doubt on one or two of those faces, I knew that by the time Gary had finished with them, a group of new actors would have been created, and a pack of confident men would leave the room, their heads held high, ready to put into practice what they knew to be true.

I took a moment, looked over at the girls, and as I did so Zlata happened to turn, catch my eye, and give me a wink. Her ladies were probably hearing similar advice. Similar, but different. But still about how to give people what they want – even if that thing is just a glass of water.

We know about that, Zlata and I. That's the business that we are in now. And even though we've been running these 'flirting workshops' once a quarter for near on five years, there seems to be no shortage of customers.

"William, I don't think you are even listening to me?" Zlata taps one of her many ringed fingers against the side of her coffee cup.

"Sorry," I say, shaking the past out of my head, and coming back to the here and now. "I was thinking."

"About what were you thinking?"

"Seizing the moment," I say. Actually what I'm really wondering is why there have only ever been two women in my life.

"Ah," says Zlata, stubbing out another cigarette in the ashtray. "They are the very wise words."

"They're your words!" I point out.

"Yes. Exactly. This is why they are wise. Now then," she says, "– *idemo*!"

I raise an eyebrow that basically says 'I teach theatrical skills, and theatrical skills cunningly disguised as flirting techniques, but foreign languages are beyond me.'

"Time to go!" says Zlata. I sigh, glance at my arm, and notice that once again my watch is gone! When I look up she's dangling it in front of me, looking very pleased with herself. I snatch it back and return it to my wrist.

"This new parlour trick of yours," I say, "is beginning to get really old!"

Today's flirting course – our *fifteenth* – is another success. Men and women gather up their belongings and go back into the world, filled with a new found confidence and self-belief that they can woo the opposite sex. Some of the guys seem so keen to put their new skills into practice that they don't even wait to get outside. Why wait when half the people in the room are single and female? Instead they're seizing the moment. Just as I've taught them. Maybe I should do the same. But there's only one woman I know of that I'd like to 'seize the moment' with, and she's married. To my ex-client's boss. She's long gone.

It takes Zlata and me a further half an hour to tidy the conference room and put it back more or less as we found it, then we head out in search of food. This is all part of the ritual: run a flirting course, break for lunch, finish up, then out to dinner. And whilst we always lunch in the same café on the other side of the park from where we run our courses, dinner could be anywhere.

Food is another of Zlata's passions, and I'd have sworn we've sought out everything London has to offer in the way of non-English cuisine – but no, here we are in Blackheath, not all that far from Greenwich. Despite the fact it's not that far from my pad on the South Bank I've only ever been here a few times before, and yet it has to be one of my favourite places in London. It's like a bustling village on the edge of the heath, with the towers of Canary Wharf visible in the distance. And whilst the heath itself is a huge sprawling mass of flat, sun-scorched yellow grass, an impressive ornate church dropped seemingly at random amongst its expanse, the 'village' seems to have been built on a series of small hills, causing the streets to duck and dive, weave and bob. It's fun, charming, quirky, and somehow slightly out of place, both in time and space, like the rest of London is somehow oblivious to its existence. Even the shops and restaurants refuse to play by the rules; whilst there is the odd high-street pizza parlour or coffee shop chain, the vast majority are small independents, thriving on the hubbub of visitors that flock here day and night, seven days a week. Take for instance *Jarad's*, which from the blackboard outside the entrance, promises the finest in Jordanian cuisine.

"This lamb thing is absolutely delicious," I say, indicating the remains in the bowl between us with my fork.

"Mensaf," says Zlata, who stopped eating a good ten minutes ago. "National dish of Jordan. Made with fermented dried yogurt, and ... other things."

"You been here before?" I ask. Zlata doesn't answer. She's finishing her wine, and moments later our waiter – a stocky man in his mid to late forties, shaven head, possibly of middle eastern descent – appears to top up her glass. They exchange smiles, the kind of smiles that indicate they know each other quite well. Perhaps even *very* well.

"A few times," says Zlata, eventually, in answer to my question. "One of the owners is special friend of mine."

I raise an eyebrow.

"How 'special'?" I ask.

"Very special."

"Was that the 'special' owner?"

"It was," she says with a smile. "Jarad. He is *very* nice man. Very gentle. But also sometimes the tiger!" She growls playfully, and as she does a light blinks on in the back of my mind, and the name 'Jarad' bounces around in my head like it's trying to connect with something. "It is very sad," says Zlata after a moment.

"What is?"

"Jarad's business partner – very nice lady, also good friend of mine – she had the big plans. A dream of many many restaurants, all over London, all serving Jarad's food."

"Why's that sad?" I ask, scraping the last of the mensaf onto my plate.

"The meeting with their business investor, it did not go well."

"I'm sorry to hear that," I say through a mouthful of food. Zlata shrugs.

"Like I say: Jarad is gentle man. Very wonderful chef. Sometimes the tiger. But in the business meetings – not so good."

"What about this business partner of his? Aren't meetings her thing either?"

Zlata takes a long thoughtful sip of her wine.

"She wasn't at meeting," she says.

"Even though it was her idea?"

"There was... the complications. She was someone else."

"You mean she was *with* someone else."

"I know what I mean," says Zlata. And suddenly all manner of bells and buzzers go off inside my brain, and I finally remember where and when I've heard Jarad's name mentioned before.

"Zlata," I say slowly, "when exactly was this business meeting?"

"Maybe three weeks ago," she says.

"Three?"

"Maybe." I count back the days in my head, and come to the same conclusion that my subconscious had already arrived at some moments ago.

"Where are you going?" says Zlata as I get up from my chair, and start putting on my jacket.

"I'm sorry Zlata – I've got to go."

"Nonsense. Sit down again. Let us order more coffee, and also cake."

"No you don't understand – I can't be here!"

"Why not?"

"Because this is the same restaurant that Nathia – and more importantly Michael and Rachel, her boss and his wife – came to three weeks ago! Don't you see? Michael was Jarad's prospective investor!"

"So?" she says.

"So I might get recognised! As Nathia's other half! As Edwin! And I'm not Edwin at the moment! I'm Roger – I mean Gary – I mean –" I shake my head. "I'm William!"

"You worry too much," say Zlata, "what does it matter who you are? Sit down."

"No, Zlata, it's too risky."

Right on cue the bell above the restaurant door tinkles the arrival of another customer, and I turn, fully expecting to see Nathia and a small army of her work colleagues, all of whom know me as her boyfriend – ex-boyfriend! Instead, slightly obscured through the enormous fish tank between ourselves and the door, I see a lone woman with her back to us. She shakes rain off an umbrella, then starts to take off her coat and headscarf. I look back at Zlata.

"'Too risky'?" she prompts.

"Right. Yes. Look – this is a case of two worlds colliding and that makes me feel uncomfortable. I'm an actor. I like the security of scripts, lines, and stage directions. Even improv has a structure. But this is a disaster waiting to happen! So thanks for dinner, but I'm outta here."

"Whatever happened to 'seize the moment'?" asks Zlata.

"I'm really more of a '*control the moment*' kind of person," I say. "See you next week." I check that my watch is still on my wrist and then, as I turn to leave, I walk straight into the woman who came in moments ago. I take a step backwards, and our eyes meet.

"Hello Edwin," she says. "Or is it…William?" My head spins.

"Rachel?" I splutter.

"William," says Zlata from behind me, "I believe you know already Rachel Richmond – *Jarad's business partner.*" I look to Zlata and then back at Rachel.

"Jarad's… *you're* the elusive business partner?"

Rachel smiles. That shy smile. "I'm many things," she says. "Most people are, I find. But no one knows that better than you, *William*, do they?"

Scene Three

"Gentlemen – welcome to my 'umble restaurant, I am Stephan LeBlanc..." I am not Stephan LeBlanc. I am William Lewis. Will to my friends. But these are not my friends. And I barely own anything more than a watch – restaurants are definitely out of my league.

I shake the hands of the two gentlemen and waiting staff step forward and offer to take their coats. I'd half expected them to be wearing traditional Arabian dress, but instead they're dressed in three-piece business suits. Savile Row, if I'm not mistaken. And I only know this because they're similar to my own, though I'm guessing that they probably own their suits, whereas mine is most definitely hired.

"It is so nice to finally meet you and put faces to names," I continue, though as I'm sure you're beginning to realise, I've never had any kind of contact with either gentleman before this moment.

"Allow me to introduce my personal assistant; Miss Taylor. Miss Taylor handles many of my day-to-day activities." Rachel steps forward and offers her hand. For a tense moment I watch the reaction of the two men. Much has been said in the previous few days about particular cultural attitudes towards women, and the reception Rachel might get as a woman working in a key role within 'my' organisation.

But the two men bow and clasp her hand much more warmly than my own.

"Also, let me introduce Jarad Hossaini, my head of catering and senior chef. It was Jarad that started me on this wonderful journey when he introduced me to his fabulous Jordanian cuisine. Shall we sit?"

Whilst waiters distribute coffees I sneak a glance at my 'colleagues'. Jarad looks like a rabbit caught in the headlights of an oncoming juggernaut. Rachel, on the other hand, seems unfazed. She smiles shyly whenever anyone looks in her direction, which they do, often, and I can see that our guests are rapidly becoming beguiled by her charms. And for the first time since I agreed to take on this role, I'm starting to believe there's every chance we might just pull this off.

Eight days ago I sat in this same restaurant, and discovered that the woman I knew as Rachel Richmond – shy and retiring wife of venture capitalist Michael Richmond – wasn't so shy or as retiring as she'd led everyone to believe. Whilst Michael spent his days breathing life (or not) into fledgling companies throughout London, his wife was secretly running a restaurant, with Jarad – a talented Jordanian chef, and as it turns out, a distant cousin on Rachel's mother's side.

"But why keep it a secret?" I asked. "It doesn't make sense."

"If you knew my husband, it would make total sense."

"But I do know your husband! Don't I?"

"You only know what you see, Will; the man who likes to put on an expensive suit, drink an entire bottle of port, and entertain you with tales of his investment exploits. But there's another side to Michael. A darker side. A cruel side. Did he ever tell you how we met?"

"Many times," I replied. "You were waiting tables. He was meeting a business associate. Your eyes met across the crowded restaurant..."

"I suppose that's one version of events," said Rachel. "It was my first job and I loved it. That quirky old building, the people I worked with, the customers – I could have happily waited tables for the rest of my life. And then Michael started coming in with his 'business associates' – first once a week, then twice, then every day.

"I thought nothing of it at first. Why wouldn't you come in every day if you could afford to? Then he started making demands: first he wanted the same table, then he refused to be served by anyone else, finally he told me he wanted to marry me."

"Crikey," I said. "That really is demanding!"

"Yes, well, I thought he was joking at first. An extension of his lewd comments, and attempts to pinch my bottom, but it turned out he was serious. He told me if I agreed to marry him he would buy the restaurant and give it to me as a wedding present. It would be *mine.* I could run it.

"Well, I was used to customers coming on to me, it came with the territory, but no man had ever offered to buy me anything more than a drink – but then, Michael wasn't your average man. He was older, wiser, more confident, more powerful. He was very, very attractive. And I was young. A little naïve. And maybe... a little greedy. I loved that restaurant so much, Will. If Michael was willing to get it for me then I figured he must really... I thought it meant..." Rachel blinked a few times, bit her bottom lip, then turned to look out of the window whilst she bunched the table cloth in her fists. I exchanged glances with Zlata.

"Meant what?"

"That he genuinely loved me," she said, so quietly I could barely hear her. I shuffled in my chair.

"Well I'm sure he did," I said. "And probably still does. Doesn't he?"

"No, Will," she said, her voice hardening. "I didn't realise it for a long time, but it turned out... he was just *buying* me. He'd figured out my price, and was adding me to his 'portfolio'." She stared off into the distance, her eyes full of the past.

"That sounds a little harsh," I said eventually.

"It's also true," she said, coming back to the here and now. "But who am I to judge? I wanted that restaurant, just as Michael wanted me. So I agreed; I married him."

"Wow," I said.

"And then I watched Michael do what Michael does so well."

"He bought you the restaurant?" I asked.

"In a manner of speaking. The owner didn't want to sell it – not even with my assurances that nothing would change. But that wasn't going to stop Michael. Within a few months he'd acquired the building, and terminated the lease on the restaurant. The brasserie closed shortly after I became Mrs Richmond, and the owner and all my old colleagues found themselves out of work.

"I told myself it didn't matter. That we'd re-open, under my management, and that I would re-employ as many of the original staff as I could, and together we would win back our old customers. It would be even better than it had been. Everybody would be happy."

"I take it that's not what happened," I said, after a long pause. Rachel shook her head. "Michael never gave me the restaurant," she said, her voice cracking slightly. "He struck a deal with a property developer, and together they tore that lovely old building to the ground, and replaced it with a block of 'luxury' apartments. And one day he presented me with a piece of paper telling me that those flats were mine – *that* was my wedding present; a constant reminder of a place I'd once loved, the people I used to enjoy working with, and how my greed had destroyed it all."

"Gosh," I said. Eventually. Though more to fill the void with something other than the sound of Zlata's rings clinking against her coffee cup. She'd obviously heard the story before, but still, I couldn't help thinking that a moment of respectful silence was called for. Whilst I glared at Zlata, Jarad came over with another coffee and set it on front of Rachel.

"For you," he said, placing a hand tenderly on her shoulder, and then taking the seat next to me.

"Thank you," she said, with a smile.

"So, how did you come to run this place?" I asked.

"I met Jarad at a family function," said Rachel, picking up her frothy milky drink. "He told me about his passion for cooking, how he'd always dreamt of owning a restaurant, and I realised that here was an opportunity to make up for what I'd done. We found this premises and together we started this business."

"And Michael doesn't know?" I asked.

"He knows the restaurant *exists*, of course – but he doesn't know about my involvement. Or that Jarad is my cousin. And that's the way I want it to stay." Something didn't make sense.

"Then how on earth did Michael end up coming here for a business meeting?"

"Ah, well – in retrospect perhaps that wasn't such a good idea," said Rachel, shooting Jarad a look.

"What wasn't?"

"The restaurant, *this* restaurant, has been extremely successful. A few months ago we started to wonder whether we could expand. Open a second restaurant. Perhaps even a small chain. But expansion needs money, William. *Investment*."

"You're kidding me. You contacted your husband! After what happened before?"

"Perhaps it was madness, but it felt like fate had handed me an opportunity. If I could get that... *miserable worm* to invest *his* money in *our* restaurant, it would, in some small way, be a kind of retribution. I wrote to Nathia, as Jarad, and asked whether her firm might be interested in discussing an investment opportunity. She came, saw the potential, and took the idea to her boss – my husband. Everything seemed to be going to plan – until, that is, the evening Michael came to see the restaurant for himself.

"I sat next to him, as his wife, and watched, helpless, as he fired his stupid investment questions at my cousin: what was his gross turnover for each year we've been in business? How much of that was net profit? What were his projections? And even though Jarad promised to provide Michael with everything he wanted, and more, by email the next day – that wasn't good enough for my husband. Eventually he wasn't even asking proper questions any more, he was just saying anything he could to belittle Jarad, my cousin, my business partner, right in front of me! I was livid, but what could I do? Once again this man had taken my dreams, and crushed them!"

Rachel sat back in her chair, exhausted. I was pretty shell shocked myself, my mind reeling at how much more there was to this melancholy beautiful woman I used to sit opposite at dinner parties.

Zlata broke the silence. "Nonsense," she said. "The dream is not over! Always there is another way to skin dog!"

"I think you mean cat," I said.

"I know what I mean," said Zlata. "And this time we cannot fail!"

"Well – possibly," said Rachel. "Zlata has this... *alternative*... idea." I was starting to feel uncomfortable.

"Why do I get the impression that this somehow involves me?" I asked hesitantly. Rachel looked at her watch, and glanced at Jarad who left the table to fetch her coat and scarf.

"There are one or two *complications*," said Rachel, getting out of her seat, taking the items from Jarad, and putting them on. "Unfortunately I don't have time to go into them now – Michael will be wondering where I am – but let's just say that we're in need of an actor who specialises in playing unusual roles in real life. You can imagine how surprised I was when Zlata said she knew someone, and even more when I discovered that I already knew you – albeit as Edwin, boyfriend of my husband's right-hand woman." I shot a look at Zlata, who shrugged.

"Yes, well, I'm not entirely sure how I feel about her telling you that!"

"Don't worry William," said Rachel, reaching across the table and placing her hand on mine, "your secret is safe with me. Let's talk tomorrow if that's okay? I'd like to become your newest client."

Not twelve hours later Zlata and I were parked in her ancient Mini Cooper, on double yellow lines, in a side street near London Bridge. Ahead of us, on the other side of a busy main road, was an austere looking coffee shop. I took a deep breath and exhaled slowly.

"So, that's the place eh?" Zlata was leaning forwards, her torso pressed against the steering wheel, her nose almost touching the inside of the windscreen. I checked my watch. It was still on my wrist, which was a good thing, but it was way too early in the morning, which was not. "Why don't we go in?" I suggested. "I could really use a cup of coffee. I was awake half the night worrying about what will happen if Michael finds out I'm not Edwin; he'll confront Nathia, my god he might even fire her, and then there will be ... 'ramifications'." I shuddered.

"That will not happen," said Zlata, without ever looking at me. "Nobody is telling anyone anything."

"You told Rachel!"

"That was different."

"No it wasn't!"

"Hush now," said Zlata, turning to face me. "Look at the cafe." I glanced back across the road, then at Zlata, who'd resumed her original position. At any moment I expected her to produce a pair of binoculars.

"Yes, it's still there!" I said. Then frowned. "Not exactly busy, are they?"

"Exactly!" hissed Zlata. "Here we sit – looking at the many peoples; all going and coming. All of them needing something to eat, some coffee, a place to meet other peoples. And yet, no one goes in. No one comes out. It is like it is invisibles."

"Too expensive, eh? It looks as if it might be quite pricey." Zlata gave one of her eastern European shrugs. "Terrible food?" She shrugged again. "Okay, so why is it empty? At ... nine-forty-five on a Monday morning?"

"It is the magic," said Zlata.

"You mean like a curse?"

"No! Not like curse – I mean it has no magic! You go in, you drink coffee, you talk, you chat, but no magic. Nothing. It is empty experience."

"Right," I said. My stomach rumbled to let me know that it too was empty.

"And not just this restaurant," continued Zlata, "all of them."

"There are others?"

"Thirteen. All over London. All dead. All empty. No magic. But we – *we* have the magic!" Suddenly everything fell into place.

"Are you proposing that Jarad and Rachel merge with these guys?"

"Exactly!" replied Zlata. "It is perfect solution." I rubbed my tired eyes.

"Well, it's an interesting idea," I mused. "But what makes you think *Café Al Muteena* would be remotely interested?"

"They will," said Zlata. I narrowed my eyes. I could tell when she was up to something. "It is owned by two gentlemens. The Tahan Brothers. Abdul and Sadaqat. They are Arabian princes."

"Princes? You're kidding me."

"I am deadly and serious. We had ... the friendship."

"The friendship?"

"Yes." I raised an eyebrow.

"The 'special' friendship?"

"Sometimes it was special."

"You and Abdul?"

"Yes. And his brother."

"Both of them!?"

"They are very close. They share everything."

I shook my head in disbelief. "Dear god ..."

"And they are very proud men. Very traditional."

"Not that traditional by the sounds of it!"

"It would be very bad thing if business fail. And so, like all business men, what they don't have, they buy. We have the magic. They need the magic. They'll talk to you." She sat back in her seat and started the ignition.

"Hang on! Me?" I blurted.

"Yes. Of course you. And now we go for coffee – somewhere else."

"But why me? Why not you?!"

"Our friendship," said Zlata checking over her shoulder, "– not so special anymore."

"Okay, well, then Jarad!"

"Jarad not so good with the business meeting. Remember?"

"Rachel then?"

"Like I say, they are traditional." There was a metallic crunch whilst Zlata went through her usual unique approach to putting a car into first gear. "Arabian business gentlemens only do business with other gentlemens."

"So because of your not-so-special-relationship, Jarad's missing business acumen, and Rachel's misfortune at being female, *I* have to negotiate with these ... gentlemens!"

"Yes. That is about the shape of it."

"You mean size!"

"I know what I mean," said Zlata. The car launched forward, approached the junction at an alarming speed, and then joined the traffic on the main road to the usual fanfare of angry car horns.

"And who exactly am I supposed to say I am?" I yelled over the noise of the engine.

"*Stephan LeBlanc*?!"

Without the hubbub of diners and waiters weaving between tables, *Jarad's* had a church-like tranquillity about it. I, however, was feeling anything but tranquil. I waited impatiently for Zlata to light her cigarette and explain what mysterious Czech logic had led her to choose such a ludicrous name. Rachel glanced nervously from Zlata to me and back again. Jarad shuffled in his seat.

"Zlata thought that was quite a good name," said Rachel.

"Zlata *always* thinks her names are good! Look, getting the name right is perhaps the most important part of developing a character. Would Macbeth have worked quite so well if the murderous Scottish general had been called..." I hunted around in my psyche for a suitably absurd name to illustrate my point. "... Bertram?"

"Well he could be, couldn't he?" asked Rachel. "Isn't Macbeth a surname?"

"My point is –"

"Never mind point," interrupted Zlata, "Abdul and his brother *already* know Stephan LeBlanc. We write them nice letter and we sign it; *Stephan LeBlanc.* It is good name! Very convincing! And we cannot change it. Not now."

"But it's French! And I am not French!"

"But you are very good actor. This will be walk in the street."

"Park!"

"I know what I mean!"

"And what if I don't agree to this... lunacy?" Zlata said nothing, just took a long drag of her cigarette.

"Well," said Rachel, "we'd have to find someone else." But I could see she wasn't convinced.

"Who? Who else is going to play this part?"

"I would play it!" said Zlata defiantly.

"You!?"

"Why not me?"

"Several reasons," I said, preparing to tick them off my fingers. "A) You're not a man, B) you're not French, C) they already know you as their ex-'special' friend Zlata! And D) ... you're not a man!"

"I will wear disguise!"

"Good god!"

"I am good with disguise!"

"Look, Will," said Rachel, reaching across the table and touching my arm, "There is no one else! We know that. So does Zlata."

"I could do it!"

"Yes, Zlata, er, possibly, but not as well as Will. That's why you suggested him. And that's why we went ahead and contacted Abdul, because we were reasonably certain we knew someone who could play the part of Stephan when and if the time came. True, we probably should have waited until you'd agreed, Will, but we had to move quickly. Abdul and his brother aren't in the country all that often." She held my gaze, those cappuccino eyes never leaving mine for a second, and though it really was lunacy, a part of me wanted to do it for no other reason than it was important to Rachel. And I liked her. I liked her a lot. If she'd put her faith in me then I wanted to show her it was justified.

"Fine," I said eventually. "Fine! I'll do it. For *you*. But on one condition!"

"Name it," said Rachel.

"None of this, *none of this*, ever gets back to Nathia and Michael. Or anyone else." I looked at Zlata. "Is that understood?"

"Of course," said Rachel.

"I could have done it," said Zlata.

Rachel is in full flow, taking the brothers through 'our' turnover figures for the past five years, our projections, all those things that business people obsess about. We've even alluded to Stephan's 'interesting' personal taxation conundrum, and why his name might not be on the bottom of any contract. A first step in removing the fictitious element from this business arrangement. And the brothers seem fine with that. In their hearts I suspect they already know that Rachel is the true business brains of this operation. And it doesn't seem to matter that she isn't a man.

"I think I speak for both of us," says Abdul, "when I say that you are a most impressive individual, Miss Taylor. Monsieur LeBlanc, you are indeed most fortunate to have Miss Taylor in your employ."

"Thank you gentlemen, I am indeed very lucky. Miss Taylor tells me much the same thing on almost a daily basis." Everybody laughs.

"Normally I'd like some time to consider such a proposal but..." Abdul looks at his brother who returns the merest of nods, "I'm not sure there is anything to consider. We would be honoured to form an alliance with you. To take what you have done here and replicate it in all thirteen of our establishments."

"Well, gentlemen," I say with a respectful bow of my head, "words cannot express how happy that makes me."

"There is just one thing we must do first," continues Abdul. "As a courtesy to our investors, we are legally obliged to run a decision of this magnitude past them." Abdul continues to talk but all I can hear is the word 'investors' echoing inside my head. This is the first time anybody's mentioned investors.

"Of course, gentlemen," I say. "Absolutely no problem." Rachel gives me a sideways glance. And I know what she wants me to ask. "But, just out of interest," I continue, "may I ask who your investors are?"

"Michael Richmond, of *Steele & Richmond*," says Abdul. Perhaps you've heard of him?"

Scene Four

Thirty seconds after our Arabian guests have left I burst into the kitchen with only one murderous thought on my mind – Rachel and Jarad are only a few steps behind me.

Zlata, meanwhile, is completely unaware that these are her final moments. She sits at the far end of the kitchen, in a haze of cigarette smoke, her feet on an upturned bucket, whilst she watches a small black and white television.

"I thought you said they were princes!" I roar.

"Hush, William," she replies, her eyes still glued to the screen, "we are coming to the best bit."

I glance at the television. "Columbo!?"

"Yes, Columbo! He is about to find out who murderer is, and always he says, 'just the one more thing'. It is my favourite part."

"I can tell you who did it, Zlata – it's the actor, in the kitchen, with," I look around me, "the frying pan!"

"What are you talking about?" says Zlata, her eyes never leaving the TV screen. "There is no actor. And the body was found in the swimming pool."

"They won't find your body, Zlata. I'm going to put you through that blender and turn you into pies!" For the first time Zlata looks up from the television, first at the blender, then at me, then at Rachel, and then back at me.

"Oh no!" she says, spinning around in her chair to face us. "Not again! The meeting did not go well?"

"The meeting went fabulously!" I say. "They want to strike a deal. Everything went according to plan." Zlata brightens. "– Except for the part where the Arabian princes aren't actually princes." She blinks.

"Of course they are princes," she says.

"No Zlata, because if they were *they wouldn't need the backing of investors*!"

"Well," she says with a shrug, "maybe not 'princes', but they have the royal blood. So 'almost princes'." I can feel the rage inside me reaching a crescendo.

"You're not listening to me, are you," I say as I lean forwards and put my hands on her shoulders. "We don't care if they're related to the King of Sweden – we only care that they don't need to involve anyone who works in investment, and by *anyone* I mean Michael Richmond! Rachel's bloody husband!" Zlata frowns, takes a long slow drag on her cigarette, and blows smoke in my face.

"I not understand," she says. "Why is this problem?" I stand up, part of me wondering whether she genuinely hasn't grasped the seriousness of the situation, whilst the other part of me can't quite believe that I haven't killed her yet and is still chomping at the bit.

"What do you think Michael's going to say when his client casually mentions that they've been in business talks with his wife?" I ask. "And that she seems to be operating under her maiden name? And is in partnership with the man he spent an entire evening ridiculing!?"

"Pfff. William. You worry too much."

"I'm beginning to realise I don't worry enough!" I reach up, take down the large cast iron frying pan that is hanging from a hook, and check the weight in my hands. Perfect.

"Will!" says Rachel. "Wait!"

"It's okay, Rachel," I assure her, "if I can convince the world that I'm the boyfriend of a woman who's clearly gay, hordes of desperate men that I'm some sort of seduction expert, and two Arabian gentlemen that I'm the French owner of a Jordanian restaurant, I reckon I stand a pretty good chance of getting away with murder!"

"No, you don't understand," she says, "Zlata's right!"

"Go ahead, William," counters Zlata. "Bash out my brains with frying pan. Personally I'd use knife. Much quicker."

"Too much blood," I reply, "and I've had it up to here cleaning up after your mess."

"What mess?" asks Zlata. "There is no mess! So they are not princes – so what? So they have the investors – so what? So investor is Michael Richmond! So what?"

"You haven't been listening to a word I say, have you?! You never do! Never mind. This ends here!" I raise the frying pan over my head.

"Will!" screams Rachel. "Taylor isn't my maiden name!" I pause, the frying pan still in the air, whilst I wait for the implications of this new information to sink in. "I picked a name at random," continues Rachel, "in case something like this should happen."

Zlata takes a final drag on her cigarette whilst I stand there frozen in thought. She flicks the dog end into the sink, where it fizzes for a brief second, and then crosses her arms in one final act of defiance.

"That doesn't change anything," I say, "As soon as Michael hears Jarad's name we're sunk."

"No! He won't remember it!" says Rachel behind me. "He's dreadful with names. Especially foreign names. I had to remind him when he was recounting the story to you and he'd forgotten it again before he'd finished what he was saying! He ended up calling him jar head! Don't you remember?" That was true. I lower my weapon.

"Okay, but what about Nathia?" I say, turning to Rachel. "She's met Jarad twice! What's to stop her reminding Michael who Jarad is?"

"And why would she do that?" asks Rachel. "She liked this restaurant. And the food. And Jarad." Jarad gives me his best 'that's true' nod. "She could see the potential – and then Michael made her look like a fool, just as he has countless times before. She's the real brains of that operation. She should have been made a partner years ago, but instead she's been held back by my husband, all while she pretends to be someone she isn't. Trust me, when Nathia realises it's the same Jarad she'll do everything she can to push this deal through."

I stand there for a moment longer, the frying pan still in my hand. You know, there's really nothing quite as irritating as getting yourself worked up enough to commit the most heinous of all crimes, only to have someone talk you down. Zlata is already lighting another cigarette.

"So," she says. "Now we will open a bottle of the finest wine – one with the sparkles – and later Jarad will bake fantastic pie, but without Zlata meat." I put the frying pan on one side.

"Well," I say, "seems like you've all got the whole thing figured out."

"William," calls Rachel as I turn and walk out of the kitchen, but I don't reply. I'm not in the mood for talking, or celebrating, or eating pie; I'm exhausted. I walk through the restaurant, grab my jacket on the way, and leave them to their victory.

All I've ever wanted in life is to be an actor. That's all. A proper actor. On a stage. With an audience. An audience that knows I'm an actor, and knows they're the audience. Just to be paid by people who want to be entertained for a couple of hours. Instead, I'm a con-man.

That's the truth of it.

And the biggest con I've pulled off in my dubious career is the one where I've convinced myself that I'm anything different. In therapy circles I believe they call this denial.

My mobile phone rings at least three times before I get home, and each time it's Zlata. I don't answer, and instead consider throwing the damn thing into the Thames, but that would be overly dramatic, even for me. In the end I just switch it off.

As I open my front door, the answering machine light dares to blink at me from across the hall – I stomp over, pull the power cable out of the back, and then yank the phone cable out of the wall. I'm not in the mood for talking, I'm in the mood for wallowing. And wallowing, as you might be aware, is best done with a bottle of cheap wine. The cheaper the better. It adds to that overall sense of suffering.

I walk into the kitchen, find an ancient bottle of wine that one of my old students gave me as a thank you for misleading them into believing that they could one day become a successful actor, pick up a vaguely clean glass from the draining board and fill it to the brim before taking a swig. Something rubs against my shin. And I look down into the eyes of my big ginger cat. He blinks back at me, then meows his general dismay that once again his food bowls are empty.

"At least you want me, eh Oscar. Even if it is only for my ability to open cans of tuna." I start looking through cupboards for something to feed my cat whilst simultaneously allowing their emptiness to become a metaphor for my life and non-existent theatrical career. If I find a tin of tuna, then the act of emptying its contents into Oscar's bowl will represent my soul being hollowed out to be devoured by an industry – represented by Oscar – that gives very little back and continually asks for more. On the other hand, should I fail to find tuna, or indeed cat food of any description, something which seems far more likely, well then, that too can take on some weighty symbolic significance which I will ponder whilst I drain the wine bottle of its contents.

Eventually I give up looking for tins, pour boiling water over some prawns I find lurking at the bottom of the freezer, and put them in Oscar's bowl. Then I grab the bottle and move to the lounge.

When I'm done with wallowing I plan to crawl into bed and dedicate much of tomorrow to self-pity, a task that will be considerably easier with the thumping hangover I'm bound to have by then.

But my wallowing plans are disrupted by thoughts of Rachel.

And her lovely long dark hair.

And those eyes.

And her shy smile.

And the way that she makes me feel.

Whilst I want to fixate on the career I've never had, all I can really think about is how much I'll miss Rachel now that my part in her ruse is over, and how I wish I'd been more to her than a stooge.

Thirty six hours later I'm woken by the sound of the door bell. I check the clock. It's barely ten o'clock.

"Hello Will," says Rachel as I opened the door.

"Rachel!" I say. "Well, er... this is a surprise!"

"Zlata told me where you live," she says. "I tried to call but..."

"Oh, er, yes. My mobile; it's ... switched off." There seems little point in lying about it.

"Right," says Rachel. "Can I come in?"

"Yes, yes of course." I usher her in. "Would you like a coffee?" I ask as I close the door and walk through to the kitchen.

"That would be lovely," replies Rachel as she follows me. I open a cupboard and look at the large empty space where occasionally I keep things like jars of coffee. When I have them.

"It appears that at present I am all out of coffee," I say. "I can offer you ... um ... water?"

"Water would be great," says Rachel. I begin opening other mostly empty cupboards where I have in the past come across clean glassware. "You have a cat?" asks Rachel, looking at the empty food bowls on the floor.

"Er yes. He's somewhere around here."

"I never thought of you as a cat person. Oh, and er, here he is." I turn, and there in the kitchen doorway stands a large black cat. It's the sort of cat that looks as if it might have been hit by a car – but the car came off worse. It should have an eye patch. Perhaps even a hook instead of a paw. It's certainly not the sort of cat you'd want as a pet.

Our eyes meet.

He knows what's coming next.

"Out!" I yell, arms flailing. "Out now!" The cat darts under the kitchen table, onto the worktops and after knocking several items off the draining board, makes his escape through the partially open window above the sink. "Bloody animal!" I mutter. Rachel looks shocked.

"That was Spot," I say by way of explanation. "It's one of my neighbours' cats."

"Oh," coos Rachel, looking considerably more relaxed. "Right. Odd name for a black cat though; Spot. Were your neighbours being ironic?"

"Oh, no. That's my name for him." Rachel frowns. "Because I'm always telling him to get out." The frown deepens. "'Out damn Spot?' It's a quote. Macbeth." Still the frown. "Shakespeare?" Finally the frown evaporates.

"Of course," she says. "Always the actor. Makes perfect sense. We actually studied that at school. Clearly it made no impression on me at all." We stand there for a moment longer before I remember I'm supposed to be finding a clean glass. "Look, Will, I need to apologise for the other day..."

"No! No – you don't," I say, resuming my search and coming across an old vase that I hope I can pass off as an oversized, ornate pint glass. "If anyone needs to apologise it's me. I was being an idiot. I just wanted to ... I was just worried that ... I ..."

"You were right," she says, "about Michael."

"I was?"

"He remembered Jarad's name. Not immediately of course, but last night he kept flicking through his appointment diary like he was looking for something. When I asked what he was doing he suddenly leapt out of his chair and yelled, 'Jar head!' Then he told me how two of his clients had been approached by 'that effing ghastly Jordanian fellow', and how he fully intended to tell them to 'stay well clear'. It was all I could do to stop him phoning Abdul and his brother right there and then." I say nothing for a moment, until I notice I'm still holding Rachel's glass of water.

"Why don't we go and sit down," I suggest. We walk through to the lounge. Rachel takes the end seat on the sofa, whilst I sit in the armchair next to her.

"So, what did you do?" I prompt.

"I asked him whether they'd said anything else, whether there'd been anyone else at their meeting, whether they'd sent him any paperwork – anything to get him to concentrate on the actual business proposition rather than his dislike of Jarad!"

"Clever," I say, as I imagine Michael all red-faced with rage as he turns the air blue.

"Maybe," says Rachel.

"Did it work?"

Rachel sighs: "I don't know. He just opened another bottle of port and sat there in silence for the rest of the evening." I nod.

"So why are you here?" I ask, eventually. She turns and looks at me. Those lovely, lovely eyes, so sad.

"I needed someone to talk to," she says. "And I didn't have anywhere else to go." I blink.

"What about Zlata?" I ask.

"Well, she's lovely, but... you know what she's like. She'd have started with one of her plans and right now I just need a friend."

"Well, I'm delighted you think of me that way," I say, though 'delighted' doesn't quite cover it.

"Of course I do," she says. "I always have."

"But you only ever knew me as Edwin. I was playing a role. Wearing a mask."

"Well," says Rachel. "We all do that, don't we? To an extent. And yet friendships blossom. And sometimes when the mask is removed they grow stronger still."

"Very wise," I say. She smiles, but the sadness is still there.

"Anyway," continues Rachel, "it's only a matter of time before my charming husband poisons the deal. He's probably putting the knife in even as we speak." She stares moodily across my apartment. And it doesn't take a mind reader to see that she's lost in thoughts of Michael. Intentionally or otherwise, this man has brought nothing but destruction to Rachel's life.

"Rachel," I say eventually, "can I ask you a personal question?"

"Of course," she says, coming out of her trance.

"Why do you stay with him? Why stay with a man who you so obviously despise?" Rachel looks down at her hands. "I assumed at first it was because you'd become accustomed to a certain kind of lifestyle, but then it occurred to me that you must have an income from the flats he gave you – so why stay in the marriage?"

"Isn't it obvious?" asks Rachel without looking up.

"Not to me," I say.

"To put it right! Undo all that damage he did when he closed my old restaurant, and turned it into flats."

"But what if you can't?" I ask. "What if you can't 'put it right'?" Rachel's face hardens.

"Then I want him to pay – in terms that cold hearted monster will understand!"

"Revenge?"

"Yes! Revenge!"

I take a deep breath and let it out slowly.

"I happen to know a thing or two about revenge," I say. "It's a popular theme in theatre. It never ends well for 'the avenger'. Death or madness are the usual outcomes." Rachel lets out a single humourless laugh.

"I can believe that," she says. "Most of the time it feels like I'm losing my mind." She goes back to examining her hands.

"You know," I say, "it occurs to me that if you really want to exact revenge on your husband for taking your colleagues' jobs – for closing the restaurant that you all loved – the easiest way would be to take something from him. Something that he treasures. Something he'll never be able to get back – no matter what price he's willing to pay."

"Yes, well, that would be wonderful wouldn't it," says Rachel. "And believe me, if I could think of anything..." she continues, her voice, soft and quiet, tailing off.

"But you're forgetting," I say gently, "this is a man who, when he couldn't buy a certain restaurant, bought the very ground it stood on! And why? So he could marry a waitress! He must have *really* wanted to marry that waitress!" Rachel looks up. "Even if he doesn't love you, Rachel, he does love showing you off. Of all the possessions he has, you must be amongst his most prized. If you really want to hit him where it hurts, walk away – and never go back."

She looks at me for a moment, and as the tears start to roll down her cheeks I can see that she's never thought of herself like that. She's so used to Michael making her feel worthless that she's completely forgotten she's the most valuable thing he owns.

A few seconds later I'm on the sofa next to her, my arms around her. And as she sobs into my shoulder, I start to wonder if some good might come of all this subterfuge after all.

We spend the rest of the day together, talking, about everything and anything: how her years with Michael have just rolled by in one unhappy blur. How she feels trapped inside that moment when the brasserie closed for the last time, and the enormous guilt that she still feels years later. But also how she *can* leave him now, how she *can* start again, how there really is nothing stopping her other than her own fears. She has the business with Jarad. They can build that together – without investors. It'll take time of course, but in the end it might be enough to make up for past mistakes.

At some point I get dressed, and we leave the apartment in search of something to drink other than water. Then we walk along the river, weaving our way through tourists, dodging the pigeons, and talking about London: our favourite landmarks. London's rich vibrant history. How *all* the theatres used to be on the South Bank. Where the original Globe Theatre used to stand. And how it had been burnt to the ground during a performance of Henry VIII.

"I didn't know that," says Rachel.

"Apparently so. During the performance a cannon was fired, but the sparks ignited the thatched roof. The whole place went up in flames!"

"How awful!" she says. "Those poor people!" And I'm about to tell her how typical it is for her to think of the people involved, and how I really like that about her – when her mobile phone rings. She scoops it out of her handbag, flips it open and claps her free hand against her other ear to block out the sound of the tourists around us. And I can tell from the expression on her face that something isn't right, and that the magic of our day together is about to be broken.

"That was Jarad," she says, closing her phone. "Our Arabian 'princes' have been in touch."

"Ah," I say. "So the deal is off?"

"Actually, not quite," says Rachel, looking across the river to the buildings on the other side. "It's a little more complicated than that. Their investors – my husband – have given the go ahead."

"He has?" I say, genuinely shocked.

"He does have just one caveat though." Rachel bites her lip, then turns to face me. "Will," she says, "Michael wants to *meet* Stephan LeBlanc!"

Scene Five

The receptionist throws me a sympathetic smile as I look up from the pages of *The Economist.* It's only a flicker, and probably better described as 'awkward'. It's the smile of someone who doesn't know whether they should be smiling, or not, and is apprehensive about what might happen next.

We've met before, the receptionist and I, many times in fact. But always I was Edwin, calling to take Nathia out to lunch, or to the theatre, or to drop off some flowers. Today – although I'm in full Edwin costume, complete with Edwin glasses, playing the part of Edwin – I have no idea how much the audience knows. And though I think it's unlikely that Nathia has admitted I wasn't her boyfriend, that for four long years she was paying me to help conceal the fact that she's actually gay, she *has* probably told them that I'm no longer in her life. Yet here I am, sitting on a couch, browsing financial magazines, in the reception area of *Steele & Richmond,* Venture Capitalists.

"Edwin!" says Nathia as she comes round the corner. "What a surprise!" So, I am still Edwin – the *ex*-boyfriend. "Caroline, if you could hold my calls for, say, ten minutes." Caroline nods rapidly, and then blushes.

"What the hell are you doing here?" hisses Nathia as soon as we're out of reception.

"What? Can't a man pop in on his ex-girlfriend when he's in the neighbourhood?"

"Shut up!" growls Nathia. "Save it for when we're in my office."

As soon as we're in the enormous room that serves as Nathia's office she closes the glass door behind us, and lowers the blinds. I open my mouth to speak, but she stops me with a hand gesture and then uses a remote on her desk to switch on an enormous plasma television mounted on the wall opposite. She turns the volume up, then perches on the end of her desk, arms crossed.

"You've got ten minutes," she says. "And it had better be good." I remove my glasses slowly, and wait just long enough to create a sufficiently dramatic effect. I am an actor, after all.

"I'm Stephan LeBlanc," I say. And I get the reaction I was hoping for.

"What do you mean you're Stephan LeBlanc!" spits Nathia, her eyes flashing with rage.

"I mean I have a client who hired me to play the part of Jarad's business partner," I explain.

"Why would anyone do such a thing?"

"You've been in a business meeting with Jarad," I continue. "You know how well that went." Nathia's lips are so thin they're in danger of disappearing.

"I mean," she says, "why doesn't this elusive business partner just start showing up for meetings! Instead of leaving it all to Jarad, or hiring a ... stooge!"

"Because they're married to your boss." I watch as Nathia's mind ticks over.

"Rachel!?" she says eventually.

"Yes."

"Rachel is in business with Jarad?"

"Yes."

"And Michael doesn't know about this?"

"Of course not," I say. "Hence Stephan LeBlanc." Nathia shakes her head in bewilderment.

"Is she having an affair with Jarad?" she asks.

"No. She's his cousin – distant cousin. Another thing Michael doesn't know."

"But why all the secrecy?"

"Well, you know; sometimes people have very personal reasons for keeping things private, and are willing to go to extraordinary lengths to make sure they stay that way." And Nathia knows *exactly* what I'm talking about.

"I take it then that Rachel is aware of *our*... 'arrangement'?" I take a breath. I knew this was going to come up.

"I'm afraid she does."

"I see," says Nathia, the temperature in the room dropping to just above freezing. "This is a breach of our contract, William," she says, using my real name for only the second time in several years.

"I'm aware of that." We stare at each other for what seems like decades, and I genuinely have no idea what's going to happen next. Part of me expects a crack team of lawyers to sweep in through the window and carry me off in chains. A more realistic part expects Nathia to command me to leave London and never return. But most of me is praying that Rachel was right about Nathia.

"So why are you here?" she asks.

"I need your help," I say. "We – Jarad, Rachel and I – need your help."

She says nothing, instead she walks round to her side of her desk and presses a button on her phone. Caroline answers.

"Edwin and I are taking an early lunch, Caroline, can you rearrange my appointments for this afternoon?" And before Caroline has a chance to reply, Nathia hangs up. She turns to me. "Let's go," she says.

"Let me see if I've understood this correctly," says Nathia, after she's checked and double checked that everyone in our immediate vicinity is either busy eating, talking, or too inebriated to pay us any meaningful attention. "You've been hired to play the part of Stephan LeBlanc, to negotiate a restaurant merger with two of my clients, so that one of the real owners, Rachel Richmond – *my boss's wife* – can continue to remain anonymous and keep her business dealings secret!?"

"Close enough," I say. Nathia takes another cursory glance around the pub, presumably to see if there is anyone who might recognise us. It seems highly unlikely. We spent twenty minutes in a cab getting as far away from her office as possible.

"But now the challenge is how you meet Michael, as Stephan LeBlanc, when he already knows you as Edwin Clarkson, *my supposed ex-boyfriend*, without him discovering that in reality you're neither of those people. Not to mention that his wife is in business with a man that he can't stand, and that you've been helping me to conceal the fact that I'm one of those 'ghastly fucking lesbian people'? Is that everything? Or did I miss something crucial?"

"You're not ghastly," I say. "A bit prickly sometimes, maybe ..." Nathia's face hardens.

"Michael Richmond is not a man to cross, William," she says, becoming almost threatening. "He's a man with fixed ideas about how the world should work, and he has the power and influence to ensure that it operates his way." I should probably be scared. Instead I'm irritated.

"Yes, and I thought you were sick of all that? I thought you'd decided you weren't going to go along with Michael's prehistoric ideas any longer? That's why you fired me, wasn't it? So you could 'come out' and be yourself?"

"And I will, William," replies Nathia. "In my own time! But the last thing I need is you interfering and outing me before I'm ready!"

"I'm not interfering," I protest. "Or at least I didn't mean to. It just got out of hand. And right now I want it all to go away!" I say. "And I don't see how that can happen without your help."

"What exactly do you expect me to do?" asks Nathia.

"Persuade Michael that he doesn't need to meet Stephan! That would seem to be the most obvious thing."

"You've got no idea, have you," says Nathia, cocking her head as if I am some strange creature inside a cage.

"About what?"

"The only reason this merger is still on the table is because Michael got me to check the figures that were given to Abdul and his brother. And guess what: they're impressive. Whoever put them together is clearly a shrewd business person. Which begs the question, why would someone with that level of business acumen want to stay in the shadows? Why would that same someone leave important business meetings in the hands of inept colleagues? Perhaps everything isn't quite what it seems? In short, William – *Michael smells a rat*!" This is all news to me. I put my elbows on the table between us, drop my head into my hands, and let out a muffled cry of frustration.

"It seems to me your only possible course of action," continues Nathia, "is to persuade Rachel and Jarad to forget the merger, and walk away." I look at her through my fingers. "Though to be honest," says Nathia, more to herself than to me, "that probably isn't an option either. Michael is unlikely to drop the matter. He *really* wants to meet this Stephan LeBlanc. And once he gets a bee in his bonnet..."

I think of Rachel, how Michael ended up buying a building just to get her to marry him. Nathia is right; Michael will pursue Stephan to the end of the world and back.

Unless he can't.

"What if," I say, an idea forming in my mind, "we killed off Stephan? Fake his death somehow?"

"Ridiculous."

"No, listen – that could work! We place an ad in the obituaries column of *The Financial Times*. If Michael thinks Stephan is dead all he'll be left with is paperwork, and the merger will go ahead." It was genius. "The FT does have an obituary column, doesn't it? Nathia?"

"Quiet," says Nathia. "I'm thinking." I sit back in my chair and stare at the bubbles in the pint before me. I'm not in a drinking mood. "Jarad said his 'business partner' was busy," said Nathia slowly. "But busy doing what?"

"Being Michael's wife!" I say, picking up my beer as a fresh bout of hopelessness sweeps through me. Maybe I am in a drinking mood after all.

"Maybe not," says Nathia, leaning forward and becoming more animated than I've seen her in a long while. "What if we turned the tables somewhat; what if a meeting between the two of them is arranged, but *Michael* is forced to miss it, due to 'unforeseen circumstances' – especially if those circumstances are of a personal nature! He might just be more sympathetic to Monsieur LeBlanc's previous absence." I raise an eyebrow.

"What are you suggesting we do?" I ask. "Phone Michael at the last minute and tell him his aunt's in hospital? Does he even have an aunt? And would he run to her bedside even if he did?" Nathia sits back in her chair. Gone is her enthusiasm.

"You're right," she says, picking up her orange juice. "It's a stupid idea; Michael doesn't care about anything other than work. The only personal life he has is Rachel and he doesn't seem to give two hoots about her." She sips her drink and then returns it to the table. "So basically you're screwed. And so am I. Terrific. Well done, William. Are you even listening to me?!"

"Hang on," I say, my head suddenly awash with thoughts of Rachel – maybe, just maybe, there is a moment waiting to be seized. "I might just have an idea."

"You want me to do what?" says Rachel.

It's taken me ten minutes to outline my plan and now all eyes are on Rachel as the four of us – Jarad, Zlata, Rachel and myself – congregate at the back of Jarad's kitchen.

"I know," I say, chewing nervously on the side of my thumb, "it's a lot to ask. But it's the only thing I could think of. We need something that Michael values more than anything else, more than his obsession with Stephan LeBlanc at least, and ..."

"It is brilliant!" declares Zlata.

"Well, I wouldn't go that far," I say. "In fact I think the whole thing is completely loony. Not to mention unethical. And possibly illegal."

"It is like banking heights!" continues Zlata.

"You mean a bank heist," I say.

"I know what I mean."

"Look, Rachel," I continue, "it's just acting. You don't have to mean it. It just has to seem like you mean it. At the time. Afterwards you can tell Michael...well, you can tell him that..."

"It's okay, Will," says Rachel, getting out of her seat and smoothing down her skirt. "I'll do it." The rest of us exchange glances.

"Really?" I ask. Rachel nods.

"Yes," she says.

Scene Six

The receptionist smiles. We've never met. She's a temp. Today is her first day after the regular receptionist, Caroline, suddenly received a surprise spa break as a 'thank you' for all her years of loyal service. Caroline's stand-in looks nervous. And I know how she feels. Nerves don't quite describe the anxiety I'm attempting to conceal. Part of me wishes that Nathia had banished me from the capital, rather than agreeing to help, but that was a week ago. It's too late to back out now – the performance has already begun.

Right on cue Nathia comes round the corner and stands directly in front of me. "Monsieur LeBlanc?" she asks. "My name is Nathia Brockenhurst – I work for Mr Richmond. Won't you come this way?"

The receptionist doesn't even blink. Why would she? She has no idea that Nathia and I know each other. She has no idea that my name is actually William Lewis. She has no idea that I'm an actor. To her, everything is just as it appears. I get to my feet, give the receptionist a smile, and follow Nathia out of the reception area.

As we enter the boardroom there's a small pile of documents at one end of the table. In the centre there's a complicated looking telephone. And at the other end there's a plate of Danish pastries, and a coffee percolator. All this for a meeting that isn't going to happen.

Nathia picks up the telephone handset.

"Michael," she says, "Monsieur LeBlanc is here, though he advises me that he does have to leave in twenty minutes to catch a plane back to Paris." She stops talking for a second whilst she listens to the voice at the other end. "I'll tell him you said that," she continues, and then replaces the handset.

"Well?"

"He's on his way. You'd better move fast." I remove my watch, pull off my tie, ruffle my hair, and take my Edwin glasses from the inside pocket of my jacket.

"Tell Rachel she's on," I say.

"Leave it to me," Nathia replies as she drags a chair to the end of the room and stands on it to reach the clock hanging on the wall.

I head out of the boardroom. Go through the doors into the stairwell and take them two at a time to the next floor. The top floor. Where there's only one office. Michael's.

Michael is standing behind his desk as I enter, putting on his jacket. He looks surprised to see me, and I can't say I blame him. We haven't seen each other in over a month and even before Nathia gave me my marching orders I was never in the habit of walking into his private office unannounced.

"Edwin!?" he says, as I close the glass door behind me.

"Michael," I say, by way of a greeting. I smile. And frown. And then smile again. "Sorry to barge in on you like this," I continue.

"Edwin – how the fuck... who let you up here?!"

"Oh, the receptionist lady," I say, walking further into the room. "She's new here, isn't she? Anyway, she looked very busy so I just came on up. I hope that was okay?" Michael's face flushes with anger. It's not okay. I never thought it would be.

"The thing is, Edwin, I've –" I don't wait for him to finish, instead my legs buckle beneath me, and I collapse onto my knees in the middle of the room. I bury my face in my hands, and cast my mind back to the Labrador puppy I had as a boy – the one that ran out in front of the car before I could do anything about it – and from the very pit of my soul I wrench up two or three great sobs of anguish. I can't see Michael any more but I can tell from the stillness in the room that I have his reluctant attention.

After a second or two I take a deep breath, remind myself that I never had a puppy, not even of any kind, wipe my nose on the sleeve of my jacket and slowly get to my feet.

"I'm sorry, Michael," I say. "I don't know what came over me. I'll leave." I turn to walk to the door, but pause just long enough to see if my little display was enough.

"Edwin! Wait!" Michael bites his lip as he wrestles with conflicting emotions. "What... what's wrong?"

"Nathia!" I reply, like there could only ever be one answer to that question. "She won't see me! She won't return my calls! She's completely cut me out of her life! I don't know what to do. I love her, Michael! How do I get her back?" Michael flushes again. But gone is the anger from a moment ago, now I can almost hear him squirm with embarrassment.

"Oh, well, Edwin," he stammers, "look, I sympathise, fuck me I do, but I'm really not..."

"But you and Rachel," I plead. "You have such a special relationship. I thought, if anyone understands women..."

"Well, er, yes," says Michael, "I can see how you'd think that. Sometimes though, things aren't always what they seem. And anyway, right now –"

"I'm a mess, Michael!" I say. "I can't get her out of my head! I haven't been to work for a week. I haven't eaten in days!"

"Right," says Michael as he casts a surreptitious glance at the schedule on his desk, "well, tell you what; why don't you wait, er, *downstairs*, and after I'm done we'll go out and get a spot of lunch. How's that sound? And you know what, maybe I can give you a few... pointers. A little of the old Richmond magic."

I take two steps forward, and I can see from his eyes that he's terrified I'm going to try and embrace him – instead, I take his hand and shake it vigorously.

"Thank you, Michael. Thank you so much. You have no idea how much that would mean to me." I keep shaking his hand, aware that I'm playing for time now. If Rachel doesn't show up soon I have no idea what I'm going to do next. "Thank you Michael. Thank you..."

"Michael." We both turn. Rachel is in the doorway. A small suitcase next to her.

"Precious," says Michael, the irritation returning to his voice. "What are you doing here? Nobody told me you were in the building."

"Your new receptionist was going to warn you," snaps Rachel. "I told her not to bother, this won't take long."

"I see. Well unfortunately, my love, I'm actually in a meeting –"

"I'm sure Edwin won't mind waiting."

"Not with Edwin, precious, I'm supposed to be downstairs in the boardroom. Right fucking now actually! So if you could just –"

"I'm leaving you," says Rachel, and once again the room is silent.

"What? Fucking what?" asks Michael eventually.

"I'm leaving you," says Rachel again. "I just thought you should know. In case you got home this evening and failed to notice my absence." I sneak a look at Michael and swear that I see his face twitch slightly.

"I think maybe I should..." I edge towards the door.

"Stay right where you fucking are, Edwin," growls Michael.

"Yes, Edwin, there's no need to go," says Rachel. "I've said everything I came to say." Michael is almost crimson now. I can actually see the veins on the side of his neck pulsating, but other than that he's completely motionless, and when he does finally speak he sounds surprisingly calm.

"Look, precious," he says. "Could you possibly *not* fucking leave me, for another," he checks the large diamond encrusted watch on his wrist, "fifteen minutes or so? It's just that there's this fucking Frenchie in the fucking building and I'm rather anxious to meet him before he gets back on a fucking plane!!"

"No, Michael. I've waited long enough. That's all I've done since we got married. Wait, for you to treat me like a human being, like your partner, an equal – rather than a trophy in a cabinet. Well, I'm not waiting a moment longer." She grabs the handle of her case. "Go and have your business meeting – don't expect me to be here when you return."

"Edwin, I wonder if you'd be so kind as to keep my darling fucking wife company for a quarter of an hour..."

"No need, Edwin."

"Fifteen fucking minutes!" says Michael, his voice beginning to crack slightly as he finally raises it another decibel. "Perhaps she can tell you how to win back Nathia!"

"Goodbye, Michael," says Rachel, and turns to leave.

I've never seen Michael move so fast. He crosses the office before Rachel's taken a single step towards the lift. But as he grabs her arm she spins round and slaps him so hard across the face I swear I hear his jaw crack.

"Don't you dare touch me!" she roars, her eyes ablaze. Michael staggers back a few steps into the office, holding his cheek, and I realise that this is the moment when he'll finally make his choice: keep Rachel, or meet Stephan LeBlanc. He stands up straight, and buttons his jacket.

"Goodbye, precious," he says, regaining his composure. And with that he pushes past her, out of his office, towards the stairs and out of sight. Rachel and I exchange anxious glances.

We've failed.

Just then we hear a scream, a cry of pain, and the unmistakeable clank of a metal bucket. As we rush into the hall Michael is on his back, clutching various parts of his anatomy. And standing over him, one foot on Michael's chest, her face red with rage, and brandishing a mop in much the same way a Kendo Martial Artist might hold a bamboo cane, is a headphone-wearing cleaning lady. She raises the mop above her head and screams: "*Ovo je za mog oca ti licemjerni, lažljivi, prevarantski gade!*" – but just before she brings the mop down on her victim I throw myself into her, rugby tackle her to the ground, and prise the weapon from her hands. Finally our eyes meet.

"He surprised me!" she says.

"Where the fuck is he?!" gasps Michael as we enter the boardroom.

"Michael!" says Nathia, getting to her feet. "What on earth ... happened?"

"Nothing! Nothing!" blusters Michael, adjusting his hair with one hand, and straightening his tie with the other. The minute or two he spent in his private bathroom changing into a fresh suit (after he'd spent a good sixty seconds swearing at the cleaner) was hardly enough to restore his usual polished appearance of ruthless capitalism; he's limping, his hair is damp, he smells vaguely of stale pond water, and the beginnings of a nasty bruise are just starting to appear on the side of his cheek. "Where's that fucking Frenchie!?"

"Gone!" says Nathia.

"Already?!" he spits. "But I can't have been more than ..." He goes to check his watch. But the chunky Rolex is no longer there. He glances at my wrist to see if I'm wearing a time-piece, but I'm not, and then finally he spots the clock on the wall. And I can see from the look on his face that his worst fears are confirmed. *Somehow* he missed the meeting.

"He said he'll try and catch up with you the next time he's in London," says Nathia. "But he didn't seem very happy about being kept waiting. What happened?" Michael says nothing. He staggers back and collapses into one of the comfy chairs running along the wall. He straightens his tie again and then stares into the space directly in front of him.

"Where's my wife?" he asks eventually. I exchange looks with Nathia.

"I'm afraid she's, er, gone, too," I say. "Though she did ask me to give you this." I take an envelope from my inside jacket pocket and hand it to him. He doesn't open it. At least not before I slip quietly from the boardroom, and out of the building.

By the time Nathia arrives at *Jarad's* we're on our second bottle of champagne. We cheer as she enters the restaurant; well, Jarad, Rachel and I do – Zlata remains curiously silent.

"Hi," I say, getting up and coming over. "Sorry – I think we're all somewhat relieved that's over."

"As am I," says Nathia. She doesn't smile, but Nathia isn't really one for smiling.

"I don't think you've ever actually *met* Zlata, my agent, have you?" I ask.

"Actually I have," says Nathia. "At a *Steele & Richmond* function. That's how we became acquainted." This is all news to me. Until this very moment I'd always assumed Nathia got Zlata's number from the internet. Slowly Zlata gets out of her seat and joins us.

"Miss Brockenhurst," says Zlata with a weary sigh, and a noticeable absence of sincerity, "it is very nice to see you again, after all of the years."

"You too," says Nathia, though I have my doubts. "Are you still in the habit of crashing parties?" she asks.

"No, no," says Zlata with the faintest hint of a polite laugh. "Now I am too old for the parties."

"I'm sure that's not the case," says Nathia. Zlata does one of her more dramatic European shrugs. This one says *that's very kind of you to say.*

"William has told me *much* about you," says Zlata, changing the subject.

"Has he indeed," says Nathia, one eyebrow climbing higher than the other.

"Not really," I add.

"You're all he talks about," says Zlata.

"Hardly ever," I chirp. "In fact never. Ever."

"I find it all very fascinating," continues Zlata.

"She doesn't mean that," I explain.

"I know what I mean," says Zlata.

"She's just stirring," I chip in, unable to prevent my voice raising an octave. "It amuses her."

"Well, you certainly created a stir today," says Nathia. "When I left the office Michael was still raging about 'that *effing* cleaning lady' and how she set about him – he's been on the phone much of the afternoon trying to find out who she was so he can make sure she never works again."

"It was the part I was born to play," says Zlata with no feeling whatsoever.

"He also sent our temporary receptionist home in a flood of tears for letting people wander around the offices unescorted, and raked me over the coals for persuading him to send Caroline away on a spa break. As dramas go, this was a fairly busy day."

"Oh, that reminds me," I say. "Zlata, where's the watch?"

"What watch?" asks Zlata.

"*The* watch!" I say. "Michael's Rolex?"

"I don't know about watch."

"Zlata!"

She digs deep into her pockets, takes out Michael's Rolex and hands it to Nathia. I stare at her, waiting for an explanation.

"I thought perhaps I keep it," she says with a shrug. "Remind him never to mess with cleaning lady!" Nathia smiles. She actually smiles.

"I'll sneak it back into his private bathroom this evening." Zlata shrugs again, then turns, walks through the door that leads to the kitchen, and lets it slam behind her.

"Was it something I said?" asks Nathia, raising an eyebrow again.

"Er, no. She's just ... a bit ... Czech," I say.

"And I am not Czech!" says Zlata from the other side of the door. I frown. And when I look back at Nathia she's looking even more bemused than usual, like we might all be slightly deranged.

"So, you're going back to the office now?" I ask, in an effort to change the subject.

"Of course – I have a merger to oversee." And now Rachel and Jarad are out of their seats.

"So Michael's agreed to the merger?" asks Rachel.

"How could he not?" says Nathia. "He can't tell his clients that he failed to make a meeting that he insisted upon. I hope it works out for you," she says to Rachel. "Both of you," she adds, and gives a nod to Jarad.

"Thank you," says Rachel, "for everything. We couldn't have done this without you."

"You're very welcome," says Nathia.

"From me too," I add. "Hey, maybe someday you'll need me to play Edwin again?" Nathia narrows her eyes and leans forward.

"Over my dead body," she whispers in my ear.

"You cold?" I ask.

"A little," replies Rachel.

"Here, take my jacket," I say, removing it and putting it round her shoulders.

"Why, thank you," she says. "But now you're cold!"

"Oh, I'll live!" I say with a smile.

"Maybe we can share it," she says, and shuffles along the bench. I put my arm around her shoulders.

"Now, this is much better," I say, as we sit in front of the National Theatre building and look across the Thames, at the buildings on the other side, at the party boats going back and forth. And though we've spent some time in each other's company during the past three weeks, this feels like the first moment we've actually been ourselves. "Can I ask you something?" I say.

"Of course."

"Were you acting?" I ask. "Earlier? When you told Michael you were leaving?"

Rachel says nothing for a moment, and just when I think I can't bear the anticipation any longer, she answers.

"No," she says. "That was the truth. Everything I want to keep is in that suitcase."

"And the envelope? What was that all about? If you don't mind me asking?"

"A copy of a letter I sent to my solicitor this morning, instructing them to transfer those flats back to Michael." I remove my arm and turn to look at her.

"But Rachel," I say. "That was your income – those are your flats!" She holds my gaze.

"I don't want his blood money, Will. Besides, Jarad and I have thirteen new restaurants to manage! And they're going to be very successful!"

"You seem very sure about that," I say.

"I have a very good feeling about it." She takes my hand. "Just as I always had a good feeling about you, Will, even when I knew you as Edwin. Even after Nathia told us the two of you had split, I wasn't the slightest bit surprised when destiny brought the two of us back together. It was somehow inevitable. Inescapable." I smile. I can't help myself. She does that to me. "And what about you?" she asks. "What are you going to do now?"

"I'm not sure," I say as I look back across the river. I put my arm back across her shoulders again and feel her move in closer still. "I was thinking about going to auditions again. I mean, it's been a while. Years, in fact. But I'm a better actor now than I was back then. Or at least I think I am. And maybe in the end, that's all that really matters."

"We make our own truth, William," says Rachel, as she snuggles her head into my chest, and I'd like to say something in reply, but all I can think about is how close she is, and how warm she feels. "I can hear your heart beating," she says. And I'm not surprised in the slightest. If it was beating any louder passers by would be able to hear it.

"So, er, where are you going to stay?" I ask, as casually as possible.

"My sister says I can move in with her," says Rachel.

"You have a sister?" I ask. It's the first I've ever heard of her.

"Older by ten years," says Rachel. "Not that I get to see her very often as she lives in Dorset. Well, that and the fact that she and Michael hate each other with a passion! She's been banging on at me to leave him for years; you wouldn't believe how many hours we've spent on the phone 'planning my escape'. When I called her this morning with the news she was over the moon! Wouldn't stop screaming for joy." But I'm struggling to hear anything with the word 'Dorset' still ringing in my ears.

"That said, Dorset isn't particularly practical," continues Rachel, oblivious to the fact she's clearly tuned into my thoughts. "So instead I'm going to use it as my *official address.* I can have my post forwarded there. Tell mutual acquaintances, that sort of thing – doubtless my controlling evil *ex*-husband is already trying to track me down, this way he'll come to the conclusion I've moved in with Heather and her kids. In reality I'm going to stay with Jarad. His flat is tiny but you know what he's like; he's already insisting that I take his bed whilst he sleeps on the sofa."

"He's a man of few words, but big actions," I say, but I'm disappointed that she hasn't thought to ask if she can stay with me.

"I'll probably kip there whilst I look for a flat share, or something."

"You could always, er, flat share with me," I stammer. "I mean, if you like. If you, if that, if..."

"If?" prompts Rachel.

"Yes, you know. If." I swallow. She sits up and looks me square in the eye.

"You know, for a man who runs flirting courses, you're really not very good at it."

"But I'm not flirting!" I protest. "I'm just, you know... offering you a place to live."

"Yes, a place, with *you.*"

"Well of course with me, it's the only place I have to offer."

"Ah. I see," says Rachel. "So if you had another place, an empty place elsewhere, you'd be offering me that instead..."

"Maybe," I say. "But I don't. I only have my place. With me. It's all I've got. Sorry about that. But you're, erm, very welcome to share it." I swallow again. "If you like." Rachel raises an eyebrow.

"You're not really selling it, William," she says, poking me in my ribs with a long slender finger, and only now do I realise we *are* flirting, and that I should be *seizing the moment.*

"Did I happen to mention it was *with me*?" I ask.

"Meh," she says with a sideways head nod. "I'm not sure that's enough now."

"Then how about this," I say, taking her face in my hands, and kissing her. A long lingering kiss that feels like it's been waiting in the wings since the beginning of act I – and even before I let go, from the way she's kissing me back I already know what she's going to say next.

"Sold," says Rachel without opening her eyes. Then she smiles. That shy smile I've come to love so much. "Can we go home now?" she asks.

Act II

Scene One

It's 2am and something isn't right.

If my life were a stage play, then right now I should be basking in the afterglow of my very own happy ever after, whilst the audience, on the other side of the curtain, gather up their coats and bags and leave an auditorium of debris for someone to clear up. But instead the curtains are still up, the house lights are down, and the audience look confused: There's a stage direction that makes no sense. The odd prop out of place. A line in the script that seems wrong somehow. To be honest I'm not really sure what it is, but something in my life isn't right and it's keeping me awake. Awake when I should be fast asleep, curled around the beautiful woman lying next to me.

I wouldn't mind so much if it were just tonight but this is the fourth night running, and my subconscious won't let up. It keeps finding new things to ask me about. And without adequate answers these queries whirl around and around and around in my mind until I could scream, were it not for the fact that I would wake Rachel.

Oh – here comes another one! Another question to which I don't have the answer, without which I will be denied any kind of rest:

Why would my agent gatecrash a *Steele & Richmond* private party?

Four days ago, Rachel and I spent a romantic evening sitting on London's South Bank, recovering from what had been a rather frantic day convincing her husband that he'd managed to miss an important meeting with a man who doesn't actually exist. This was all so that a merger between a chain of unsuccessful coffee shops, and a restaurant that Rachel part owns (but her husband doesn't know about), could go ahead unencumbered by her husband's racist paranoia. During the course of those shenanigans Rachel walked out of her marriage, and a few hours later, as we watched the sun setting over London, I suggested that she might like to move in with me. And just so she was in no doubt as to what I meant by 'moving in', I punctuated my offer with our first kiss.

That was quite a day.

As we entered my apartment a little later I was somewhere between completely and utterly exhausted, and walking on air. I closed the door behind us, and as I did so a stocky ginger cat walked out of the lounge to see who was entering his domain, and more importantly whether they'd brought anything with them in the way of food.

"So this," I said to Rachel, "is Oscar."

"Well hello Oscar," said Rachel, squatting down and instinctively scratching Oscar's head, "it's lovely to finally make your acquaintance." Almost immediately Oscar started to purr. "Has that big bad Spot been eating all your food again?" asked Rachel in that voice that people reserve for animals and small children. "Has he? *Has he*?" Unsurprisingly Oscar said nothing. He just pushed his enormous ginger head into her hand, whilst I was far too beguiled by this beautiful woman and the affection she was showing my cat to answer on his behalf. "And how did Oscar come to get his name?" asked Rachel, looking up at me. "Another Shakespearian quote?" I tugged on my ear.

"Er, no actually. He was a stray. I found him living in a bush outside the entrance. A tiny feral kitten – all teeth and claws, with enormous ears. Took me forever to actually catch him and bring him in." Rachel frowned.

"Right!" she said, the penny dropping. "He was *wild.* Oscar Wilde. Cute." I smiled.

"Would you like some ..." I hesitated, "tea?" Rachel stood up and came closer.

"Do you actually have any?"

"Possibly," I said.

"And milk?"

"You know, black tea is a highly underrated beverage."

"And what about clean mugs, or will we be drinking out of vases again? Perhaps a saucepan, or other receptacles?"

"You really do want the world on a stick, don't you!"

Rachel poked me in the ribs.

"You know Mr Lewis, perhaps you and I should embark on a little late night shopping trip to get some provisions. If I'm going to be living here we might need something more to sustain us than *black tea.*"

"Sorry," I said with a frown, "I know not of this '*shopping*' of which you speak."

"Then it would be my pleasure to introduce you to its delights."

I pulled her closer. "You know, I really have everything I need right here."

"Really?" asked Rachel, putting her arms around my waist. "Everything?"

"*Everything.*"

"Are we still talking about food items?" she asked, her eyes locked with mine.

"Not even remotely," I replied.

The next two and half days were a delightful blur of domesticity. In sixty hours we went from being *dinner party acquaintances* who'd become *friends* and *co-conspirators* to a full-on *co-habiting couple.* Put like that I'm surprised either one of us didn't try and make a break for it and run for the hills – but we didn't. It felt right. More right than anything that had happened to me in a long, long time.

And after that first night together, and an obligatory trip to the shop the following morning, and a day of subtle negotiation over drawer space, wardrobe space, bathroom space, and various other (largely empty) spaces that had really just been waiting for someone to come along and make them feel loved again, it was starting to feel as if Rachel and I had always lived under the same roof. As though all those empty spaces were really just fragmented parts of much a larger space – one that was Rachel-shaped.

Come Monday morning, a new daily routine was beginning to emerge. I awoke to find her side of the bed empty, and when I plodded into the kitchen to look for her, I discovered that Oscar had already been fed, the dishwasher was already humming to itself, and there was a note waiting for me on the kitchen table:

Morning sleepy head!
Gone to work – will call you later.
☺ *xx*
PS. We need more milk

"More milk," I repeated, scratching my head aimlessly. So this was my challenge for the day. I reckoned I could handle milk.

By 10am not only had I completed the milk mission, but I'd also managed to pick up a copy of *The Stage*. I made myself a cup of tea – *with* milk – and settled down for a day of scouring the pages for an audition, one that might lead to a *real* part, in a real play, or on a film set – anything – I didn't mind.

Nor did I mind how big the part was. I mean, okay, obviously I wanted something a little more substantial than 'extra' work – I wasn't *that* desperate (yet) – but I'd have honestly considered absolutely anything; Doctor Chasuble's understudy in a Theatre In Education production of *The Importance Of Being Earnest*, Security Guard Number Three in an episode of *The Bill... anything*! And surely, in the four or so years since I had last looked for acting work, the world must have moved on and the task of securing some sort of *paid* theatrical work must have become easier? No?

No.

Nothing had changed.

After an hour or two of scouring the pages, all my old fears and loathing and desperation about trying to forge a career in an industry that limps from day to day, whilst simultaneously having the nerve to exude this bullshit veneer of prestige and glamour, started to creep back into my head.

Nothing had changed. *Absolutely nothing*! In fact, if anything, the entire theatre community appeared to be in a worse state that it had been the last time I checked! Fewer theatres, fewer productions, no jobs. At all.

When I'd finally accepted that the mythical ad I was looking for *wasn't* printed in a microdot amongst an article on the growing number of theatre companies applying for charitable status, I tossed the paper in the bin and chewed on the side of my thumb for inspiration. What now?

Maybe it wasn't the industry. *Maybe* it was the lens that I chose to view the industry through, i.e. *The Stage.* Perhaps there were in fact countless jobs out there, but for whatever reason, our nation's favourite theatrical newspaper didn't know about them. I entered the mysterious cavern that was my spare bedroom, moved a dozen boxes of junk, unearthed my ancient computer, and switched it on.

Something *had* changed.

In four years the number of websites where desperate souls such as myself could upload their acting resume had more than doubled. And the larger ones that I was familiar with now offered a wealth of services "*guaranteed*" to enhance your chances of making the big time. For instance: for a "small" monthly fee your profile could appear somewhere near the top of the search results, surrounded by blue flashing stars and a yellow box. And *that,* apparently, could make all the difference when a casting director with money to burn comes looking for the next Tom Cruise.

Something about this situation felt very familiar. And moments later I realised that here I was again, living with a girlfriend who had a job, whilst I played the part of the desperate out of work actor trying to prove to himself that four years of drama school hadn't been a complete and utter waste of time. Okay, so the girlfriend was different, and the flat was different, but there wasn't a single part of me that wanted to return to that fruitless existence. Which is when I remembered that I didn't have to. Looking for work wasn't my responsibility; *I had an agent!*

"Zlata – it's Will. You probably realised that. Okay." Voicemail. I hate voicemail. "Look, I wondered whether we could have a chat sometime about you finding me some acting work. Real acting work. On stage I mean. Or film.

I mean, obviously the flirting courses, are, er, real – but I think maybe it's time I did something I could ... well, that I could tell people about frankly. That would be nice." I bit my lip whilst I considered what else to add. Then a thought occurred to me. "Oh, and talking about flirting courses, can you confirm the date of the next one. I've got the 13th of September in the diary, but that's a Saturday and I thought we'd decided Sundays were better. Okay. Well erm – give me a call." I hung up.

It wasn't really like Zlata not to answer her phone. She was one of those people who relished in taking a call no matter how inopportune a moment it might be. Even when I did seemingly get Zlata's voicemail, it was usually just Zlata messing about.

In fact, thinking back over all the years we'd known each, I couldn't recall ever having to leave Zlata a message, ever before.

The day continued its downward spiral.

I called up an old mate of mine over in Wapping to see if I could twist his arm into taking a fresh set of publicity photos for me. I was expecting some resistance. Last time I spoke to Dave he was spending most of his days being paid not insubstantial amounts of money to photograph naked and near naked women for girlie calendars and every top shelf men's magazine I'd ever heard of. It was difficult to see what I could possibly offer that might persuade him to squeeze me in between 'glamour' shoots. But after some initial small talk – and a few awkward moments as I reminded Dave who I actually was – I broached the subject of having some head and shoulders shots, which I'd be happy to pay for, obviously – and then suddenly the deal was done, and we were putting an appointment in the diary for the coming

Thursday. Clearly the glamour photography industry wasn't as lucrative as days gone by either.

I followed this with a call to anyone and everyone I could remember from theatre school. Of those I did manage to contact, not one was earning a living as an actor – most had given up on finding acting work years ago. Only *two* of us, according to ex-classmate-turned-estate-agent Janice, were actually working in theatre; Carol Brown (and we all know what happened to her), and James Henderson. And whilst it was a shock that out of a group of perhaps thirty of the most talented people I know, only two had forged a career, I wasn't surprised that Jim was one of them; he's one of those actors who had spent a lifetime perfecting his art even before he got to drama college, because for Jim – and the many other actors like him – the only way to interface with the world is to develop some sort of socially acceptable mask to conceal the jumble of insecurities and oddities that would otherwise be on full view. He's the sort of actor who you never really remember simply because when he's playing a character, that's all you see. Just the character. What he has isn't talent, it's how he makes it through life. So if anyone other than Carol was going to make it, it was always going to be Jim.

Annoyingly Janice didn't have his number, but she did have an address. I scribbled it down and then sat and looked at it for a full minute and a half. What was I going to do? Rock up, claim to be just passing by, and then casually ask if he could help me get some work? Yes. That's exactly what I was going to do. I put on my jacket.

My overwhelming thoughts, as I squeezed through the gap that had taken on the ambitious role of 'door', was that for an abode it really wasn't all that secure – tucked as it was down a side road, off the less salubrious end of Brick Lane. I'd stood outside for some minutes checking and double checking that this was the address Janice had given me. But it was. This was the place. Though 'place' was quite a generous term for what was actually a twelve foot gap between two old warehouses, transformed into a premises by the cunning use of corrugated iron. And whilst I was absolutely positive that people did *live* in 'places' like this, I'd had higher hopes for a classmate who apparently now worked in theatre.

"Hello?" I yelled into the darkness, whilst I waited for my eyes to adjust. "Is anybody in here?" One thing was for certain; this wasn't anyone's home. Couldn't be. All around me were shelves and shelves of what, to the untrained eye, appeared to be...junk. Old furniture, shop dummies, hat stands, seventies crockery, framed photos, posters, paintings, rolled up rugs, boxes of records, CDs, newspapers (all labelled by decade), briefcases, trunks, stuffed animals, swords, fake machine guns, pistols...

"Can I help you?" said a voice. I span round to see a serious looking man in his mid thirties, around five foot four, sporting a big black paint-speckled bushy beard, and wearing an old equally paint-splattered moth eaten cardigan, knee length khaki shorts, and a pair of moulded rubber sandals. And he was holding a gold sceptre. Complete with emerald jewel. If you'd plucked Moses out of history, rolled back his years, and then dropped him in East London in the twenty-first century, this is exactly what he would look like.

"Hi," I said, as I waited for my brain to give up making sense of everything, "I'm looking for Jim."

"That's me," said the man.

"Jim?"

"Who are you?"

"It's Will. From LAMDA?"

"Will?" asked Jim, after a pause so pregnant it had given birth to another pause.

"Hi," I said again. I couldn't resist; "Do you… *live* here?"

"Here?" asked Jim, like there might be another 'here' I was referring to. "Of course not," he said. "This is my workshop." Before Jim could elaborate, there was a muffled pop, and something wet hit me in the face. I recoiled, wiping whatever it was out of my eyes and – when I looked at my fingers, they were covered in blood.

"Bollocks!" said Jim, looking down at the gaping gun shot wound that had appeared in his chest. "Typical, just typical."

"Props?"

"Yep. Whatever you need – I'll find it. And if I can't find it, I'll make it," said Jim. The kettle clicked off and Jim began pouring hot water into two ornate china cups, whilst I continued to sponge fake blood out of my clothes and looked around at what functioned as his office. It was like sitting in a fairy tale, or a place where fairy tales were made. In the middle was a table covered with small pots of paints, tubes of glue, bottles of this and that, brushes, tools, a washing up bowl that looked as if it were part fossilized – whilst surrounding us on all four sides were more working areas, and more shelves, only this time stacked with smaller objects than the rest of the 'workshop'; toys, telephones, spectacles, badges, jars, tins, fruit (fake), flowers (also fake) – and from every era too; next to the art deco Tiffany lamp, which was on and working, was an ancient looking PC with a built in tiny green screen monitor that flickered occasionally in a manner that suggested it was about to breathe its last, and next to that a robust bottle-green cast iron typewriter that would probably continue to work even if you dropped a bomb on it. The entire workshop was like a pinch in the fabric of time itself.

"So give me an example," I said. "What's the weirdest thing you've ever had to make?"

"Weirdest?" asked Jim, handing me my coffee. "Nothing really. I usually end up making run of the mill items that are hard to come by."

"Like?"

"Police badges," said Jim with a world weary sigh. "They're always in demand. You won't find many of those lurking in charity shops."

"How on earth do you make a police badge?"

"Plaster of Paris and silver paint. I got a mould from somewhere."

"Right," I said. "And your exploding chest?" Jim gave another weary sigh and examined the sticky red hole, prodding it with a finger.

"New type of squib I've been working on. Remote control. Though clearly it needs some tweaking. I reckon something else must have set it off."

"Doesn't it... hurt? When it goes off?"

"Oh! Stings like a son of a bitch! Looks good though. Just need to get the bastard to go off when it's supposed to."

It was fascinating, and at the same time, deeply depressing. Jim had been top of our class. A real talent. And here he was making exploding blood capsules, and fake police paraphernalia.

"So what about you?" asked Jim. "What are you up to these days?"

It was early evening when Zlata finally got back to me. And when she did, it was via text message. Which was odd in itself. In all the years I've known her, I'd never seen Zlata send a text to anyone – not when a simple phone call offered so much opportunity for loud talking and expansive arm gestures.

The message read simply this: *course cancelled.*

So here I am. Lying in bed. At just gone two-thirty in the morning.

You know when you're watching a particularly sub-standard action-movie, and sometimes there's that 'hang on a minute' moment when the plot kind of unravels inside your head and you realise that nothing you've seen makes any kind of sense? Or it does make sense, but only if you're willing to accept that a staggeringly unlikely – and often extremely convenient – event, has taken place?

So it is with my life.

The events of the previous four weeks, perhaps even longer, just don't add up. And this isn't merely a case of my 'actor's paranoia' on overdrive, fuelled by almost a week of insomnia. This is a full-on bona fide conspiracy, with facts and figures and everything.

Let me talk you through the thoughts that are currently buzzing between my ears: I have no idea how many theatrical agencies there are in London but I'm willing to bet it probably runs into the hundreds. Neither have I any idea how many investment companies there are, but I'd stake the entire contents of my spare bedroom that they outnumber theatrical agents 10 to 1. And restaurants; just how many quirky independent brasseries must there be in the whole of London? If you told me there were half a million I wouldn't be the slightest bit surprised.

So given these facts, what are the chances that Zlata's restaurant owning 'special' friend, Jarad, happens to the be the cousin, of the wife, of the boss, of her – flirting courses aside – one and only real client, Nathia.

It's a bit of a coincidence.

More so when you consider that *two* of Zlata's ex-lovers – granted, they're brothers, but they're ex-lovers nonetheless – also *just happen* to be *clients* of Nathia and her boss.

Now I'm no statistician, but I'd gamble my non-existent career that the likelihood of Zlata meeting any of these people by *accident* must be bordering on ... 'impossible'.

But it goes deeper than that. There are Zlata's reactions.

90% of acting is *reacting*. It's not enough to be standing in the right place waiting to say your next line, you must continually react to the events around you in a manner that's in keeping with your character. And Zlata isn't doing that.

In the original plan, Zlata's remit as 'cleaning lady' was merely to prevent Michael from getting downstairs by getting in the way and, in the process, use her watch stealing skills to remove his Rolex. She wasn't supposed to beat ten bells out of him with her mop! Granted, Michael 'surprised' her – that was also part of the plan, hence her headphones – but wouldn't the normal reaction be to jump or perhaps let out a single scream? It's a rare person indeed whose natural flight or fight response is to grab the nearest object that can be brandished as a rudimentary weapon and fight to the death!

And then, later that same day, whilst Rachel, Jarad and I were popping champagne corks, Zlata seemed to be more than a little withdrawn. Sullen, even. Like our bonkers plan hadn't succeeded at all.

And what about that whole business about not wanting to return Michael's watch?

And her off-the-cuff comment about not being Czech.

I don't care what time it is, there's not a hope in hell of ever getting another night's sleep until I've got to the bottom of this. I slip out of bed, get dressed as quietly as I can, kiss Rachel softly on the forehead, and leave the flat.

Zlata sighs as she opens the door. She seems both surprised and not-surprised-in-the-slightest to see me. She stands there in jogging bottoms and a moth-eaten jumper, a tumbler of something pungent and intensely alcoholic in one hand, and a cigarette in the other.

"Now is not the good time," she says.

"You don't know why I'm here. Now might be an excellent time."

"Are you here maybe for the sex?" I'm gobsmacked, but then I remember it's Zlata.

"No!"

"Then I have sleeping to do, and I do not want to talk to you." She starts to close the door. I put my hand against it to stop her.

"Do you mean you don't want to talk to me now – or do you actually mean you don't want to talk to me ever again?"

She gives me that weary look again.

"I know what I mean," she says, and tries again to close the door.

"Zlata, wait! There's something wrong, isn't there. I don't know what exactly, but I'm pretty sure it has something to do with you, and me, possibly Rachel, Michael, maybe even Nathia. Maybe even Jarad. I don't know. But I do know it's making you miserable, and that possibly I'm supposed to *know* what this thing is – but I don't. So I need you to tell me. I'd *like* you to tell me. Because, whatever it is, maybe I can help. And that's what friends do. Isn't it?" She looks at me intently – and I know, deep in my soul, that I've said the right thing, and that any moment now I'm going to discover that I've forgotten her birthday, or the anniversary of our first meeting, or her Czech name day (even though she's apparently not Czech) – or something. Then I can make it right, and we can all move on.

"Very nice speech, William," says Zlata. "Well done. But it is still the night time and you still can't come in." This time she succeeds in closing the door. It slams in my face.

"Zlata! For god's sake!"

"Goodbye William," she says.

"Five minutes! Just give me five minutes!"

"Go home!"

"No! I'm not leaving! If necessary I'll stay here all night!"

"Whatevers. You can please yourself."

"Good, because at some point tomorrow you're going to have to leave that flat in order to get a cup of the sludge you call coffee and a fresh pack of cigarettes, and when you do I'll still be here, having read your post and chatted to your neighbours." There's a long pause.

"I now no longer drink coffee. It is bad for you. I only drink water from the tap."

"Oh really. And the cigarettes?"

"I have thirteen cartons of duty free. My sister brought them for me from Istanbul. It is very nice place. Maybe I go and live there with her. I will sell carpets."

I shake my head, sit down on her door mat, and lean against the door. We're talking at least, though I'd have preferred there not to be an inch-and-a-half of wood between us.

"You don't even have a sister!" I say when I'm comfortable, at which point the door opens and I fall backwards.

"I think you know not even the one jot about me, William," says Zlata, looking down at me lying on her carpet.

Zlata Ruzencova was born Zlata *Ivanović* – not in the Czech Republic as she'd always led me to believe, but in Dubrovnik. Croatia. Back when Croatia was part of Yugoslavia.

Life for young Zlata was a good one; her father – Dragan Ivanović – was a successful entrepreneur, with a small hotel just outside the walled city, and a couple of bars and restaurants near the harbour itself.

Back in those days whilst the Yugoslavian economy was sluggish at best, the tourist industry was booming, and holiday makers from all over the world flocked to the medieval city in search of cheap Mediterranean sunshine.

I have no idea what any of this has to do with the events of the past month – nothing I suspect – but at least Zlata's talking to me again. And that's a good thing.

I'm sitting opposite her on an ancient two-seater sofa, trying to ignore the springs that are poking me in places that I don't want to be poked, and I nurse a tumbler of lethal looking liquid that Zlata poured for me without asking whether I wanted it or not. She's on her third since I entered her flat, and there's a cloud of cigarette smog floating just above our heads. I'm trying to ignore that too.

"You know, my parents were very fond of Yugoslavia," I say in an effort to re-start the conversation.

"And we probably welcomed them with the arms open," says Zlata – though more to her drink than to me, and with an edge that suggests the welcome may not have been as genuine as it might have appeared. "We welcomed lots of peoples," she continues. "Especially British peoples." For the first time in perhaps five minutes Zlata looks at me. And I can tell from the weight of her stare that we've finally reached a point in the conversation where things might start to make sense. I hold the eye contact.

"There was one man," says Zlata. "An English man. He came to stay in our hotel, and he was very charming, and very handsome. He used the long words, and always he spoke in the big voice." She takes the bottle from the side table, and empties the contents into her tumbler. "And I was stupid young girl," she adds, and I notice that her hands are shaking slightly.

"How old were you?" I ask.

"Old enough," she says. "But not wise enough. He would sit in our bar, in the evenings," continues Zlata, "and discuss with my father anything, and also everything. And I would stay and help with the English words. Stupid," she says, and takes a sip of her drink.

"Why was that stupid?" I ask. "It seems like a nice thing to do."

"My father didn't need help." Says Zlata. "His English was like mine, also very good. But I wanted ... I wanted to be near this man. This handsome man. This charming man." Her voice cracks ever so slightly.

"Wait a minute," I say as I remember who I'm talking to. "Did you ... did you and the man ... *did you*?"

"One night he came to my room, yes."

"To your bedroom?"

"He had run out of soap."

"Right!" I say. "Well that's perfectly reasonable. Knocking on the door of the proprietor's young daughter, in the middle of the night, in search of soap!"

"He stayed for the long while."

"Well, I'm sure the soap was very hard to find!"

"And the next night, I went to his room." She takes another sip of her drink. "And the night after that. Like I say," continues Zlata, a coldness in her voice that wasn't there before, "he was the charming English businessman." Somewhere an alarm goes off in my head.

"Businessman?"

"Yes. Like my father. And it was not long before they were doing what businessmen always do. Hatching the deal. Striking a plan."

I started to say something, and thought better of it.

"This man have big English tourist company with strange name. I remember it my whole life: *Vanadium Global.* Many customers. Many English peoples looking for lovely holiday. And for just the small investment, they could come to our hotel. Our home in Croatia. And we would be able to charge the bigger prices! And we would build bigger hotel! It was the lifetime opportunity!"

"How small was this investment?" I ask

"Everything we had." My heart sinks. "And after my father make the investment the big tourist buses, they never arrive. And the peoples, they never come. And our hotel is still small."

"I'm sorry to hear that."

"There is no need," says Zlata with a snort. "*I* did not mind. *My mother* did not mind. We did not want big hotel full of English peoples, wanting their chips and their tommy ketchup. But my father, he is proud man. He call the English man, and he says 'Where are my customers? We have the business deal! You are the English man; English men are honourable.'"

"And what did the Englishman say?"

"There were the many apologies. And the many reasons: it was recession. It was competition. It was new British holiday legislation. But, for just the one more small investment..."

"He asked for more!?"

"And my father paid. And again. And again."

"More than once?"

"More than once."

"But where did he get all this money from?"

Zlata shrugs.

"From other 'businessmen'. The sort you hope never to do the business with."

A shiver runs down my spine, followed by a wave of melancholy from across the room. A part of me doesn't want to know the end of the story, but Zlata is sitting there, staring into her empty glass, waiting for me to ask her.

"So..." I say, "what... happened?"

"What happened to all of us," she says without looking up. "The war! One day there was shooting in the streets and my home wasn't safe place. My mother put me on boat, and told me to flee."

"She sent you away?"

"Just for few days. To be safe. It would be for me like holiday. But every day it get more crazy. More fighting. More death. Until soon I need new home, in new country, to start new life."

"So you were basically... an asylum seeker?"

"Yes."

"But you've been back? I mean, since the war – to visit?"

"Once. To see my mother."

"Not your father?" I ask, but regretting it almost the moment the words pass my lips. Zlata shakes her head.

"Shortly after I left, he went missing. He was member of communist party. And it was not the good time to be communist. We think maybe... he was executed," she says, her voice wobbling just a little. And I'm stunned.

"For being a communist?"

"Perhaps," she says. "Or maybe, he make the one business deal too many."

"You mean... with the people who lent him money?" Zlata nods. "Why didn't you all flee?" I ask. "If it was that dangerous?"

"My parents had money just enough for me. Nothing else. Just big empty hotel and two empty bars. In a warzone.

The charming English man, he stole from us our options." And in that moment, all the revelations of the previous few minutes, and the odd little occurrences for the past month or longer, all start to make sense.

"Zlata," I say. "Why England? Of all the countries you could have chosen to seek asylum – why here?"

"To steal from you the good jobs," she says bitterly. "Like all asylum seekers." I ignore her sarcasm.

"Then why change your name?"

She says nothing.

"Did you come here to find the English businessman?" I ask. "Your *charming* English businessman?"

"Yes," she says.

"Is it Michael?"

"Of course," she says.

I close my eyes and shake my head.

"I need drink," says Zlata, getting up from her armchair, and leaving the room. From my place on the sofa I can hear her going through kitchen cupboards in search of another bottle, and though the chair is uncomfortable, staying in it would have definitely been the better option. Instead I feel like I should be *doing* something. Pacing, at the very least. I stand up, take a step or two towards Zlata's chair, and notice the open book on her side table laying face down. It's a play. *Hamlet.* And though I should leave it where it is, I pick it up – just out of curiosity, just to see which scene she's reading. Which is when I discover the gun.

Simply lying there.

On the table.

I've never seen a real gun before. I've seen some pretty convincing fake guns – props, toys – but there's something about the object I'm staring at now that leaves you in no doubt that this is not a prop. Or a toy. This is most definitely the real thing. Even without touching it I can sense its weight – both metaphorical and physical. I can smell it too. A faint, almost odourless vapour that glides down the back of my throat and leaves a metallic taste in my mouth. Without really thinking I reach out to pick it up...

And then stop myself.

I have no idea where this gun has been or what it's been used for. Nor, for that matter, where it might end up. And as I'm pretty sure that hand guns are still illegal in this country, there's no way I want my finger prints on any part of it.

Which is when Zlata comes back into the room.

"What is this?" I ask. It's possibly the most stupid question I could have come out with, but surprisingly Zlata doesn't berate me or give me any backchat. She just does what she always does when she doesn't want to answer a question, or the question within a question: she shrugs.

"Where did you get it?" I continue. It's a better question, but it still doesn't remotely scratch the surface of what I want to know.

"It does not matter," says Zlata.

"Is this thing loaded?" Perhaps my most intelligent question so far, but still Zlata doesn't answer. Instead she lurches forward and snatches the gun from the table. Our eyes lock.

"Zlata," I say, stretching out my hand slowly, "I need you to give that to me."

"Why?" she asks. It's a perfectly valid question. Particularly as only seconds ago I was concerned about finger prints. But everything's changed now.

"Because it's a gun," I say. Which isn't really the reason, but I'm hoping it'll do for now.

"So?" asks Zlata.

"Because... I'm not sure you're in a particularly good place... and I don't want to see anyone get hurt." Zlata frowns.

"I am not planning to shoot you!" she says.

"Okay, well that's good to know. Although until you said that I didn't think you were! But now that you have, I'm a little worried! So, for *both* our sakes ... *gimme the gun*!"

She's still frowning. "I am not planning to shoot me either!"

"So ... why do you have a gun?" I ask. And though it's probably my best question of the evening, the answer is in my head almost the instant I've said the words, and Zlata's silence is all the confirmation I need. "Michael!?" I ask.

"Of course Michael!"

"Have you gone completely mad!?"

"You do not understand!"

"Try me!"

"When I was standing over him ... face to face with that ... monster ... this devil man, it was like my father was there with me – and finally, I had the chance to make sure he would never again take from anyone!"

"You'd have beaten Michael to death with the mop if I hadn't intervened?"

"Of course not! It is too hard! I need something better."

"So you got a gun!?"

"Next time I want to be ready."

"Next time? What *next time*? It's over!!"

"It's not over!" says Zlata, raising her voice.

"Of course it's over!"

"My father was executed!"

"Yes, but Michael didn't pull the trigger!"

"He took our options, William!"

"Okay, yes, sort of, in a way – but your father had choices! He *chose* to give his money to Michael!"

"There were no choices!" says Zlata, stamping a foot. "Only lies!"

"But –"

"There is no 'but', William! You ask why I come to England? I come to make Michael Richmond pay!"

And I've heard these words before. Albeit from Rachel's lips; another woman hell bent on revenge, and for a brief second I wonder how many other bitter souls are desperately waiting for their opportunity to put right what karma seems to have forgotten about. But the sight of tears running down Zlata's face pulls me back to the here and now.

"Zlata," I say as softly as my racing heart will allow. "Don't you remember what I told Rachel? If there's one thing theatre teaches us, it's that revenge is never enough. You will never fill that seething cesspit of anger inside you! And the more you try to satisfy that thirst, the more it will consume you. Sure – you could walk into Michael's offices with your gun, blow out his brains in some twisted homage to your father – but you'll spend the rest of your days behind bars. And that will be *another* life wasted, and who will pay for that?"

"Then help me, William!" pleads Zlata.

"Do what?" I ask. She says nothing for a moment, but it's long enough for her tears to stop, and for her face to harden.

"Let us take from him all of his money!" she says. "Just like he take from my father!"

"And how are we supposed to do that?"

"We will find a way!"

I shake my head.

"And what about the people who work for Michael?" I ask. "And all the people connected with his company? And all their jobs? What about Rachel and Jarad's restaurant merger that's being managed by *Steele & Richmond*? What about that?"

"There will be other mergers," says Zlata. "And other jobs. We will help them all!"

"Help!?" I'm gobsmacked. "The past few weeks have been one long train wreck. And all because of you and your secret quest for revenge! Without you poking around in people's lives Rachel and Jarad would never have approached the Arabian brothers! And all that nonsense with Stephan LeBlanc could have been avoided!"

"Yes, and maybe you would never have met me," says Zlata, waving her arms around in that way that she does, only this time with a deadly weapon in one hand. "Or Rachel, or Nathia, and you would be working in the Woolworths, not being actor, and selling the pick and mix!" And that hurts. More even than bullets.

"But I'm not an actor, Zlata," I say. "I haven't set foot on a stage in almost *seven years.* In fact – thanks to you – I am nothing more than an elaborate con-man. I'm sorry about what happened to you and your family – really I am – but enough is enough. It's time for us – you, me, Rachel – to put the past behind us and get on with our lives! Do something we can be proud of!"

"And what about Michael Richmond?" asks Zlata. "We let him carry on taking from people? Destroying lives with greed?" I pick up my jacket and put it on.

"I'm not so sure the greed was his and his alone, Zlata. True, the man is a monster, and true, without Michael I'm sure things would have turned out very differently for you and Rachel, but there will always be monsters, Zlata. Always. And sometimes what the world needs isn't fewer monsters, sometimes it just needs us to be better people."

"Did you learn that from theatre also?" asks Zlata, her face now red with rage.

"No Zlata, that's common sense." I walk to the door, and open it. Zlata stamps her foot behind me.

"William!" she says. "If you walk away I will never ever speak to you again."

"I'm sorry to hear that," I say, and close the door behind me.

Scene Two

It's funny how much your life can change in just a few days. A little over a month ago I'd been earning not an inconsiderable amount of money by pretending to be my client's boyfriend.

Four days ago I still thought of myself as a single man who officially shared his living space with no one other than a big ginger cat.

And an hour ago I had a theatrical agent. Someone who I also considered to be my best friend. But one late-night confrontation later and I'm now reasonably certain that I am agentless, and minus a BFF.

I'm sitting in a cab, the angry Slavic whine of Zlata's voice still reverberating between my ears, and although recent events should tell me that nothing stays the same, and everything must change – it's difficult to believe that I'll feel anything other than pain ever again.

The sun is just starting to reclaim the horizon as I arrive home. I ease myself back into bed, trying carefully not to wake Rachel. With a bit of luck she'll never even know I've been gone.

But when I wake, and plod through into the kitchen there's a note on the kitchen table:

Morning gorgeous.
Gone to see my solicitor.
Be back as soon as I can.
☺ *xx*
PS. Hope you're OK

"Hope you're okay?" Clearly my late night activities hadn't gone as unnoticed as I thought.

It's around three when I hear her key in the lock. Oscar, who has been sharing the couch with me, snoring his little head off, is awake and by the front door in less time than it takes to say the word 'tuna'.

"I'm home," says Rachel.

"I'm in here," I reply.

"Hi," she says as she enters the lounge. "You okay?" I smile back.

"Sure," I tell her. "Good day?" Rachel wobbles her head from side to side, grimacing slightly.

"Frustrating," she says. "You?"

"Oh, er, not so bad," I reply.

"What you doing?" she asks, glancing at the pad of paper on my lap.

"Writing an ad," I say.

"Like a newspaper ad?"

"Exactly. For *The Stage*."

"Oh," says Rachel with a nod. "What for?" I look down at the pad and tap it aimlessly with my pen.

"Acting classes," I say.

"You're going to run a class?" she asks.

"That's the plan. Gotta do something whilst I wait for an audition to come up."

"Where are you going to run these classes?"

"Oh. I know this pub a couple minutes' walk from Elephant and Castle. It has an upstairs room that can be hired by the hour."

"Right," says Rachel with another nod. "So how far have you got? With your ad?" I take a deep breath, compose myself and prepare to read what I've written.

"Acting classes. Tuesday & Thursday. 7–9pm."

"I like it," says Rachel. "Very... direct."

"You don't think it's too wordy?"

"Well," continues Rachel, "towards the end I was beginning to lose interest. If I'm being brutally honest."

"Yes," I say, the tone of my voice draining the humour out of the situation like a hole in a bucket. "Unfortunately, that's exactly what I'm afraid of." Rachel comes over, sits down next to me, takes the pad out of my hands and sets it on the coffee table.

"Will," she says, looking me square in the eyes, "where were you last night?"

I tell Rachel everything. About Zlata's past; how she isn't Czech, how Michael conned her father out of everything, how she'd been the only one in her family able to flee a war-torn country, and how she'd ended up in England looking for asylum... and revenge. And oddly, Rachel takes the whole thing in her stride.

Maybe it's the shared female logic, but to Rachel it all makes some sort of weird sense; befriending her, Nathia, Abdul, his brother, all so Zlata could get close to Michael – Rachel says she'd have done exactly the same. She understands it all. And she tells me not to worry. I just need to give Zlata time, that's all. We'll be friends again. Eventually.

But two days later, and I'm beginning to feel like things between Zlata and me will *never* get better. No one, including

Jarad, has heard a peep out of her. And I find myself making considerable effort to think about *anything* else to prevent my mind chewing over those last moments together.

For instance, I'm sitting on the Tube, on the way back from having my mug shots taken, and whilst I glance around the carriage looking for things to occupy my Zlata-obsessed brain I notice that the only other passenger in the carriage – who appears to be *hiding* behind his newspaper, rather than reading it – bears a striking resemblance to an overweight weasel in an ill fitting suit. Small beady eyes, a neck roughly the same circumference as his head, sparse but prominent whiskers, large sticky-out ears, a nose that's taking up far more than its fair share of face – other than a general lack of cuteness the similarity really is quite uncanny. I'm slightly irritated that I don't know anyone who is casting a production of *Toad of Toad Hall*.

That said there is another reason for my heightened observational skills; I'm pretty certain this is the same man I saw lurking outside Dave's just a few hours ago.

Dave Fells lives and works in Wapping. If you've ever been to Wapping, near the tube station and the river, you'll know there really isn't a great deal going on. A post office, a baker's, an off licence, the odd pub, a smattering of houses and warehouse after warehouse – most of which have been turned into luxury, and not so luxury, apartments or offices. A short, rotund man standing in the street tends to stick out simply because there's no real reason to stand in the street. There's nothing to look at, no parking meters to feed, no windows to peer through – not at eye level anyway. There are hardly any doors to knock on, or buzzers to push – if you're in the street you're usually en-route to somewhere else, you're not *just standing*.

"You're not expecting any visitors this afternoon, are you Dave?"

"Don't think so," said Dave from the other side of a roll of paper, in the middle of his huge open-plan apartment/studio. "I mean, I might be yeah? Buggered if I can remember to be honest. Forgot you were coming over till you showed up. One of these days I'll wake up and won't know who I am. Tilly darling, come and stand on this corner for me will ya?" From the other side of the room the short Chinese girl who had been lying on Dave's couch, doing absolutely nothing, got up and shuffled over to where Dave was still trying to set up a huge roll of paper as a backdrop. Only then did I notice that aside from an old sweater – that looked as if it might belong to Dave – she didn't appear to be wearing anything else. "Cheers doll," said Dave, "now be a babe and find something to put on the other corner will ya." I went back to looking out of the window. The man hadn't moved, and was now looking up at us. As I caught his eye he looked away, stuffed his hands in his pockets, and wandered off down the street, very slowly.

"Probably an estate agent, yeah?" said Dave, coming over and looking over my shoulder. He fumbled around in his pockets, found a pack of cigarettes, put one in his mouth and then proceeded to do even more fumbling whilst he searched for a lighter.

"He doesn't look like an estate agent," I said.

Dave was still fumbling for his lighter. "Maybe it's the stuff I was smoking last night but he don't half look like one of those rat like things. With the long necks. Yeah?"

"You mean a weasel?"

"Do I? Yeah. Probably. I don't know what I mean most of the time."

"If he were a foot or so taller, and a stone or two lighter, I'd put money on him being a plain clothes copper."

Dave peered over my shoulder again.

"Yeah!" said Dave, his eyes narrowing. "Bloody rozzers. Can't flippin move these days without bumping into someone from the Old Bill. I wouldn't mind but all they're flippin' interested in doing is nicking ya for smoking the odd bit of weed! Why can't they get out there and catch your actual tea leaf! Tossers. You seen my lighter?"

"Those things will be the death of you," I said, still watching the man who'd got as far as the corner and had stopped. It was as if he was waiting for me to move away from the window.

"Yeah, probably," said Dave with a sigh. "That or this sodding industry. If I don't start selling some mucky pictures soon I'm gonna be out of here and on skid row. I'll have to get a proper job and I'm buggered if I know how to do anything else. Anyway – I'm ready when you are!"

I stood at the window just a second or two more, just long enough to see whether the man was going to turn round. And then he did.

"You're right," I said, "he really does look like a weasel." I turned away from the window. Tilly was still standing on one corner of the paper, her weight on one leg whilst she idly played with a lock of hair. On the other corner was the sweater. And I was right; she hadn't been wearing anything else.

It's a peculiar and oddly distressing thing to try and open your front door, only to find your entrance impeded by a heavy object. Thoughts such as *is that a body on the other side of this* or *I really need to put Oscar on a diet* go through my head, but once I've managed to squeeze through the crack I discover that it's neither a body nor Oscar. It's an armchair. An ancient, leather armchair whose tired cushion is permanently concave from the many bottoms that have sat on it over the years. Keeping it company in the hallway is a battered fridge freezer (still sporting the fridge magnet from the one and only foreign holiday Isla and I ever went on). Also in the hallway are half a dozen cardboard boxes, and an equally ancient computer, monitor, and keyboard. My ancient computer. From the spare room.

"Hello!?" I say.

"Oh ... shit," comes a muffled female response. "Hello! I'm in the spare bedroom." That much I've worked out for myself.

Rachel is getting up off the floor when I enter the room, which is now considerably more spacious than when I'd been in here a few days ago. Not surprising really, given that half its contents are now in the hall.

"What are you doing in here?" I ask. "And what's that?" I say pointing at the sleek grey metal box, flat screen monitor, and glowing keyboard that now occupy the space where my dirty beige computer hardware used to live. Rachel bites her lip.

"It was supposed to be a surprise," she says, straightening her skirt, and brushing her messed up hair out of her face.

"Well, it worked. I am ... surprised."

"Yes, but the plan was to get it all set up and ready for when you got back! Unfortunately it took me longer than I expected to clear some of the, erm ..." she glances around the room as if looking for a collective noun lurking amongst the contents. "Stuff," she says eventually.

"There is quite a lot of 'stuff'," I say with nod.

"You know Will, I do find it fascinating that a man who struggles to stock his kitchen cupboards with food and other *essentials* still manages to completely fill quite a spacious spare bedroom with…"

"Junk?"

"I was going to use the word 'memorabilia'," says Rachel, still gawping at the assorted items on top of other assorted items, on top of other assorted, and very possibly crushed, items. "What is all… this?" I sigh, and then join in with the visual tour.

"Most of it came from my old bedsit," I say, "which – as all good bedsits should be – was a squalid seedy dive that in hindsight should probably have been burnt to the ground as I left. When I moved in here none of my old furniture really seemed to suit the apartment, so I got the removal men to dump it in the spare room whilst I figured out what to do with it all."

"And what did you 'figure'?" asks Rachel.

"I decided to buy new and give this all away."

"Right," says Rachel. "And that was when?"

"Four years ago," I say. "Give or take. When I started working for Nathia."

"But it's not just furniture, is it," says Rachel. "There's like every single copy of *The Stage* ever printed, and… is that a pantomime horse?"

"Well," I say, "you know what it's like."

"Not really," says Rachel, giving me a look of complete bewilderment. I sigh again.

"The moment you declare a room as a *junk room* – however temporary an arrangement you intend that to be – well, that suddenly makes the room an extremely convenient place to… put… more junk." We exchange glances again. "Which of course makes the job of actually getting rid of it all the more onerous."

"Well, how would you feel about getting rid of it today?" she asks. "Together?" The question hangs in the air like a helium filled balloon and I find myself looking around, not just at the gargantuan task she's suggesting, but to see if there's an object I can use to ignite the imaginary symbolic balloon before anybody starts taking it seriously.

"That sounds like a lot of fun," I say. "Really, really seriously good fun. And normally I'd be the first to join in when it comes to lugging smelly old furniture to and from the lift, however now I come to think of it, I can actually think of many *other* activities – that we could do together – that are just as strenuous, but, extraordinary though it might seem, could be *even more* enjoyable." Rachel smiles. "Would you like me to list them for you?" I ask hopefully.

"No," she says, taking hold of the lapels on my jacket. "I'm sure I can guess what you have in mind."

"Well then," I say, "shall we move from this somewhat crowded bedroom, to the much nicer, less crowded alternative, across the hall?"

"The thing is Mr Lewis," continues Rachel, her voice becoming almost a purr, "none of the activities you have in mind, tempting though they may be, result in a functioning spare bedroom, slash *office*."

"That is regrettable," I say, pulling her closer and starting to undo whatever buttons my fingers can find.

"And much as I like the way your mind's working..."

"Good, good," I say, nuzzling her neck.

"I think an office takes priority."

I stop nuzzling.

"Not so good," I say.

"Will, the thing is, I wanted to understand what you're up against – with the whole job hunt thing? So I went looking at those websites you told me about and there are *lots* of auditions available. Did you know that?" She puts her hands on my shoulders and pushes me away enough that she can look me in the eyes. "Admittedly not for anything particularly exciting," she continues, "but it would be a start, wouldn't it? It's got to be better for your career than teaching an evening class twice a week?" I sigh and let go of her, feeling both annoyed that a bucket of metaphorical water has been thrown over my less than metaphorical passions, and guilty that I'm not reacting more positively to my girlfriend's obvious interest in my fruitless efforts to find work. "So I thought maybe if you had a better computer, and somewhere to work other than a junk room, it would be easier to apply for some of those jobs?" Rachel cocks her head on one side whilst she waits for me to reply, and when no response is forthcoming she takes a step back towards the dreaded new machine. But rather than switch it on she picks up an old brown envelope. "Now I know you've just had new mug shots taken but I found these old photos in a drawer." She slides half a dozen near identical black-and-white photos out of the envelope and hands them to me. There I am, all wide-eyed, innocent and full of naïve hopes and dreams. "And, well, I think you look kinda cute. And you haven't changed that much. So I thought you could use one of those pictures on your online profile, just until your photographer friend sends you the new ones."

"Actors do have a tendency to use really old photos," I admit.

"Well there you are then. So I've scanned them in –"

"Scanned?"

"The printer has a built in scanner," says Rachel. Her eyes narrow as she reads the expression on my face, and I can see that only now is she realising that my entire computer 'knowledge' could probably be fitted on a single floppy disk. By which I mean the floppy disk label. "Things have moved on a little in the world of computers since you last, erm ... since whenever it was that you acquired that dinosaur sitting in the hall. Not that this is the best machine in the world," she says, caressing the monitor as a car mechanic might caress an old MG, "but it is a *lot* faster. Especially after I'd replaced the graphics card and put some more memory in it. Plus I removed your old hard drive and installed it in here as a secondary volume – if you had anything important on your old computer you should still be able to find it with a little hunting around." I blink.

"There was a card game I quite liked," I say. "And a sort of unexploded bomb logic puzzle."

"Okay," says Rachel with a nod, and an expression on her face that makes me wonder whether she's regretting making quite so much effort. "Well, software-wise it's a little more up-to-date than you've been used to, but it is a lot more secure and well ... I'm sure you'll get the hang of it. But I'm happy to help with anything that you're not familiar with." She gives me a weak smile, glances at the computer and then back at me. "Sorry," she says. "Is this interfering?" And all at once I realise I'm being a total idiot. An ungrateful clot. Whereas this woman – this wonderful, beautiful woman – is doing anything and everything she can to be a part of my life.

"No," I say, moving closer and once again taking her in my arms. "I love that you're helping," I say. "It means the world to me." She lets me hold her for a full thirty seconds before she gently eases away.

"Then let's get lugging," she says.

I spend most of Friday and part of the weekend 'mastering the new computer'; reluctantly putting myself forward for parts that I would never seriously have considered a few years ago. But it's hard to procrastinate when your girlfriend keeps coming in with fresh mugs of tea, bucket loads of enthusiasm, and cheerful enquiries as to 'how you're getting on'. By Sunday I'm actually feeling relieved that I placed that ad in *The Stage* and am looking forward to the opportunity my acting class will give me to get away from the dreaded computer screen. Tuesday evening can't come soon enough.

I even use the impending class as an excuse to take a break from job hunting, and instead stretch my fledgling technology skills to their limit to knock up some sort of a register, but this only encourages Rachel all the more and we spend much of Monday evening creating a grid thing called a 'spreadsheet' to keep track of which student has paid, and how much.

By a quarter past seven on Tuesday evening – whilst I'm glad to be out of the house, and away from the computer – it's becoming very clear that the need for a register, and spreadsheet, was optimistic to say the least.

"So, who have we here? Kate?" I look up from my clipboard at the gum-chewing teen slumped in the chair before me, dressed in a variety of black or near-black, ripped or threadbare clothes. Thick black eye liner. Jet black lipstick. Fingerless black leather gloves. Enormous black Doc Martens boots. The only colour about her person is the occasional strand of multi-coloured hair in a headful of otherwise jet black curls. She twirls a purple lock around one finger, whilst she fixes me with a look that could freeze fire. I'm not fazed. We had our fair share of goth girls when I started drama school. By the time we graduated most of them had morphed into something entirely different, but I already know that I'm not going to get anything out of her.

Not yet anyway. I have to earn her trust. That's okay. In a way that's what acting is all about.

I look back at my register and frown. "Dee Jay Zed," I say, reading out the initials before me. The tall skinny black youth on the seat next to Kate draws himself up to his full height, opens his legs, puts one hand on one knee, an elbow on the other, and rests his barely-bearded chin on his fist.

"Dee Jay Zee!" he says, stressing each letter.

"Right," I reply. "What does the ... zee ... stand for?"

"You can call me DJ," he replies. I frown.

"So ... do I detect a hint of an American accent?" I ask.

"Yo'," says DJ with a nod, as if this somehow passes for a response, then he leans back in his chair in a similarly over-dramatic manner, and continues to nod like a plastic dog in the back of a car. Even Kate is having a hard time not looking at him like he isn't a complete berk.

"We may have to work on that accent a little," I say, "if you're planning on keeping it." Kate smirks.

I turn my attention to the enormous forty-something bald man on the end, who is quivering like a life-sized jelly sculpture of an adult rhino.

"And that leaves us with Ray," I say. Just as the chair beneath his right buttock gives way.

I'm not in the best of moods when I make the trek over to Wapping to pick up my mug shots from Dave. And the more I think about the previous evening's class, the more bitter I become.

Three students barely covers the room fee. Factor in the tube ride and I am definitely out of pocket. But what's really bugging me is that usually with drama clubs and the like, there's a high percentage of natural talent in the group. Even those who come along because their parents, parole officers, or therapists think it might be a good idea – or because there's literally nothing else to do, and it's cheaper than spending two hours in the pub – often find that underneath all the angst, depression, or self-loathing, there's an actor fighting to get out.

But not, so it seemed, as far as Kate, DJ and Ray were concerned.

My usual battery of warm-up exercises had taken almost the entire first hour due to Kate's lethargy, Ray's inability to move in any way that was unbecoming to his vocation as hired muscle, and DJ's constant questions about why we were doing them, and whether this is what Samuel L Jackson or Will Smith would do, on set, before someone yells 'Action!'

After the break we tried our hands at some simple improvisation, and I'd watched, in horror, as I witnessed three people who hadn't just lost touch with their inner child, but had probably moved away, in the middle of the night, changed their names, and had plastic surgery to boot. Metaphorically speaking.

By the end of the evening, there wasn't a single cell in my body that wanted to do it all again, and the thought that I might be doing this every Tuesday and Thursday for the next few weeks, perhaps even months, whilst I wait for a miracle to change the course of my life, is deeply depressing.

As Dave lays out my photographs on his light box all I can see, staring back at me, is a tired no-hoper. It's hard to imagine how anyone would ever want to offer that man an audition, let alone a part in anything. Still, one deep breath later and I manage to step into the role of 'delighted client'. I enthuse about the pictures, hand Dave a fistful of notes, slide the prints inside an envelope and give him a cheery wave from the street as I leave the building. Which is when someone calls my name.

Or at least, a name that I was once known by.

I spin round and on the other side of the road is a jet black car. The sort that pops into your head when you hear the word 'statesman'. And sitting in the back, with the mirrored window wound down, is Michael Richmond.

"Edwin," he says again, with a smile, and a small wave. "Need a lift?" I stand for a moment, rooted to the spot, unable to do anything other than listen to the blood rushing in my ears and the distant echo of my heart beating far faster than it should. All actors have moments like this. A point in their career when a fellow actor delivers a line, and you *know* that this is your cue, that you *should* be doing something but you're buggered if you can remember what. And all the while the audience is sitting there. Waiting.

One of my tutors once told me that when this happens, the best thing you can do is simply to *move*; the very act of movement not only buys you time with the audience, but it distracts your brain, causes you to concentrate on something other than the panic, which allows your instincts to kick in and –

"Michael," I say, as I'm crossing the road, wearing my biggest broadest Edwin smile, "what brings you to this part of London?"

"Oh, business. Just business," says Michael. "What else should bring anyone anywhere?"

"That almost sounds like a quote."

"Come on," says Michael. "Jump in."

"That's very kind," I say, my smile never faltering for a moment, despite the hammering of my heart inside my chest, "but are you sure you're heading in my direction?"

"Where are you going?" asks Michael.

"Back to the office," I say. "Just off Commercial Street." Four years of researching Amnesty International's comings and goings had, amongst other things, branded the location of their London office on the inside of my skull, and thankfully Commercial Street was a good twenty minutes in the wrong direction for Michael, maybe more.

"I'm sure we can make a slight detour," says Michael opening the door and shuffling along the seat. I broaden my smile even more and get in.

"Commercial Street, John," says Michael addressing his driver.

"This really is very kind of you," I say as the car sets off, though in my mind I'm trying to figure out how long the journey might take, as well as how likely it is that Michael's appearance is nothing more than an enormous coincidence.

"Really, it's not a problem," says Michael. "What you got there," he asks, giving a nod to the envelope in my hands.

"Just photos," I answer, with a smile.

"Anything interesting?"

"A selection of images we're considering for a forthcoming press campaign," I say. "Hard hitting stuff."

"Mind if I take a look?" asks Michael. Our eyes lock. Is he calling my bluff?

"They're a bit... sensitive," I say. "It's why I had to come and collect them in person."

"Ah, right," say Michael, facing forwards. "Say no more. So how are things with you, Edwin?"

"Oh you know, same old same old."

"Right," he says.

"And you?" I ask.

"Oh yes. Never better," he says. "Now that I'm footloose and fancy free." My beating heart stops.

"Yes. I'm sorry about that," I say, as warmly as possible, whilst also trying to ignore the fact that my throat is now so tight I can barely breathe, let alone talk. "And... well... I never did get an opportunity to apologise for barging in on you like that. My timing could not have been worse." Actually, my timing was pretty darn perfect, though that isn't anywhere near as comforting as I need it to be.

"Oh, think nothing of it," says Michael wafting away my apology. "You know what I've learnt, Edwin? Sometimes you need a day like that to come along and fuck with you. Shake things up a bit. Cause you to take a good hard look at your life, assumptions you may have made, people that you've put your trust in."

"Right," I say, a familiar bead of sweat forming under my hairline.

"Keeps you sharp, Edwin. Know what I mean?"

"I'm not sure I do."

"Take for instance my dear darling wife," says Michael. "Now why would she choose *that* particular moment to walk out on six years of marriage?"

"I've no idea," I lie.

"Well I've been thinking about that a lot these past few days, and you know what I think?"

"No," I say.

"She was fucking someone else." Michael catches my eye, and I fight the urge to look away or swallow.

"Really?" I say, injecting as much disbelief into my voice as I can get away with. Michael breaks off eye contact, looks straight ahead and curls his bottom lip

"Can't think of any other reason to explain it, Edwin." he continues. "I mean, I gave her everything she could ever want: money. Nice house. Expensive holidays. But in the blink of an eye, with no warning whatsoever, she gave it all up. Doesn't that seem fucking... odd," he says. "To *you*?" I feel the first trickle of perspiration start to run down the side of my face.

"There weren't any... signs?" I ask. If Rachel were here right now I'm sure she'd have a thing or two to say about the state of their marriage.

"Not a fucking thing," says Michael.

I take my biggest '*Well, who'd have thunk it*' deep breath, then blow it out slowly.

"Right," I say, with a nod.

"But d'you know what, Edwin?" says Michael, slapping a hand on my thigh far harder than I would have thought necessary.

"What?" I ask, though I really, really don't want to know.

"I don't give a fuck. Not one single fuck. Fuck her, Edwin! That's what I say. *Fuck her*! Fuck her and her new fancy man – they can both fucking burn in hell for all I care! And if there's any truth in what my enemies say about me, Edwin, I'll make sure that's exactly what'll happen. They'll burn, Edwin. For all eternity." I swallow, as slowly as possible, whilst I try to think of something to say, but Michael isn't finished. "And there's this other thing that's been fucking bugging me," he continues. "Can't get it out of my mind: that fucking Frenchie. Just who the fuck is he? Nobody seems to know. Nobody." Michael shakes his head, and turns to gaze out of the window. The seconds roll by.

"Stop the car, John," says Michael, coming out of his trance, and obediently his driver pulls over despite the double red lines. "Can't take you any further I'm afraid Edwin," says Michael. "Just remembered I have a meeting this afternoon. Can't afford to miss another fucking one, eh? But there's a tube station just down there if memory serves."

"No problem," I say, keeping my voice as level as possible whilst I wait for a huge sense of relief to wash over me. "I appreciate the lift anyway."

"Look after yourself, Edwin," says Michael, a noticeable edge to his voice. "Ain't nobody else going to do that for you. There are some nasty fuckers out there."

"Thanks Michael, I will." I get out of the car.

"Oh, and Edwin," says Michael, winding down the window.

"Yes Michael?"

"We never did get to discuss that business opportunity."

"Er, no," I say. "No we didn't."

"Still interested?" he asks. I shake my head slightly.

"I'm not sure business is really my kind of thing," I explain.

"Well," says Michael. "It's not for everyone. It's an instinct really. Maybe you just don't have it. Take care."

"Yes," I say. "You too. All the best."

I stand on the side of the road – my head full of questions, but barely the energy to do anything other than watch the car disappear out of sight.

I arrive home, fully intending to tell Rachel about my meeting with Michael and his cryptic threats, but before I get the chance she bounces out of the spare bedroom and throws her arms around me.

"Guesswhatguesswhatguesswhat!!" she says as she showers me with kisses.

"Whoa! You seem happy!"

"I am!" she says. "And you have to guess why!"

"Okay," I say, glancing in the direction of the 'spare bedroom slash office', "you've found that card game I liked?" Rachel rolls her eyes.

"No," she says. "Better than that."

"You've ... sold the computer and put the money towards a really nice holiday?"

"No!" she says, thumping me in the chest.

"You've –"

"Will," says Rachel, accompanied with more bouncing and more kisses, "you have an audition! Tomorrow!"

"T ... Tomorrow?"

"Yes!" she screams, throwing her arms around me again, and her legs – and whilst she isn't particularly heavy, moments later we collapse on the floor with her on top of me. "Let's go and celebrate," she says after a long, passionate kiss.

"But I haven't got the part yet," I say, "... whatever it is."

"No, but I have a very good feeling about it," says Rachel, and then she kisses me again.

Maybe the news about Michael can wait.

It's with mixed feelings that I enter the lobby of a particularly shabby hotel, in an even shabbier part of North London, twenty four hours later. On the one hand I am delighted that I had indeed got an audition, that there are still auditions in this world to have, and that I have a girlfriend who is extremely supportive and unencumbered by all the cynicism I managed to accumulate in earlier years. On the other hand, the role of 'perplexed customer' in a television commercial for a high-street building society isn't exactly what I had in mind when I pictured the first rung on the long, long ladder to international theatrical stardom.

But, as Rachel had said, it's a start. So let's call it that. And I might be able to dredge a little more enthusiasm from the bottom of my soul if it isn't for fact that this audition appears to be following a very similar pattern to those that I'd attended many years ago.

As I look around for directions to *The Cumberland Suite*, I'm dimly aware that there are at least two other men doing exactly the same, and that they are roughly the same height, and build as myself. We even have the same colour hair. And by the time we've found the room and introduced ourselves to the harassed assistant, there are at least two dozen more of us. Two dozen near-identical male actors. What little enthusiasm I have is starting to wane rapidly. I can see where this is going already.

"Take a seat outside," says the assistant, indicating a row of conference room chairs lined up against the wall. I sit between two men who look like they might be not-so-distant relatives, and as the back of my head touches the wall it feels as if we're part of some sort of a police identification parade.

"Alright fella?" says the man to my left. "I'm John." He sticks out a hand and we do that awkward sideways handshake you do when you're sitting side by side.

"William," I reply. "Will to my friends."

"Will," says John, placing himself firmly amongst those people I consider my nearest and dearest, "gotcha."

"Been to a lot of these?" I ask. I don't want to, but it's what you do. It's a reflex. It's like asking a cabbie if he's been busy. It's just the done thing.

"Oh yeah," says John. "Third this month."

"Right," I say. That seems like a lot.

"Last month I did half a dozen, I reckon."

"Half a dozen," I muse. "Blimey." Then a thought occurs to me. "No joy though?"

"Nah," says John. "I mean I fought I might get a call back on the last one, but you know – nothing happened."

"Sorry to hear that," I say, genuinely sympathetic but also a tiny bit relieved that getting work is still every bit as hard as it always has been. I'd hate to discover that I could have got proper acting work a few years back had I applied more effort.

"Yeah well," continues John, "they needed someone who could read apparently?" My thoughts grind to a halt whilst I make sense of what I've just heard.

"Right," I say. "I see. That's ... annoying."

"I know!" says John. "But it 'appens more often than you'd fink."

"Really? Well, that is ... surprising." The door to the conference room opens and the assistant sticks her head into the corridor.

"John Wright?" she says

"Oh, that's me," says John. "First up! Must be my lucky day. Good luck mate," he says followed by another awkward hand shake.

"Yes," I say, "Er, you too." And in that moment my hopes rise. Just a tiny bit.

Two and a half hours pass. Two and a half hours whilst I try, in vain, to read the book I've brought with me rather than notice each and every time another of my clones is called into the room. Sometimes they're in there for five minutes, sometimes it's more like fifteen, but always they emerge either grinning like an idiot or the epitome of smugness; both strategies intended to exude confidence and let everyone else know that the role we're waiting to audition for has, in all likelihood, just been cast – so why don't we all just toddle off home? But I'm too long in the tooth to be taken in by such nonsense. I know how these things work.

"William Lewis?" asks the assistant. I resist the urge to look at the empty chairs around me, and instead give her a warm smile that I hope will make the crucial difference when the choice between twenty four identical looking actors is being made.

I take off my jacket, put it on the back of the lone chair in the middle of the room, sit down and beam my enthusiastic smile at the two people behind the table in front of me, neither of whom acknowledged my presence as I walked in and show no signs of doing so now that I'm mere feet away. The assistant joins them and begins shuffling sheets of paper.

"And finally we have?" asks a man wearing a jazzy cardigan, a pink shirt and a pair of glasses on a fluorescent green cord.

"William Lewis," says the assistant. Cardigan Man puts on his glasses, and then proceeds to look over the top of them.

"Ah yes. William. Thanks for coming along. Sorry to keep you waiting."

"Quite alright," I say, my smile still intact, but softened slightly to communicate my empathy with the *terribly challenging* task of picking just one actor from two dozen near identical hopefuls.

"Okay, well hopefully we won't need to keep you too much longer," he says. "All we really need you to do is read the words highlighted on your script." All at once my blood runs cold.

"Script?" I ask as pleasantly as I can.

"You don't have a script?" asks the woman sitting beside Cardigan Man.

"It's okay," says the assistant, "I have a spare." She shuffles more paper, then leans across the desk as far as possible and waves a single sheet at me. I get up and take it from her, before returning to my chair.

"Just the words highlighted?" I ask, fighting the urge to frown.

"If you would," says Cardigan. "I'll cue you in when you're ready." I scan the two lines, put the script on the floor next to me and look directly at Cardigan. He raises an eyebrow, adjusts his glasses, then looks down at the paper in front of him.

"'So, how can I help you?'" he reads with a breathtaking lack of expression.

"I've come about a mortgage," I say. Nobody looks up.

"'Well you're in luck,'" Cardigan continues. "'We've got hundreds here.'"

"Could you tell me about them?" I ask, as genuinely as possible ... and coming to the end of my allotted words.

"Well, that's terrific. Thanks Will." Cardigan shoots me a hollow, meaningless smile.

"William," I say.

"We'll be in touch if we want to see you again."

"Do you know when that'll be?" I ask after I've let half a dozen violent thoughts come and go.

"Shouldn't be longer than a week or so," says Cardigan. "Though if you don't hear from us then I'm afraid you can assume you weren't lucky this time. Thank you for your time though." I give a short sharp nod, get up, put on my jacket and walk out of the room.

As I step back into the corridor I notice my paperback, still lying on my chair. I walk over to retrieve it, and as I do so I can hear the three of them through the door that's still ajar.

"Was that the last one?"

"I think it was, yes."

"You know, I think we'll just use Jeremy."

"Oh yes, I think so. Are you seeing him again tonight?"

"Right then. Good to see everybody. Again. Still just us then? Nobody's got any ... friends? Or acquaintances? Anybody else who might be interested in ... ? No. Of course not." Ray slowly raises his hand, as though he's afraid a passing pterodactyl might swoop in and bite it off. I sigh. "Ray, there isn't any need to raise your hand – not when there're only four of us." He puts it down and looks as if I've just questioned his parentage. I shake my head, and try to remind myself that it *isn't their fault*: it isn't *their* fault that I've decided to start teaching again. And it isn't *their* fault that in the whole of South London there are only three people who are vaguely interested in being taught what I still laughingly consider a craft. And it isn't *their* fault that the one and only audition I've had in the past four years... I push that thought out of my head. "Did you have a question?" I ask. Ray shakes his head, whilst avoiding eye contact, then shuffles uneasily in his seat. The chair under his left buttock creaks pathetically – despite sharing the job of supporting Ray's bulk with an identical chair next to it. It's probably only a matter of time before it buckles under Ray's enormity and joins the growing pile of broken furniture in the corner of the room.

For a man who spends his afternoons in a spit-and-sawdust gym, and his evenings guarding the doorway of a small Soho Night Club, he is, quite possibly, the last person – *on the planet* – who anyone would consider *shy*. "Why did you raise your hand then?" I ask. Ray shoots a sideways look at DJ.

"Don't look at me man," says DJ, his arms and legs crossed so tightly he looks like he might be using his new found theatrical skills to improvise a plaited Danish pastry in a purple shell suit. "I ain't doin' yo' askin' for ya! It got nuttin' to do wiv me, yeah? I just here to learn from the boss! An' I dun care about no cer-tif-i-cate," says DJ, punching out the syllables like they have some sort of individual significance. I look at Kate, who is engrossed in some very important texting.

"Ray wants to know if we get some sort of qualification at the end of term," she says without even looking up.

"I see. You mean like a BTEC? Or maybe even your LAMDA level one? Or some other worthless piece of paper that won't make a jot of difference when it comes to finding work?"

Ray says nothing, just continues to look sheepish and embarrassed. Kate shakes her head in despair.

"Something like that," she says, on behalf of her timid classmate. I nod.

"No," I say, matter of factly. "Okay, right. Thanks for that Ray. Any other questions? No? Then let's start with some warm-up exercises – on your feet." The group stand up like this is the first time their legs have had to support their weight in many, many years, and, as usual, they stand pretty much in front of their chairs. "Find a space in the room," I say, making as much effort as possible not to sound as if I'm going to explode or go on a murderous rampage at any given moment. Ray takes a step forward, Kate a step to the left, whilst DJ positively slinks, using every part of his anatomy, over to the wall, whereupon he leans against it in a manner that suggests he might offer you some drugs were you to join him. I close my eyes, *again*, count to three, and pray, *hard*, that I can make it through the rest of the lesson without having to dispose of three corpses. Then I open my eyes, and no one has so much as twitched. "Somewhere you can move about without touching anyone else," I say. "Or anything else. Such as the wall. DJ. DJ? DJ, step away from the wall. Great." I force a smile. "So – same as Tuesday, let's start with the Rubber Chicken ..." Though there are only three of them, the groan is worthy of a much bigger group.

We manage to get through the warm up exercises in half the time and, flushed with this small victory, I decide to teach them the rhyme *There'll Be A Tattoo At Twenty To Two,* and after several excruciating attempts of getting everyone to say it together, we move on to saying it 'in the round'.

This turns out to be a mistake.

By break time we still haven't nailed it and I'm seriously beginning to doubt my ability to teach a four-year-old how to tie his shoe laces, let alone three misfits how to remember a tongue twister. I'm this close to breaking my *no-alcohol-whilst-working* rule, but soldier on into the second half, fuelled by caffeine and a grim determination to instil *some* sort of acting skills into my talentless trio. I introduce them to the concept of theatrical games and ask them to improvise a television advert, in the style of a western, whilst one person is sitting, one person is standing, and the third person is lying down. And therein is my downfall. Whilst Ray does an excellent impression of a night club bouncer frozen solid by his own lack of imagination, and Kate reluctantly puts herself on the floor only to discover that it might be a great opportunity to have a nap, DJ pushes away from his place on the wall and slinks towards them.

"I am *wall-king* through a door," he says, without the slightest indication that he's doing anything of the sort. "You know, like a swing-door, in those cowboy movies. And I is carrying a heavy box. It's so heavy, yo' – I can barely lift it."

"Okay, you can stop now," I say, getting up and collapsing my chair in one fluid movement. "And I think we'll call it a night." Kate moves into a cross legged position and takes her phone from her pocket.

"It's only just gone eight thirty," she says as she stares at the screen.

"Yep, I know," I say, gathering up other chairs and all but throwing them against the wall.

"But we've paid till nine," she says. Ray's still standing motionless in the middle of the room.

"And you also paid me to start teaching you from seven, but for the second time I was here, on my own, till at least ten past. DJ didn't breeze in until seven fifteen."

"Yo bro, that ain't fair," says DJ. "I was *biz-zee.* I had important business to take care of."

"I really don't care why you were late, DJ. You could have been *hanging with yo' bitches* for all I care – all I know is that none of you seemed that bothered that we didn't start on time, just as none of you seem the slightest bit interested in putting in any real effort. So let's see how bothered you are now that we're finishing early!"

"But dude..." says DJ.

"Don't dude me, DJ!" I say. "I spent four years at the London Academy of Music and Dramatic Art, graduated second highest in my class, and this afternoon I spent several hours sitting outside a hotel room, waiting to spout two lines of badly written dialogue to three people who, as it turns out, had already decided to give the part to someone else. I wasted an entire day letting people treat me like garbage, and I'll probably do it all over again, and again, and *again,* because all I want in this life is the opportunity to act, and those ignorant bastards, and people like them, are the only ones who can make that happen! But *you* can't – so I don't have to take that kind of bollocks from you!" The room is silent, and not a single one of them has the guts to meet my eyes. "Turn the lights off when the three of you have finished bad mouthing me," I say, "and maybe we'll see each other on Tuesday. Assuming I have nothing better to do." And with that I walk to the door, gallop down the stairs, push through the bar, and –

He's here.

Sitting by the door, munching his way through a packet of Twiglets, an empty pint glass on the table, a half full glass next to it – but it's definitely the same man. The man from the tube, the man from outside Dave's, the weasel man. This can't be a coincidence ... can it?

I look over at the bar and catch the eye of the landlord. I raise my hand in a cheery wave. "See ya next time Jerry," I say as loudly as I can get away with, and I feel all eyes in the bar turn to look at me. I take a breath, and walk calmly out through the door making sure it closes behind me, then I walk slowly down the street.

Seconds later I hear the familiar bar noise again as the door re-opens. I keep walking, but glance into the wing mirror of a parked car to confirm what I already know to be true.

Weasel Man *is* following me.

Scene Three

Losing Weasel Man turns out to be surprisingly easy. His little fat legs are no match for my stride, and once I enter Elephant and Castle underground station – only to come out again via a different exit, hail a passing cab and jump in – I am both impressed with myself and intensely frustrated; what have I actually achieved? So I've given The Weasel the slip – so what?! Wouldn't it have been smarter to confront him? Ask him why he's been tailing me?

Though is that actually necessary?

I'd bet the remains of my savings that Weasel Man is working for Michael.

Which just leaves the question of why?

"You're not divorced by any chance, are you?" I ask my cabbie. He reaches up and adjusts his wing mirror so he can see me.

"No mate," he says. "Why d'you ask?"

"I've, er, got this friend," I say, "who's being tailed by a private detective."

"Blimey," says the cabbie.

"Yeah," I continue. "I told him I reckoned it was his girlfriend's husband trying to prove adultery."

"Could be," says the cabbie.

"But I'm not sure whether doing so actually makes any difference in a divorce settlement these days."

"Buggered if I know mate," says the cabbie. "I've been married almost thirty years. The missus says she's thought about divorcing me but apparently I'm out working so much it wouldn't make much difference."

"Right," I say. That was no help whatsoever.

"My sister got a divorce though."

"Really?" I ask, brightening. "Did she cite adultery as the reason?"

"Tried. But apparently you can't cite the entire Arsenal football team." And again, no help whatsoever. I shake my head, and decide to get home and chat it over with Rachel. She'll know what to do.

When I get in Rachel is already in bed. Or rather on the bed. Fully clothed but fast asleep.

"Tough day for both of us then," I say to myself.

I remove her shoes, pull a blanket over her, then undress as quietly as I can before slipping between the covers next to her. But I can't sleep, and it's the small hours of the morning when I eventually drift off.

By the time Oscar comes and wakes me, Rachel has already left. A cheery little note in the kitchen reminding me that she has an appointment with her solicitor to chivvy him up about her divorce and the restaurant merger, before going on to say that once again we are out of bread, milk, cheese, cat food, and anything to drink other than water.

I wash, dress, and head out in search of provisions, and – more importantly – evidence that I'm *not* being paranoid, and that I really *am* being tailed. But Weasel Man is nowhere to be seen. Which means that either my fertile imagination created the whole thing, *or* Mr Weasel has got what he needs.

Which is what exactly?

Doesn't he need pictures of Rachel and me being intimate together? When would he have got those? More to the point – *how*?

A normal person might be able to shrug off thoughts like these – but actors are not *normal* people, and my head is a jumble of paranoia. So when – as I'm keying in the code to the ground floor entrance of my apartment building – someone behind me breathes my name against the back of my neck, I let out a rather unbecoming scream for a man in his mid thirties and throw both bags of shopping into the air.

"Jesus, Will!" says Kate, "It's only me!"

"Kate! What the hell do you think you're doing!?" she looks confused, "– sneaking up on people like that!" I add.

"I wasn't sneaking!" she protests. "I was just waiting."

"Waiting where!?"

"Over there," she says, indicating the wall by the river. "You walked right past me."

"Right, right. Okay," I say, my heart rate slowing to something approaching reasonable. I crouch down to pick up my groceries. One carrier bag is now swimming in milk, granulated sugar, and half a dozen broken eggs, whilst the other has split completely and sent its contents bouncing back down the stone steps and into the street.

"Let me help," says Kate.

"Thanks," I reply grumpily, "I can manage." But she ignores me, and gathers up my misshapen bread, cheese, dented tins of cat food and a cracked jar of coffee whilst I pick up the bruised fruit, scuffed vegetables, and semi squashed tomatoes. I add them to my carrier bag of sugary, soggy items, and deposit the lot in the dumpster near the entrance.

"How did you know where I live?" I ask.

"I phoned the paper," she says.

"What paper?"

"The one with your advert? *The Stage*?"

I frown. "They wouldn't give you my address."

"I told them I was a reporter. That I was following a lead."

"What... lead!?"

"I was kinda vague about that," she says with a side toss of her head. "But I promised to throw them the story if it panned out." I blink.

"And that worked?"

"I'm here, aren't I?" I shake my head in astonishment.

"Forget acting," I say, "you should pursue a career in journalism." I held out my hands to take back the remains of my shopping.

"Can I come in?" asks Kate.

"That depends."

"On what?"

"On whether you like your coffee black, and with a possible hint of glass."

"Why don't you do anything like that in class?" I ask as I make two mugs of coffee. Black. Kate sits at the kitchen table playing with a lock of multi-coloured hair.

"How d'you mean?" she asks after a moment.

"Pretending to be someone you're not. The whole investigative reporter thing. That's improvisation – *improv.* That's what I was trying to get the three of you to do last night!" Kate shrugs.

"It's different on the phone, isn't it," she says. "You can be whoever you want when you're just a voice at the other end of the line. But when people see you in real life – well, they kind of make up their minds before you've even said a word." I sit down opposite. She takes her coffee with both hands. Hands that are sporting flawless black painted finger nails. Hands that are still wearing fingerless gloves, even in July. And I realise that I am wrong about this girl; anyone who puts this much effort into looking like they don't give a damn has plenty of potential.

"You can change that, you know," I say leaning back to observe my pupil. "You can be whoever you want to be in real life. I can teach you. If you let me. And you're willing to put some effort in." Kate says nothing, just plays with a lock of her hair.

"Don't give up on us, Will," she says eventually. "I know we're pretty crap, and I know we've been late and stuff, but Ray and Derek, they're all right. And even though we're different ages and things, it feels like we have something in common. We kinda need each other."

"Derek?" I say after a moment.

"DJ," says Kate. "Derek Jacobs."

"So, he's not an actual DJ then?" I never thought for a moment that he was. Kate shakes her head.

"He works for his dad. Car and van rentals. Don't tell him I told you."

I smile.

"So is that why you're here? To ask for a second chance?"

"I guess," she says. I smile again. And then a thought occurs to me.

"Kate – how old are you?" I ask.

"Seventeen," she says.

"Seventeen? I thought you were older."

"What difference does it make?" asks Kate.

"It matters because I should really have a consent form from your mother or father." Kate slumps back in her chair, her gaze remaining fixed on the coffee cup in front of her.

"That might be tricky," she says, "They're both dead."

"Oh! I'm ... I'm sorry to hear that."

"Don't be," she adds. "Mum died when I was very little. Cancer. Long time ago now."

"Even so. That must have been tough." Kate says nothing. "And your Dad? What happened to him?"

"Dad was an arsehole," she says matter-of-factly. "He shot himself when I was fifteen."

"Jesus! That's ... awful."

She gives a half hearted shrug, though this time there seem to be great invisible weights resting on those young shoulders.

"So who do you live with?"

"No one."

"But ... how?"

"I work in a toy shop. The pay's crap – but the owner lets me stay in a bedsit at the back." Questions are queuing up in my mind about the legality of her situation and how she seems to have fallen through the cracks in society – but she isn't on the streets, and she seems in good health, and she's taken it on herself to sign up to a drama class. If nothing else, this girl is a fighter.

"Shit happens, doesn't it," says Kate, as though reading my mind. "You just have to get on with it."

"Maybe so," I say, "but no one should have to go through what you've been through. Especially at your age."

"Happens all the time," says Kate.

"Hardly," I say, with a shake of my head.

"Maybe not *exactly* the same," says Kate, "but I'm not the first girl in the world to lose everything before she's old enough to vote." And as Kate draws invisible spirals on my kitchen table with a painted finger nail, my thoughts wander to the other ladies in my life, and how they too have suffered losses, and suddenly I want to fix it! Fix it all! But what can I do?

It's three days later when I see The Weasel again.

I've spent the entire weekend bouncing between the paranoia induced from *not* being followed, to making plans and promises in my head about how I can help Rachel and Jarad launch their new restaurants, patch things up with Zlata, and turn South London's most unlikely trio of would-be actors into theatre pros.

When Monday morning arrives I decide to take a break from my quest to find real acting work, and elect instead to drop in on my *girlfriend* – as we've now agreed she is – and surprise her with a bunch of flowers, in the hopes that it will take her mind off the fact that the merger with our Arabian friends has seemingly ground to a halt, and for no apparent reason.

Also, I'm kinda hoping that having a happy girlfriend might alleviate some of the guilt I'm experiencing about Zlata. Specifically the fact that Jarad hasn't heard from her since *that* night and I haven't the heart to tell him that I am probably the reason. But despite these 'trifles', Jarad knocks us up a superb lunch, and the three of us are in good spirits as I leave and make my way back down to the station. And then, reflected in a shop window, I see him.

I spin round and across the road, back turned to me, looking intently into a bakery in a weasel-like manner, is my stalker.

In a moment of confusion and semi panic I take my phone from my pocket, put it to my ear, wait a moment or two, then let out a loud laugh and a cheerful, "How are you?" whilst I think about what to do.

There are, in my mind, only two options: walk across the street and confront him, or see just how far he's willing to pursue me and what I can find out in the process.

I let out another laugh, wish my imaginary caller all the best, and opt for the latter course of action.

Doubling my walking speed I head off down the road, but instead of turning left for the station, I turn right and head up the hill. I don't look behind me, I don't stop along the way, I walk as determinedly as possible until I can almost see *The Crown*, at which point I cross the road, stop outside a charity shop, and make a rather grand point of assessing its exterior before walking inside.

It is, as I'd hoped, extremely busy, as these places always seem to be these days. And typically the clientele of this particular flea market are your more interesting types: students, single mums, pensioners, the thrifty, the arty, the downright weird. I grab whatever I can see that might come in handy; a dirty beige raincoat, a cloth cap, a feather boa, a walking stick, a rather sad faded suit jacket, a baseball cap, a raggedy pair of cords, a beaten up pair of gigantic brown shoes, an ancient game of *Mouse Trap*, an old shopping bag... and finally, after a heart-stopping few seconds looking for the one item I need more than any other, a powder compact! I try not to make eye contact with the grandma behind the counter and instead dart to the back of the small shop, and into one of the changing rooms. I draw the curtains behind me.

Sitting on the floor amongst my items, I open the powder case and am relieved to see that the mirror is still intact.

Carefully I position the compact on the floor so that I can see under the curtain and back into the shop – and there he is; slightly out of breath, and standing in the doorway. For a fleeting second I'm delighted at my ingenuity, and then the reality of the situation kicks in. As I'd walked up the road this had seemed like a fine plan. But now, huddled in the cupboard sized changing room of a small charity shop it's clearly utter madness. But then, what have I got to lose? Really?

It isn't me who emerges from the changing room several minutes later, but a hunched over eccentric old man in a cloth cap, overcoat, and feather boa, carrying a striped shopping bag, and under the same arm a boxed board game. In his other hand – my other hand – he grips a walking stick with which he stabs the ground in front of him as he makes his way slowly to the door, in shoes as big as flippers.

I shuffle past my tail. I even dare to growl a, "Scuse me young man," as I pass, and he doesn't even look at me. I'm already out of the shop when I finally hear the grandma yell something.

From inside Costa Coffee next door, I watch the old dear waddle into the street, and a moment or two later The Weasel. Both of them suitably perplexed, looking up and down the road for either the young man who'd entered the charity shop, or the old fella who'd left it. But neither of them are looking for someone in a baseball hat and suit jacket, which is what I'm wearing now. I wait a little longer, watch as they flap their arms in frustration, and then as the old lady goes back inside her shop, and my tail walks back down the road. I wrap my stolen items inside the raincoat, tuck it under my arm, and casually leave the coffee shop.

I keep my distance, reasoning that although I'd spotted my tail, anyone who is in the habit of tailing people probably knows how to tell if they themselves are being tailed. So I am slightly disappointed when my nemesis shows no signs whatsoever that he knows I'm behind him; he doesn't stop to look in shop windows or to tie his shoe laces, just keeps walking, past the station and left into Bennet Park. I lean nonchalantly against a parked van and use the compact again to spy on him as he gets into a car, removes the 'Doctor On Call' sign from the dashboard, and drives away. Only now do I wish I'd made a note of the registration. All I can remember is that the car is blue. And old. An old blue BMW. In Blackheath they're almost ten a penny. Clearly my detective skills need some work.

Though I'd be lying if I said that the afternoon's events hadn't been, at least on a theatrical level, quite exhilarating – as the day progresses and the adrenalin wears off, my initial excitement has once again given way to anxiety.

Weasel Man had tailed me from *Jarad's*, which means there's an excellent chance he saw Rachel and me inside the restaurant, and probably now has the 'intimate' photos he needs for his client. And whilst I am quite proud of my amazing ability to give him the slip, it has, yet again, been a completely pointless exercise! So he drives a beaten up BMW! Blue! So what!

Still, at least I know for certain that I'm being followed, and as soon as Rachel returns home I fully intend to tell her so that she can ... what exactly? Get cross with me for not telling her sooner? With Michael for assuming that her leaving couldn't have had anything to do with him? What else can she actually do with the information? Other than phone her husband and tell him to cite whoever he damn well likes in the divorce papers and just leave us the hell alone!?

"What do you think, Oscar?" Oscar lifts his head from my lap and gives me one of his looks. This one clearly says: *you're talking to me again aren't you? Talking when you should be stroking me or feeding me. I think we both know that talking's not an acceptable alternative.* I sigh.

"Fat load of help you are," I say as I tickle him behind the ear. Oscar purrs, but his affection is short lived. As soon as he hears a key in the door he launches himself from my lap to see whether the intruder might have brought something edible with her. Just over two weeks and Oscar has already decided that his new human flatmate is far nicer than the old one.

"I'm in here," I shout. There's no reply. So I get out of my chair and wander into to the hallway – and there is Rachel, crouched on the floor, rubbing Oscar's ears between her thumb and forefingers. He's almost beside himself with joy, whereas Rachel ... has been crying.

"Rachel?" I say. "What's wrong? What's happened?" She looks up at me, panda-like eyes and mascara streaks running down her cheeks.

"They've closed us down," she says with an unladylike sniff. "It's that bastard – I know it is!"

"They" turns out to be a man from Greenwich Council Environmental Health Department.

Shortly after I'd left he'd made an impromptu visit following – so he'd said – a number of complaints that his department had received about the cleanliness of *Jarad's* and the quality of the food. After a cursory inspection of the kitchens he declared that the restaurant remain closed until a fuller inspection had taken place. Typically Jarad had said very little, whilst Rachel had completely lost her temper and, in her fury, thrown a wine glass at the man.

Fortunately she'd missed – but he had threatened to report the incident to the police.

"The thing is, we only had our annual inspection the other week – and we passed with flying colours! There's no way that anyone could have made a complaint! None!"

"It does seem odd," I muse, as she paces up and down. "Can Environmental Health even do that? Close you down without any actual evidence? It doesn't seem very...well, likely."

"You're not listening to me, Will!" says Rachel. "It's Michael! I know it is! That bastard has paid someone to put the boot in!"

"But why would he do that?" I ask from my place on the sofa. She stops pacing, looks at me as though I have finally lost the plot, and then throws her hands in the air in despair.

"Because he's a complete and utter bastard!?" she cries. I look down at the carpet and shake my head in frustration – my life seems to be full of hysterical females.

"Okay," I say slowly, "that's true – but can I just remind you that he has two Arabian clients who are trying to merge with *Jarad's* in order to boost their failing coffee shop business, and your husband –"

"*Ex*-husband!"

"– has his most trusted assistant managing the deal. It doesn't make any kind of sense, business or otherwise, that he'd put the boot in!"

"It hasn't got anything to do with business, Will," says Rachel. "It's revenge!"

"For what?!"

"Leaving him!!"

"He would do that?"

"Yes!!" she says, and suddenly all I can hear are Michael's words echoing inside my head: *they can both fucking burn in hell for all I care! And if there's any truth in what my enemies say about me Edwin, I'll make sure that's exactly what'll happen.*

"No," says Rachel, her bottom landing in the armchair in front of me, "maybe you're right. Perhaps I am being paranoid. After all, there's no reason to suspect he knows about my involvement with the restaurant. He hasn't a clue where I am." And suddenly the events of the previous few days start to make much more sense.

"Crap," I say under my breath. How can I have been so bloody stupid? "Rachel," I say, "there's..."

"But if it isn't Michael," she continues, "who else would do such a thing? It's not like there's a queue of people out there hell bent on revenge! Who else would want to hurt us in this way?" The word 'revenge' bounces around inside my head until it finally connects with the only other thing that makes any kind of sense. Kind of. I get up.

"Where are you going?" says Rachel as I come back into the lounge with my jacket.

"To sort this out. Maybe."

"Wait! Will," says Rachel getting out of her seat and taking my arm, "you can't go confronting my husband! Especially at," she glances at the oversized clock on the wall, "ten thirty at night!"

"Relax. I'm not going anywhere near Michael – but there is someone else who might know something about this."

"Who?" asks Rachel. I bite my lip. It can't be Zlata – can it?

"Zlata! Open the damned door! I know you're in there; I can smell cigarette smoke wafting under the door."

"There is no smoke! I am not smoking! And there is no space under the door for it to do wafting, even if I was smoking! Which I am not!"

"Okay, but you are talking – and that's pretty compelling evidence that *you might be in there*! So open up! Now!"

"Go away William! We are not the big friends any more!"

"No, you're absolutely right! We're not! Which is why this time I won't have the slightest problem with kicking down this door! So it's your choice. You can either let me in, or I'm coming in anyway and you'll need a new lock and chain – but I'm not leaving until you've told me why someone has reported Jarad's restaurant to Environmental Health, and why they've closed him down pending an investigation!"

Five seconds later Zlata opens the door. She stands there defiantly, her eyes ablaze with rage – and a half-smoked cigarette in her hand.

"It is Michael Richmond!" she declares, to me and the two or three neighbours who have opened their doors to see what the commotion is at this time of night.

"Dear god – not you as well."

"Who else could it be?"

"Well ... *you*!?"

"Me!?"

"Yes, you! Who else in this situation is acting like the spurned lover!?"

"I am not the *spermed* lover!" said Zlata, stamping her foot for emphasis.

"Not sperm! Spurn – ... never mind!"

"I am deadly and serious! Why would I report Jarad to the environment?"

"Because you're angry?"

"Yes! I am angry! At *you* I am angry!"

"But Jarad says you haven't been answering any of his calls, and he hasn't spoken to you in over a week! That sounds like a very angry woman to me."

"Yes! At you! And I do not want the big discussion with Jarad about why I am angry at you – but I am not angry at Jarad!"

"So you haven't spoken to Jarad ... because you're angry with me?"

"Yes! So maybe now I report *you* to the environment!"

I squeeze my eyes closed for a second or two then shake my head to try to make sense of the Zlata logic at work.

Zlata shifts her weight onto her other leg and takes a drag of her cigarette. "This all made so much more sense in my head," I say eventually.

"Would you like to come in?" asks Zlata.

I sigh.

"Yes please," I say.

I'm sitting on Zlata's couch, whilst she stands in front of me, pours the tiniest dribble of lethal liquid into a tumbler, and then hands me the glass.

"Thank you," I say, the aroma assaulting my nostrils before I've even taken a sip.

"So let me see if I understand this," says Zlata, one hand perched high on her hip.

"Go ahead," I say, as I work up the courage to try my drink.

"Someone has reported *Jarad's* to government officials, who have closed down restaurant."

"Local government," I say. "And it's more likely a bribe. There's nothing to report. The place is spotless."

"And you want me to be this bad person?"

"No!" I protest. Zlata raises an eyebrow. "Well, okay, yes I did – but only because I thought that if you'd paid a 'special friend' in the council to temporarily throw a spanner in the works, well, maybe we'd be able to work it out." Zlata narrows her eyes. "More to the point though," I continue, "it wouldn't be Michael – and Rachel would have less to worry about." I tip the entire contents of the tumbler down my throat, and regret it instantly.

"It *is* Michael!" says Zlata.

"I realise that now," I rasp. "Well – it's a strong possibility."

"He is devil!" says Zlata.

"He's not the devil!"

"Of course he is! He is monster!"

"But he doesn't have anything to gain from closing down the restaurant – he might even lose two of his clients!"

"But he might get back Rachel!" says Zlata. I frown.

"How does closing down the restaurant get Rachel back?"

"Maybe it is like the big threat! 'Come back to me Rachel – or I close down your restaurant'."

"That's ridiculous!"

"Oh, but *me* closing down restaurant – that is so much more biological."

"You mean logical," I say.

"I know what I mean," she says, and raises an eyebrow again.

"Pour me another drink," I say, passing her my tumbler. "I think my life just got a whole lot more complicated."

I'd fully intended to go home. To wake Rachel and tell her everything. But instead I wake up around nine, on Zlata's couch, with a stinking hangover, and no sign of my Eastern

European friend. Not even a note. But at least we're friends again. That's something.

So I phone my apartment, and Rachel's mobile. When I get no reply at either I grab my jacket, and head to the restaurant – the only other place she could be.

It's taken most of July for the summer to get its act together, but as I emerge from Blackheath station, aside from one lone storm cloud that looks like it might toddle off and cause mischief elsewhere, the sky is blue and clear, and the temperature is beginning to soar. Which might lighten the mood were it not for my hangover and the fact I'm wearing yesterday's clothes. And then, as I walk around the corner and head for the restaurant the first car parked in Montpelier Vale is a dark blue, rusty old BMW.

And it's *the* same car.

I'm sure it is.

I kick myself for not previously making a note of the number plate – I'm not going to make that mistake again and repeat the letters in the registration over and over in my head, trying to think of famous actors or playwrights that they could stand for.

KWR, KWR, KWR...

There's no-one in the car which means, as usual, its owner is probably lurking in the shadows. Which leaves me with a simple choice: do I walk brazenly past the BMW, up the road and into *Jarad's* – as I normally would – or do I continue on, as if heading for *The Crown* or *The Hare & Billet*, but cut in through the alleyway, climb over the fence and enter the restaurant through the back?

I opt for the latter.

It's only as I pull a muscle in my groin, and tear a hole in my jacket on a protruding nail, that it occurs to me this might have been a bad idea. And once I've picked myself up from the ground, brushed off the odd piece of rotting vegetable that was in the cardboard box that failed miserably to break my fall, I realise there's no question about it. It *was* a terrible idea. A point that's underlined when I reach the back door and find it locked.

And then it starts to rain.

Heavily.

Usually this door is unlocked. Usually Zlata, or a waiter, or another member of staff, is standing where I am now, adding to the pile of fag butts at my feet, but the restaurant is closed, the staff are probably at home, and I have no idea where Zlata is.

Which is when she opens the door.

"Thank god! I thought I was going to drown out here!"

"Why are you not coming in through the front door?" asks Zlata as I push past her. She closes the door behind me and locks it again.

"Because he's back!" I say, grabbing a tea towel from a shelf to dry my hair. "And I didn't want to be seen entering the restaurant."

"Who is back?"

"The Weasel! The man I told you about last night!" I say. "The owner of the BMW! Is Rachel here? I need to tell her and Jarad everything."

"No need," says Rachel, coming into the kitchen. "I think I already know." Her face is ashen. She looks as though her world has finally fallen apart, and I wish to god I'd said something sooner.

"Rachel! There you are! Thank god. Are you okay? I'm sorry I never came home last night. But you were right about Michael –"

"I know."

"No, listen, you don't understand. For the past few days there's been this man, and he's been following me. I was going to tell you, but then –"

"It doesn't matter," she says. "Come through to the restaurant. There's someone I think you should meet."

Rachel's turned her back and is walking into the restaurant. I follow her, with Zlata in tow. "It's not Michael, is it?" But Rachel says nothing, just holds the door for me. And as we walk into the restaurant he's here, standing by the fish tank, peering in, as if at any moment he might hook one out and swallow it whole. The Weasel.

I glance over at Jarad, who's leaning against the unit with the condiments and cutlery. He looks nervous, as usual.

Weasel Man turns, and smiles. A wide, sardonic weasel-like smile that seems all the wider given that his beady, watery eyes are too close together. I already want to punch him and I don't even know what he wants.

"Mr *Clarkson*!" His voice sounds not unlike an oak table being dragged across a stone floor, and he's exaggerating my surname in a manner that suggests he knows my name *isn't* Clarkson. "So nice of you to join us." I almost expect him to bow, but instead the smile widens another inch and I find myself bunching my fists. "I wasn't expecting you to be here, but I doubt my client would mind you being privy to this conversation."

"Your client?"

"Michael," says Rachel. "Mr Boot works for Michael. He's a private detective."

"I am many things," rasps Mr Boot. "Today I'm merely a humble messenger. And please, call me Archie."

"I will do no such thing," says Rachel. "In fact I can think of plenty of other names which I plan to start using if you don't get straight to the point."

"And I'm sure they're all very colourful," says Archie. He gives a small hiccup of a laugh, and then another, and then all of a sudden he's bent over, coughing so violently that I'm convinced we're going to end up with a bloody lung on the restaurant floor. Jarad stands up and takes a step forward but Rachel puts her hand out and prevents him from going to Mr Boot's aid. Eventually the coughing stops.

"I do apologise," wheezes Archie, his smile fading as he gasps for breath, "laughing tends to bring on my asthma. Along with mould spores. And dust."

"You should have been a tax collector," says Zlata. Everyone looks at her, she just shrugs. "Tax is not a laughing matter."

"And who is this charming lady?" asks Archie.

"None of your damn business," I say before Zlata can introduce herself. The less this man, and therefore Michael, knows about the people in the room, the better. "Why don't you just cut to the chase?" Archie looks offended for a moment, and then, after checking the faces of everyone else in the room, the grin reappears.

"Fair enough," he says with a nod. "I'm here, as Mrs Richmond has already stated, representing my client."

"Michael Richmond – yes, yes, we know – what does he want?" Archie's thick wiry eyebrows climb his forehead in mock surprise.

"He wants his wife back, Mr Clarkson."

"Then he's going to be bitterly disappointed," says Rachel, the colour returning to her cheeks, along with the fire in her eyes. But I'm more confused than angry. Six days ago I'd sat in Michael's car and he'd told me himself that Rachel could burn in hell for all he cared. Yet now he wants her back? It doesn't make sense. But I decide to keep this to myself.

"I'd think carefully before you decide on a course of action, Mrs Richmond. My client has instructed me to tell you that due to the unfortunate closure of this restaurant by the local authorities, he has had no choice but to inform his clients – the joint owners of *Café Al Muteena* – that to proceed with the proposed merger between themselves and Mr LeBlanc's restaurant would be unwise, and one that he could not possibly support."

"Then to hell with it," says Rachel. "We'll find other partners, and other investors. My husband isn't the only financial big shot in this city, and he's dabbled with my life for long enough!"

"*Pi ka ti materina*!" shouts Zlata, quickly followed by a complicated arm gesture. I shoot her a look that says 'shut the hell up' in any language.

"Do I take it, Mrs Richmond, that you're able to speak on behalf of your *employer*?" There's silence in the room, as we jointly wonder the same thing – is the cat out of the bag about the fictitious Stephan LeBlanc?

"I am," says Rachel, wearing her best poker face.

"In that case I will pass on those sentiments Mrs Richmond, but I ought to tell you that your husband anticipated that this might be your initial reaction, and instructed me to inform you that this closure by the Environmental Health department, whilst nothing more than an inconvenience at the moment, could quite easily become *permanent*. It really is your choice: return home, proceed no further with your divorce, have nothing more to do with this catering venture, the mysterious Monsieur LeBlanc – or the charming Mr *Clarkson* – and your husband gives you his word that things will return to how they once were. Including this fine establishment." The room is silent again. "Alternatively, stay, and prepare to face the consequences."

"That's not much of a deal!" I say. "Either way Rachel has to leave the restaurant!" And I'm expecting Rachel to agree with me, or at the very least voice her objections. Instead she stares at the floor.

"But if I return to Michael," she says, "at least the restaurant will remain open. And this time, everyone gets to keep their jobs."

"Exactly," says Archie, with a slight bow. Nobody says anything in response. "Well," continues Archie. "I can see you have much to think about. I'll leave it with you for a day or two. Lovely to meet you all." He nods. Nods at me. Nods at Zlata – who raises her fist and takes a step forward to do god knows what; I block her with my arm. He nods at Jarad and Rachel. And then finally, he leaves, the bell on the door tinkling ironically as he closes it behind him. I want to rip it from the wall, run after him, and shove it down his weasely throat.

But instead we all stare at the floor, and when I eventually find the courage to look up at Rachel's face, and the tears running down her cheeks, I can see in her eyes that she's already decided what to do.

Scene Four

It's not such a bad deal. Jarad gets to keep his restaurant. With a little help from Zlata he'll probably be able to run it without any problems. He'll be fine. It won't ever be the culinary Jordanian empire that Rachel promised him, but Jarad won't mind really. That was more Rachel's dream.

And me – well things will carry on as before. I'll run the occasional flirting course with Zlata now that we've patched things up. And I've got my evening classes – other people are bound to join. Eventually. Maybe. Perhaps I'll get a private client or two. That'll help with the finances. And one day, if I keep plugging on, going to auditions, I'm sure to land a part in a play, or a movie. It's just a matter of time. But I'll finally get that thing I've wanted my whole damned life, and everything will be exactly how I hoped it would be.

At least that's what Rachel's telling me.

For the umpteenth time.

As she packs her bag.

And tries not to cry.

She's leaving in the morning. And when I get back from class there's going to be no more discussion – no more debate about possible alternatives. We've spent the best part of forty eight hours talking about this. But we're done now.

We're beat.

Two days ago I was full of fight. I made a list of things we could do to prevent Michael closing the restaurant. It wasn't a particularly long list. It mainly involved going to the police, or a solicitor, or Greenwich Council – but the more we phoned people or met with them, the more we discovered our only chances of survival revolved around being able to *prove* that someone at the Environmental Health department was accepting bribes to close us down – and without proof no one was willing to even entertain the notion that we were anything other than the owners of a cockroach-infested restaurant who were doing whatever we could to stay in business.

"For god's sake, Will," said Rachel as I followed her into the bedroom sometime in the small hours of Wednesday morning, "this is what Michael does! This is how he works!"

"But no one's beyond the law!" I countered. "All we need to do is prove..."

"How? How are we going to do that?" asked Rachel as she began pulling off items of clothing as though they were made of chainmail. "Even if we could find some shred of evidence to support our claims, it wouldn't make a jot of difference! You can't fight Michael with court orders, Will. Have you any idea how many times my husband has received a court summons? I used to place them in the same pile as the household bills." She slid in between the sheets and let out a long weary moan as her head finally hit the pillow. I wanted to say something, but I had nothing new. So I undressed.

"Michael doesn't respect truth or justice," she continued, her voice nothing more than a drone, her eyes still closed. "To him they're just meaningless concepts. And so long as legal processes are run by people, he'll find someone. Someone greedy. Someone flawed. And then he'll exploit that flaw. Zlata was right. He *is* the devil. Her father's greed, my greed – it's where he gets his power from."

I said nothing. Just slid in next to her, and switched off the light.

And so it continued the following day, and on into Thursday. Our talks getting ever more desperate, Rachel getting more and more frustrated with my reluctance to accept what she saw as the inevitable, and eventually, because I didn't want to argue with her any more, I remained silent and she told me how – hard though this may be – her returning to Michael was the best thing for everybody.

But it isn't, is it. How can it be? Because even though Jarad gets to keep the restaurant, she has to return to the man who's taken everything from her, and I'm about to lose the only woman I've ever wanted more even than a life in theatre.

Right now I'd do anything, trade anything, to keep her in my life.

Anything.

But I'd already played my one and only trump card yesterday evening.

It was Tanya who'd eventually opened the door after I'd spent several minutes standing in the hallway with my finger on the buzzer. She wasn't smiling. Neither was she wearing very much – which might have been the reason she wasn't smiling, except that in all the time I've known her I don't think I've ever seen her smile, so it was impossible to tell.

"It's your *boyfriend*," growled Tanya with as much venom as the word would allow. From somewhere inside Nathia's apartment I heard someone curse and then, after a moment or two, Nathia came to the door, in a towelling bath robe.

"William," hissed Nathia, "You've got a bloody nerve coming here!"

"I tried phoning," I said, "but you've been ignoring my calls!"

"You shouldn't be phoning me! Have you any idea of the shit storm that's been raining down on me this past week?!

"No," I said. "But I think I can probably guess."

"Then I suggest you turn around, delete my number from your phone, and never, ever, *ever*, come anywhere near me, again! Have I made myself clear?" I gave an impatient sigh and shifted my weight onto my other leg.

"Not really."

Tanya rolled her eyes, turned and walked back into the flat.

"I beg your pardon!" said Nathia, in that tone of voice that suggests 'death may be imminent'.

"Look I get that you're angry," I continued, "and although I'm certain it has something to do with me and the events we set in motion, I need to know the details."

"*You* need to know?"

"Yes. For instance, does it have anything to do with a weasel-looking private detective –"

"Archibald Boot? How do you know –"

"He's been following me! *Was* following me. As well as Rachel I shouldn't wonder. And probably Jarad – and anybody else connected with the restaurant."

"Following *you*?" said Nathia. "Wait a minute. So that means Michael must know about... you and Rachel?"

"Yes. He does."

"So he might also know that you're not Edwin?"

"It's a strong possibility."

"William! This is terrible!"

"Oh, it gets worse, believe me."

"I don't want to hear this, William!" said Nathia, putting both hands into her hair and beginning to pace on the spot. "This is not what I need right now!" Her selfishness knew no bounds.

"You and me both!" I said.

"Were you followed here?!" she asked.

"I don't think so. To be honest I don't think Mr Boot is particularly good at blending into the background, and I think he's probably unearthed everything his client wanted to know."

"If Michael knows I hired you to be my boyfriend –"

"There'll be 'ramifications' – I know! You've told me a hundred times! Look – can I come in?!" Nathia stopped pacing and looked at me.

"You are kidding!"

"Why would I be kidding? Clearly we're both up to our necks in it! So now would be a very good time for us to pool our resources and tell each other what we know!"

"There are no 'resources' to pool, William," said Nathia, "and if you have *anything else* to tell me, that could possibly make this situation worse, there's a very good chance I'll break both your legs and throw you down the lift shaft!" She glared at me with such intensity I swear the stubble on my chin began to singe.

I soldiered on: "Right, fine! Then can you at least spare me five minutes to tell me what *you* know so I can pass that on to Rachel, who is also up to her neck in it. Then you can break whatever you want... as long as I'm still able to make a phone call or two." Nathia huffed and puffed for a moment or two, glanced over her shoulder in the general direction of Tanya, and then tightened her robe around herself, stepped to one side, and gave me a curt sideways nod to indicate I could come in.

I sat in Nathia's kitchen, watching Nathia pace as she regaled the events that had taken place since our one-off production of 'The Meeting That Never Was', and it became clear to me that we'd overplayed our hand. Faking a meeting between Michael and the fictitious Stephan LeBlanc was one thing, having Zlata beat him up in her guise as 'surprised cleaner' was another, but Rachel walking out on her marriage – *actually* leaving Michael – *for good* – that had been a step too far.

Archibald Boot had been called in to the offices of *Steele & Richmond* the very next day, and whilst Nathia had no idea what was being discussed behind those glass doors, it seems obvious now that Michael was arranging to have Archie track down his wife.

"I still don't understand how he actually found her. She told everyone she was living in Dorset," I mused – though more to myself than Nathia. "London's a big place, you can't just bump into someone ..."

"Does it matter?" spat Nathia. "He's a detective. It's what he does! He probably found out where her phone was being used!"

"Is that even possible?" I asked. But Nathia glared at me again, and it was a moot point anyway. Clearly Archie had tracked Rachel to the restaurant, and that's when our troubles had really begun.

"I've spent the last fortnight being either ignored completely, given orders, or cross examined on at least three occasions!"

"Cross examined how?"

Nathia held up her hand and with the other, ticked questions off on her fingers.

"Do I have any contact details for Stephan LeBlanc? Why not? Do I know where his wife is staying? Has she attempted to contact me? Have I been in contact with her? And finally – and this is when I knew the shit had really hit the fan – when was the last time I saw *you*? He also demanded to know exactly where you work, where you live, and how you could be contacted."

"And what did you say?"

"What do you think I said! I told him that I didn't have details for Stephan LeBlanc. That for tax reasons the restaurant was in Jarad's name. That I hadn't seen his wife since the meeting that never happened. Or you, for that matter. That I hadn't been in contact with either of you – and that it was none of his damn business where you worked, or lived, unless he could give me a very good reason why he needed that information."

"And?"

"After several showdowns I was eventually told that the merger between *Jarad's* and *Café Al Muteena* would not be going ahead, and I was not to work on any accounts, or contact any clients, without his express permission." Nathia stomped over to the fridge, took out a half full bottle of wine, removed the stopper, got herself a glass, and filled it to the brim. She didn't offer me one. "My life is unravelling in front of my eyes, William! If I wasn't as useful to Michael as I am, I swear I'd be out on the street. I told you that Michael wasn't a man to be messed with – but mess with him you did." She took a seriously large swig of her drink. "This," she said punching out the words, "is – all – your – fault!"

"How is this my fault? And how is your life unravelling?? All you've had are a few awkward questions and oh – a bit less work to do! Meanwhile Jarad's restaurant – *his livelihood* – is closed, pending an investigation by the corrupt local environmental health department! Whilst Rachel is seriously considering returning to the 'loving arms' of her controlling husband, who will probably keep her under lock and key now that he knows she has a tendency to do more than your average trophy wife! It seems to me, *Nathia darling*, that on balance you're the only one coming out of this unscathed!"

Nathia's eyes narrowed. "Apart from you, you mean."

"Oh, I'm scathed," I said. "Just not in a way that seems to matter to anyone!"

"It's still your fault!" she spat. "You're at the centre of all of this. Who else is possibly to blame?" I squirmed. There was someone else. Someone who was *really* at the centre. Though making Zlata the focus of Nathia's rage wouldn't necessarily achieve anything.

And anyway, was it Zlata's fault? Hadn't she only been trying to right a wrong, in much the same way that Rachel had? And hadn't they both been victims of Michael's greed? If anyone *was* to blame, if there really *was* a 'centre', an eye to this storm, then wasn't it... Michael?

"Have you ever heard of *Vanadium Global*?" I asked, impressed that after two weeks I could still recall the name of the company that Michael had persuaded Zlata's father to invest in.

"Are you changing the subject?"

"Have you?"

"The name rings a bell," said Nathia. "But what's that got to do with anything?" I bit my lip for a second or two. Despite what Nathia may have thought, I've never been in the habit of betraying confidences, but perhaps given the circumstances she deserved to know the bigger story. Everything. Right from the start.

I told her about Zlata.

In the end it hadn't made the slightest bit of difference. Oh sure, Nathia had calmed down – a bit: she didn't break my legs or throw me down the lift shaft, but she did tell me that an *every-man-for-himself* strategy was her favoured option from here on, and that she didn't ever want to hear from me ever again.

I walked down rainy streets in the small hours of Thursday morning, desperately trying to think of a way out of our predicament – although actually, it would have been more accurate to say that all I really wanted was Rachel to stay in my life. To pick *me*, over everything else. To hell with the restaurant, and anything else that Michael might try and destroy to get her back – they were just *things*. Jarad could find alternative work. So could the waiters and waitresses. But I'd never find another Rachel, not if I lived a dozen lifetimes. And though Shakespeare warned otherwise, I desperately wanted a happy ending to our *Romeo and Juliet* story. We could call it *Love's Labours Won* – after the Bard's lost play. But maybe there's a reason why that particular work of literature has been mislaid. Maybe it never really existed in the first place.

"What's bugging you, bro?"

"Don't call me bro, DJ," I say as I set out two chairs, back-to-back, in front of the trio.

"But there's something though," continues DJ. "You cancelled Tuesday's class, and even though we all like made a special effort to be here on time and t'ings, you're still acting like you're mad with us." I ignore him. I'm not mad with them. I have far better things to be mad about than three wannabe actors. True; I had cancelled Tuesday's class – but so would you if you'd had the day we'd had. And the only reason I hadn't cancelled tonight's was because, despite my protests that this was, in all likelihood, our last *ever* evening together, Rachel had more or less pushed me out of the door, and promised that she'd still be there when I got home.

"Leave him alone Derek," says Kate. She's perceptive, that one.

"Right then," I say. "I thought we'd start with something a little different tonight. Still improv. In a way. DJ, come and sit on this chair. And Kate, if you'd like to sit behind him." The two do exactly as I say, and whilst I wouldn't go so far as to use the word 'enthusiastic', there's a definite absence of slinking and shuffling that normally follows requests such as this. "Now, DJ; I want you to imagine that you run the advertising section of a local newspaper."

"Why?" asks DJ.

"Because that's what I've asked you to do."

"Okay, but like – what's my motivation? Am I like an *evil* advertising executive?" I sigh.

"No. You're just a regular guy. Doing a regular job. And in a moment you're going to receive a phone call from someone you've never spoken to before, and I want you to deal with it exactly as you would, if you were that regular guy. Do you think you can handle that?" DJ screws his face up, folds his arms and crosses his legs. If there's any truth in what my mother always told me, one day he'll get stuck like that. I'm hoping it's today.

"I dunno bro," continues DJ. "Sounds a bit lame. I'd never take a job like that."

"That's why we call it *acting*, DJ."

"Okay, okay, I hear ya. But what if I was like a *super* villain? I could be hanging in my secret lair, right? And Ray – he could be like one of my henchman, yeah? An' he could pretend to have one of those dome-shaped hats, you know? With like, razor blade rims, yeah? Dat would be so –"

"Derek," says Kate, and with that DJ stops talking, faces front and looks like someone just put him on the naughty step.

"Okay," I say. "Good chat. Glad we got that sorted out. So now, Kate – you can be anybody you like."

"Okay," she says.

"But whoever you are, it's your job to convince DJ here –"

"Brian," says DJ.

"I'm sorry?"

"Brian. Dat's my name. I am Brian, the world's most dullest Advertising Executive. I'm like, winning awards for my epic dullness."

"Excellent. Brian it is," I say with a nod. "So Kate, I want you to imagine that you've seen an advertisement in last week's paper. And for reasons known only to yourself, it's your job to convince Brian to give you the name and address of the person who placed that ad, even though Brian isn't supposed to divulge that information. Do you think you can handle that?" Kate smiles. And for a glimmer of a moment, during the worst week of my life, it feels like something is going my way.

It doesn't last.

She's gone when I get home.

Well of course she is.

Just a note left on the kitchen table: *I'll always love you*, it says. And then, as if that declaration might be enough to fuel my inner Romeo, and send me galloping to her abode, to stand under her balcony and throw pebbles up at the window, she adds, *but it's better this way*. And I realise we're a long way past the balcony scene. This is the tragic end Mr Shakespeare predicted, the one I prayed would never come. The only woman I've ever loved more than theatre is gone.

I sit down at the kitchen table, and weep.

Act III

Scene One

You know what I've finally figured out about life? It's pointless. This isn't much of a revelation, I admit. Many people – most of them smarter than me – have said similar things long before I had my epiphany, and they will probably continue to say such things long after I'm gone.

Anyway. Given that there is no real purpose to our being here – that mankind is nothing more than the natural consequence of a particularly unlikely set of cosmic criteria falling into place – the only logical course of action is to find someone you particularly like, someone who likes you back, and for the two of you to hunker down on this rock we call earth and enjoy the ride.

Sure, go ahead and build stuff, write stuff, paint stuff, perform stuff... if that gives you a buzz then knock yourself out! But don't do it out of some misguided notion that you're *advancing the development of mankind*, or that it's another step on the path to enlightenment, because mankind was pretty advanced before you and I got here, and beyond knowing that life's completely and utterly pointless there is no enlightenment to be had! Most of all, don't do any of that writing, building, acting or painting shit if there's even the tiniest, remotest chance that the special someone who walked into your life suddenly doesn't realise how special they actually are. That, my friend, is idiocy of the highest degree.

"Hello?"

I look down at the phone in my hand, and then hold it to my ear again. But there's nobody there.

They've hung up.

Well, who can blame them? I'd only phoned to tell them that the Tuesday and Thursday night class is postponed until further notice – by which I'd meant *cancelled, permanently, without the slightest chance of ever being resurrected* – and then, in order to fill the deafening silence of disappointment that my announcement had been met with, I'd started on a bitter drunken rant about how the class was a pointless waste of time anyway – not just for me, but for all of us, really. Particularly Ray. And even he, being a man of very few words, had to admit that was true, surely? When he hadn't replied, I'd naturally moved onto the meaning of life.

Because that's what you do when you're drunk, heartbroken, and standing in the middle of your lounge in your dressing gown, a bottle in one hand, and a phone in the other.

But Ray – like Rachel – was gone.

I stab buttons with my forefinger, find Ray's entry in my phonebook, and delete it. Then I go to the call log and clear it.

There's a kind of clarity that you can only experience with a bottle and a half of wine inside you. Decisions that are difficult when sober become surprisingly simple when drunk. And sometimes it's necessary to take precautions whilst under the influence in order to prevent your sober self from doing something really stupid in the morning. Like changing your mind. His mind. The mind you share. Whatever.

I stagger to the bedroom, and pass out.

There really is only one person who could be hammering on my door at 7am, and the longer I lie in bed with my head under the pillow, the more I wish I'd had the forethought to paint a large red X just below the spy hole, pin up some *POLICE LINE DO NOT CROSS* tape, or erect a *BEWARE OF THE SABRETOOTH TIGER* sign. Anything, to discourage people – and by people I mean one person in particular – from trying to enter my lair of personal misery.

"Go away!" I say from my side of the door, once I've dragged myself out of bed, and found my dressing gown from the pile of assorted clothes on the floor.

"Open up William!" says Zlata.

"I don't want to talk to anyone," I say as I lean against the wall.

"I am not anyone," she says. "I am Zlata."

"Yes, and I especially don't want to talk to you!"

Zlata doesn't reply; instead she starts hammering her fists against the door again. "Stop that! Please!" I plead, covering my ears in an effort to stop the noise echoing inside my throbbing head, as I slide down the wall until I'm sitting on the floor. "Why are you knocking? I'm right here!"

"You said you did not want to do the talking, so I am instead doing the banging."

"Can't you at least come back at a decent hour?"

"It is the decent hour. Unlike you, I do not turn up in the night-time," she counters.

"It's 7am Zlata! That *is* the night-time!" But Zlata doesn't answer. Instead I hear the muffled sounds of a conversation from further down the corridor, and by the time I've struggled back to my feet there's the sound of a key in my lock. The door opens and there, also in his dressing gown and looking extremely worried, is my elderly neighbour, and behind him a triumphant Zlata.

"William!" she says pushing past my neighbour and throwing her arms around me, "you are not dead!"

"No," I say, "I am very much alive. Still."

"Your neighbour," whispers Zlata, "is very nice man. I think he likes me." She takes a step back, her hands still on my shoulders, and gives me a wink.

"Sorry to bother you Mr Fogden," I say, looking over Zlata's shoulder. "But thank you, so much, for your... concern." Mr Fogden gives me a nod of bewilderment, looks Zlata up and down, and then shuffles back to his flat. I make a mental note to change the locks and give a spare key to a *different* neighbour, one who can be trusted not to let loopy women into my apartment. "Are you going to close the door?" I ask Zlata.

"What are you doing here?" It's a stupid question, but a small, ridiculous part of me hopes that Zlata has some sort of news about Rachel. Specifically good news. Or Michael. I'll accept news about Michael too. Specifically very, very bad news. I walk through to the kitchen.

"I am the concerned friend," says Zlata as she stands in the doorway and watches me open kitchen cupboards in search of something amongst the emptiness.

"Well I'm touched," I say, "really I am. But I'm fine."

"You are not fine William," declares Zlata. "You have not been answering phone."

"That may well be the case," I say, "but I am still fine."

"Your home smells of socks," says Zlata.

"Still fine."

"And you have not left flat in five days." Finally I find what I am looking for.

"Not true," I say rinsing out a pint glass and filling the bottom third with water. "I've been to the off licence at least twice." I drop two large tablets into the glass and watch as they fizz.

"Why are you taking the pills?" asks Zlata. Sometimes her stupidness knows no bounds.

"Because I have a hangover?"

"But you do not drink."

"I drink!" I say, offended by the accusation that I might be incapable of drowning my sorrows. "... Occasionally."

"Yes," says Zlata, "but you are not very good at it."

"Well then, all the more reason for me to get some practice in – which is exactly what I intend to do, once I've got rid of you!" I tip the contents of the pint glass down my throat. Zlata shakes her head.

"This is not good plan," she says. "Instead you will have shower, put on nice clothes that do not smell, and spend the day with Zlata!"

"Doing what?"

"Exciting things!" she replies, becoming more animated. "We will visit the museum of science and press all the buttons!"

"Thrilling," I say.

"And then we will sit in park." It's sounding worse by the moment.

"Lovely."

"And we will make the better plan."

"What sort of plan?" I ask.

"The plan to get rid of Michael Richmond!"

"Oh no! Not this again!" I put the pint glass on the side and walk out of the Kitchen. "Zlata, go home ..."

"William!" says Zlata as she follows me into the lounge. "Do you not have the love for Rachel?!"

"Of course I bloody do!"

"Then you must fight!" she says, clenching a fist. "Fight to get her back! And I will help! Together we can do it!" I stand in the middle of my lounge, and look back at my idiot friend – all heels and hair and hell bent on revenge. She just doesn't get it. She's as crazy and deluded as she is passionate and determined. I glance down at Oscar, still laying on the sofa in pretty much the same spot where he's been for the last few days – somewhere he can watch the front door, even though his body language tells me that he too has given up all hope of ever seeing his mistress again.

"Zlata," I say. "Come with me." She follows me out of the lounge and round the corner to my bedroom. I walk to the other side of the bed and open a wardrobe door. "See this wardrobe?" I say.

"Of course," says Zlata.

"It's empty."

"Everything is always empty," says Zlata. "You are like the old Mother Humbug."

"Hubbard."

"I know what I mean."

"The point I'm trying to make is that five days ago they *weren't* empty. Five days ago this wardrobe was full of clothes; Rachel's clothes. Down here were her shoes. Over here; more shoes. This drawer; stuffed with all manner of exotic underwear." I walk back to my side of the bed and open the door to the ensuite. "In the bathroom; barely enough space for my toothbrush – and instead of the rank pong of old socks, there was once the sweet scent of rose perfume, and other, girly... odours."

"There is no need for pong," says Zlata. "Just open window."

"I don't care about the pong!" I say, making no attempt to hide my exasperation. "I care about Rachel! But she's gone, Zlata. She packed up her bag, and left. *Voluntarily* returned to a man she can't stand. And why? Because in all the years she's been married to Michael she *never* once found a way to 'win' – and god knows she tried! There's a restaurant in Blackheath that's currently empty, and going out of business, thanks to her last misguided efforts to get one over on her husband!

"Yes, I love her, Zlata. More than life itself. More than theatre! More than fucking anything – but this is not a fight I can ever hope to win. I am defeated before I've even begun!"

"Nonsense!" says Zlata. "We just need the right plan!" I drop my weight onto one leg.

"Zlata! How long ago did you come to this country?"

"Many years," she says.

"And in all those years of scheming, and planning, and coming up with ways to worm your way into Michael's life, and the lives of those associated with him, what exactly have you achieved? Let me summarise it for you in one word: *Nothing*!"

"It is *not* nothing!" says Zlata, stamping a foot.

"It is *precisely* nothing!" I say, raising my voice and my arms in despair. "This man can not be beat! He has eyes everywhere, knows everyone, and will not stop at anything to get what he wants! You should know that by now Zlata, because god knows everybody else does!" It's too much. I sit down on the edge of the bed, and try desperately not to let my emotions bubble over, but my eyes are already filling with tears.

"William," says Zlata, crouching in front of me and taking my hands in hers, "do not do the despairing. There is always hope."

"No, Zlata," I reply with a shake of my head, "I don't think there is."

"You just need to find it."

"I wouldn't even know where to start looking."

"I said it already," says Zlata with a smile. "In the museum of science. And then the park." I shake my head again.

"I really don't want to leave the house."

"You have to," says Zlata. "You have acting class tonight."

"Not any more," I say. Zlata frowns.

"Why you have no class?"

"Cancelled it," I say with a shrug. "Phoned my students – *all three of them* – and told them it was postponed. Until further notice."

"Then we will phone and tell them you start again!"

"Can't," I say. "I've deleted their numbers." Zlata stands up and puts her hands on her hips.

"Why would you do this thing?" she asks.

"Because the class is a complete and utter pointless waste of time! That's why!" Zlata cocks her head on one side.

"But you write numbers in book."

"In a register, yes."

"Good," she says. "Now where is register?"

"Threw it out yesterday morning with the empty wine bottles and all the other trash." Zlata walks out of the room.

"Where is phone?" she asks over her shoulder.

"What are you doing?" I whine.

"I will get back numbers!"

"You're wasting your time," I say, following the sound of her voice back into the kitchen. "I have spent five drunken evenings deleting text messages, call logs, everything and anything that might remind me of my stupid arse ambitions to pursue a career that I no longer want."

"Of course you want," says Zlata, my phone cradled in her hands. "Everybody want something, if only glass of water."

"But that was before something better came along. Someone better. With a better life. But like the cliché I am, it wasn't until I lost her that I finally realised how much better life with Rachel really was! Zlata! Are you even listening to me? I told you you're wasting your time –"

"You have new text message," she says, holding out the phone, and I can see in her eyes it's something important. I snatch the phone back, but whatever hopes I have that it might be a message from Rachel are instantly quashed when I see the number: Nathia. In four years I'd learnt many things about my previous employer but there is one characteristic that stands out amongst the rest: Nathia is never the bearer of 'good news'.

Still, the message is intriguing: *There's been a development,* it says. *Come over tonight. 10pm.*

I glance at Zlata. Six hours to sober up. I can do that. And it's hard not to let my hopes rise, just a little.

Though I'm still nursing a hangover I am at least sober when I present myself on Nathia's doorstep. Which is more than can be said for Nathia.

"Here he is!" says Nathia, as she opens the door and almost knocks me over with her alcohol-breath, "William Lewis. Destroyer of worlds!"

"Destroyer of worlds?"

"Please William, enter – and do take a good look around – a good look at the luxurious home I worked so very hard to obtain, because I have no idea how much longer I'll be able to afford this place." I slide past my bottle-wielding host, into the hallway. This isn't the greeting I was hoping for.

"You okay?" I ask.

"Peachy," replies Nathia with a nasty little smile.

"You seem a little ..."

"Drunk?"

"Just a tad," I say. Nathia snorts and staggers into her dining room, and over to the sideboard.

"I'm emptying the liquor cabinet," she says, picking up a glass that's already half full and topping it up with the contents of the bottle she's still holding. "No point in having a liquor cabinet if you've nowhere to put it. Besides I'll probably need it as firewood when I'm living on the streets."

"Right," I say, "Okay." I shove my hands deep into my pockets and rock back and forth on the balls of my feet. "And why exactly is that going to happen?"

"Haven't I told you?" slurs Nathia.

"No."

"Because I'm out of a job, William!" The words rattle around in my head.

"What?" I say eventually.

"Yes – that's right! Dear Old Lesbian Nathia is out on her ear. Fired. Redundant. Call it what you will. I've been chucked on the scrap heap of life." She picks up her glass, and in one slug creates more than enough space for a refill. I'm dumb struck. I open my mouth to say something, but no words come out. "Cat got your tongue?" asks Nathia.

"I ... that's ..."

"Not what you were expecting?" continues Nathia. "I'm intrigued William, just what exactly did you think I'd drag you all the way over here to say? Ah! Were you hoping for some news about the lovely Rachel? Of course you were! Let me guess – something along these lines perhaps: overjoyed by the return of his wife, Michael has suffered a huge myocardial infarction, leaving everything to his darling wife – *your girlfriend* – thereby giving her the opportunity to resolve everything, and for the two of you to ride off into the sunset? No such luck I'm afraid, William. No such luck."

I shuffle uncomfortably on the spot. That is, more or less, exactly what I'd been hoping for.

"Would you care for a drink?" continues Nathia. "Arsenic perhaps? Don't be offended, I was thinking of pouring a large one for myself."

"Er, not for me thanks," I mutter. "I did all my drinking last night."

"Good for you William! *Good – for – you!* You know, it occurs to me that I was probably a little hard on you on ... Wednesday was it?"

"Wednesday."

"Right, well, there was I, blaming you for turning my life into a circus when really – it's me, isn't it! It's *all me*."

"I don't follow."

"It's simple: if I'd just 'come out' all those years ago – been a proud lezzer, and to hell with what the rest of you might think – well, I'd never have met you, would I? Or Zlata! You'd have never met Michael, or Rachel. There'd have been no *Stephan LeBlanc* – none of 'this' would ever have happened. *If I'd just had the guts to be 'out'*."

I say nothing. And then, partly to fulfil my need to be doing *something* other than just standing and watching a drunken woman self destruct, I pull out a chair and sit myself at the table. As the silent moments roll by I find myself replaying the events of the previous four years in my mind – only this time with Nathia in full Gay Pride mode, and without the need for her fake boyfriend.

"Actually, I'm not entirely sure that's true," I say after the alternate years have rattled past in my head. "Zlata would *still* have befriended Rachel. Rachel would *still* be in business with Jarad. Together they'd have hatched the same hare-brained scheme to strike a deal with the Arabs. And they'd still have needed someone to play Stephan." Nathia staggers closer, puts a newly opened bottle on the table, and uses her now free hand to steady herself.

"Ah – but, lovely boy, you're forgetting one thing: you wouldn't have been able to come to *me* for help, would you? So all that drama we had three weeks ago? That would have been avoided. And besides, I wouldn't even be working for *Steele & Richmond*! There's no way Michael would ever have employed 'one of those fucking dreadful lesbian people'." She's right, of course, but I can feel myself getting more and more irritated by the conversation, and my appetite for another round of 'if only' waning considerably.

"Nathia, are you going to tell me why you're out of a job, or did you just get me here so you could wallow?"

"Oh, both!" she says. "But thank you for reminding me! Let me furnish you with all the gory details before I get back to my self pity; although later," she says, her voice dropping into a low growl whilst she puts a hand on my shoulder and leans forward until her lips are barely six inches from mine, "if you get me drunk enough, maybe you could ply me with your flirting skills. See if there's a hetero woman in me after all."

"Okay," I purr, moving forwards as much as I can without actually making contact – whilst at the same time reaching across the table to take the bottle, "–that's enough booze for you!"

"I say when it's enough!" snaps Nathia, but her drunken lunges are no match for my jaded sobriety, and I hold her back with a free hand.

"Fair enough," I say, "but why don't we take a break from the bottle for a minute or two, just until we've established exactly what sorrows you're trying to drown!" Nathia slumps into the chair opposite, and gives me a snarl before draining the contents of the glass she still has. Then she leans across the table, hooks a single sheet from the top of a neat pile of papers with a long bony finger, and slides it across to me. I pick it up.

"What's this?" I ask.

"All the companies *Vanadium Global* has had dealings with over the past twenty years. That's as far back as I could go. Give me back my drink."

"In a minute," I said with a frown. "First explain this list."

"The company that Michael claimed to own, all those years ago when he met Zlata's father? It still exists. And curiously enough, it seems to have dealings with an awful lot of *Steele & Richmond's* clients. Even *Steele & Richmond* is a client of *Vanadium Global.*"

"I don't understand," I say, my frown still in place. "So what? How is that significant?"

"I've managed to piece together some of *Vanadium Global*'s accounts from what I have access to, but they're a blizzard of transactions, back and forth, between *Vanadium Global* and the people or companies on that list. Significantly large payments – going back decades."

"I'm still not following you. That's what company accounts should look like, shouldn't they?"

Nathia sighs.

"Yes William, they should – but *Vanadium Global* doesn't *do* anything. It's a company in name only. Its registered offices are the same as *Steele & Richmond*, and yet, until you mentioned it on Wednesday evening, I had only the vaguest recollection of ever hearing its name before."

"Nathia, you're going to have to spell this out to me, because I still can't see where you're going with this. People have invested money in *Vanadium Global*? So what? Maybe it's a tax avoidance thing."

Nathia leans forward. "I thought so too at first, but the more I looked at it, the more it appears to be an elaborate Ponzi scheme." I raise my eyebrows in a *that-could-be-a-type-of-pasta-so-far-as-I-know* kinda way. "A scam!" says Nathia. "Where money from new investors is used to pay existing ones, so that the existing ones invest further still!" I frown again. "It's a kind of corporate robbing-Peter-to-pay-Paul. Fraud, William! It's fraud!"

"Fraud?" Nathia reaches across the table, grabs the remaining sheets of paper and starts laying them out in front of me. Meaningless tables of numbers with company names next to them. Meaningless that is, to the likes of me.

"Even doing the basic amount of digging that I have," continues Nathia, "coupled with what you told me about Michael's activities in the past, there are grounds here for a full criminal investigation."

"For fraud?"

"And possible money laundering. Not to mention a host of other financial irregularities. Now give me back my drink!" It still doesn't make sense.

"But if you've uncovered this in less than a week how comes no one's blown the whistle on him in twenty years?"

"Because, William, contrary to what you might have heard, there *aren't* small armies of fraud investigators trawling through company returns, looking for things to investigate."

"But aren't accounts supposed to be audited?"

"Auditors," says Nathia, in a tone of voice that suggests her next few words are ones she's uttered many times, "are only responsible for ensuring that a company's financial statements show a true and fair record of the company's financial position. It is not their responsibility to detect fraud!"

"It isn't?"

"No!"

"Then whose job is it?"

"Depending on the industry you're talking about it's either 'everybody's' or 'nobody's'. There are a few checks and balances in place, the odd legal requirement for people to flag anything that seems suspicious, but those clients who've invested in *Vanadium Global* aren't exactly squeaky clean. They're unlikely to want their own dealings to come under too much scrutiny. Which means that if this gets out, there could be dire consequences for some very wealthy people." I looked at the list again.

"So all of these people, are in some way, crooked?"

"Oh, like you're so perfect!" snaps Nathia. "Mr *Stephan LeBlanc,* Mr *Flirt Coach...*"

"I might make a living deceiving people, but no one's getting shafted!" I retort. "Unlike anyone who has to deal with ... these ..." I scratch around inside my head for the right word, "idiots!"

"*Idiots* is the one thing they're not, William! Did you know they've done studies into honesty amongst children? Those little darlings who are prone to playing fast and loose with the truth always test as more intelligent than the honest kids – and that is a list of some of the smartest people in the land!"

"It's a wonder they can sleep at night," I muse. "How do they ever learn to trust anyone?"

"They don't!" scoff Nathia.

"No?"

"Most of my clients wouldn't recognise the truth if it came with a certificate of authenticity from the Pope himself! That goes double for Michael." The word 'truth' flashes inside my head like a motorway information sign on the fritz, and despite Nathia's black mood it feels as if the universe might be trying to throw me and Rachel a lifeline.

"How dire?" I ask.

"What?"

"You said there could be dire consequences if this gets out."

"Well, it's hard to say without being able to see the full financial picture, but in all likelihood we're looking at the end of *Richmond & Steele,* and a possible prison sentence for Michael."

"Jesus!" I say.

"Basically, William, this has cost me my job, and the job of everyone who works for that bastard. *Now* – can I have my drink back *please*?"

I hand her back the bottle, and watch as more booze glugs into her tumbler. "Hang on," I say, a thought occurring to me, "so you *haven't* lost your job?"

"As good as. It's only a matter of time."

"But you just told me that there's effectively no one else looking into this. Didn't you? I mean, right now, we're the only people – other than those perpetrating the fraud – that actually *know*."

"You really don't listen to anything I say, do you!" snaps Nathia after she's quenched her thirst.

"I heard every word!" I say irritably. "Which part did I supposedly miss!?"

"That I'm legally bound to report it, *dumb arse*!"

"Why?"

"Because it's the law!"

"Yes, but, if you do that..." I stall. I actually haven't any idea what would happen next.

"Investigators will swarm into *Steele & Richmond,* freeze the company's assets, and we'll all be out of a job within a matter of weeks, possibly days."

"Okay," I say. "So ... don't. Don't tell them!" Nathia looks at me in utter bewilderment.

"It's the law, William. I have to!"

"No you don't! Well, okay, yes you do ... but still, no you don't!" Nathia shakes her head.

"Even if it wasn't the law, William," says Nathia, "it's still the right thing to do." Her shoulders slump. "It seems to me that Michael Richmond hasn't exactly enriched the lives of those he's come into contact with. I think perhaps it's time he was stopped, and that those who want to should finally get the opportunity to put the past behind them, and live the life they've always wanted."

I feel a lump in my throat. She isn't talking about Zlata, or even Rachel, but herself. And in my head I can hear the sounds of metallic prison doors echoing as I imagine Michael being carted away in chains. His business empire will come crashing to the ground. Zlata will finally get her wish. And Rachel will be beyond his grasp.

At least until they let him out.

Which could be how long? How long is a typical stretch behind bars if you've spent your life defrauding everyone around you? Five years? Ten?

I feel a shiver run through me as I realise it will never be long enough.

Michael will be right back where he started within months of being released – and that's assuming he doesn't have a fancy lawyer to keep him from going to prison in the first place, which seems far more likely. Another Weasel-like associate to pay off the authorities or make sure someone else takes the fall. Sure, an investigation from the fraud squad would be inconvenient, and potentially devastating to lots of people – Nathia might indeed lose her job – but my gut instincts tell me Michael would *still* come out on top. We'll never be rid of him. Not now. Not ever.

"...And are you even listening to me?" asks Nathia. "William?!"

"Yes! Er, No. I was thinking."

"Oh dear god, please don't do that again."

"Nathia," I say leaning forwards, "I couldn't persuade you to hold off – reporting the fraud I mean – just for a few days. Could I?"

"No," says Nathia. And then: "Why?"

"Because I have an idea."

Nathia slaps her hands over her ears. "No, no, no, no –"

"Nathia, listen – I need you to trust me –"

"Trust you?!"

"Yes. Trust me! Have I ever let you down before?"

"Really?" spits Nathia. "You really want to go there?"

"Oh come off it, Nathia!" I say, getting out of my seat and taking to my imaginary stage. "Four long years I played the part of your doting boyfriend and in that time did anyone, ever, suspect that I was anything other than who I appeared to be?" Nathia's mouth moves from left to right and back again whilst she considers this.

"No," she says eventually.

"Right! And everything that's happened to us in the past few months has been as a direct result of *other* people trying to straighten out the past, or get their revenge. But I'm not interested in any of that. I only want to sort out the present. And the future. And I think I can. Well, some of it. Not all of it. Probably not your job to be honest, but... well maybe..."

"Get to the point, William," said Nathia crossing her arms, "before I throw you off the balcony."

"Does Michael still want to meet Stephan?"

"Possibly. Why?"

"Probably best you don't know."

"William!"

"No, Nathia – maybe you're right: maybe I have been toxic. To your life, I mean. Not intentionally, but maybe hiring me wasn't one of your better ideas. I think perhaps it's time you were more honest with the world about who you are. So the less you know about anything I do from here on – well, the less you'll have to lie about if it all goes pear-shaped. Just do me this one favour," I continue, "hold off on reporting the fraud for a day or so. At least until after the weekend. And maybe the Monday. But, in the meantime, find out if Michael still wants to meet Stephan, and if he does I'll let you know where and when." Nathia's eyes narrow.

"That's at least two favours," she says.

"Okay," I admit. "Two favours. Two small favours – and then that's it. I promise. You'll never have to see or hear from me ever again."

Zlata says nothing. She stands there, with her weight on one leg. And whilst the off the shoulder t-shirt, boxer shorts, and wild unkempt hair suggest that I might have got her out of bed, the half-smoked cigarette in her hand tells me that she didn't exactly rush to answer the door.

She blows a cloud of smoke in my face, and then watches as I waft it away irritably.

"This is becoming habit," says Zlata. "You are like my 'midnight caller'."

"I know." I say. "I'm sorry." Zlata takes a long drag on her cigarette.

"Are you here for the hot sex?" she asks eventually. I sigh.

"No."

"Then why?"

"Zlata, I think we can make Michael go away. For good."

"Really?" she says after another long pause.

"Really," I reply. "But we might need to enlist some help."

"Are you sure you want to park here?" I ask Zlata, looking over my shoulder at the traffic swerving to avoid us.

"I am not parking," says Zlata. "I am pausing. You will get out, I will drive round and round." I peer out of the passenger window at the shop we've screeched to a halt in front of. To a casual passerby it looks as if it might be a junk store, or perhaps a charity shop. Only the dirty, fading sign above the entrance, gives any real indication of the 'delights' that await patrons.

"Actually Zlata, you might as well go home. This is the last shop in the book. I can find my own way back."

"What do you mean last?" asks Zlata.

"I mean this is it," I say, pointing at the listing in the directory on my lap. "We've visited every toy shop in the area."

"But maybe there are the shops that sell toys and also the other things?" she suggests.

"She said 'toy shop'. That's pretty specific. If she's not here ... well, I don't know what we'll do."

"Then this must be the place!" declares Zlata. "You will go inside, and I will drive round in the circles."

Outside there was still a semblance of hope that *Marbles & Marshmallows* might be a cornucopia of childhood delights, hiding behind a shabby exterior. But as I open the door, hear the angry buzz of what passes for a door chime, catch a nasty whiff of acrid stale tobacco smoke, and peer into the gloom through a haze of dust, those hopes gasp their last, shrivel up, and die.

This isn't a toy shop. It's a mausoleum. The final resting place for the innocence of youth. But for the first time since I've known her, Kate – dressed in black from head to toe and looking sombre as ever – doesn't look the slightest bit out of place.

"Can I help you?" she asks as I approach the counter. This isn't the reaction I'm expecting, and for a fleeting second I wonder whether there could possibly be another gum-chewing seventeen-year-old goth girl, living and working in a ropey South London toy shop. I open my mouth to reply, but close it again under the intensity of her stare. She gives me a very slight, sharp sideways nod, and I turn my head, slowly, in the direction she's indicated. Sitting at the other end of the counter, which runs the entire length of the shop, is a wiry wisp of a man who I'd completely missed when I came in. Skinny to the point of looking under-nourished, his threadbare cotton shirt hangs from his shoulders like it's still on a wire coat hanger. Greasy hair, yellowish pitted skin, tobacco stains on his fingers – this is not the sort of person you'd expect, or perhaps want, to find working in a toy store. Not even one as run down and off the beaten track as this. He looks up from his magazine and I give him a warm, cheerful smile. He doesn't smile back.

"I'm looking for a gift," I say, turning my attention back to Kate.

"Who for?" asks Kate after some more intense eye contact.

"My niece."

"Is it her birthday?"

"No. It's... kind of an apology gift," I say. "I haven't been the most attentive of uncles recently. You know how it is. I've been caught up in my own nonsense." Kate says nothing.

"I was hoping to get her something that would enable us to ... connect. Again."

"I see," says Kate, after some gum chewing.

"She's quite creative," I suggest.

"Really," says Kate with a slight nod. Then she walks to the far end of the counter, lifts the hinged end section, and crosses to the other side of the shop. I follow her, aware that her colleague is watching our every move. "These are quite popular," says Kate, taking what appears to be a brightly coloured plastic picture frame from a shelf. "You can draw on it with any object," she says, and uses her finger nail to write on the matt grey surface. She hands it to me. The words *RING ME!* are scrawled in large letters. "And then you just slide this across to clear it."

"Ah yes," I say, "I used to have something very similar when I was a kid." I erase her message and write one of my own: *LOST NUMBER*. Kate rolls her eyes, before shaking her head.

"How about something more *permanent*," she says, erasing the board and putting it back on the shelf. "We've got drawing pads, colouring books, crayons ..." She walks further into the shop, behind a shelf, and out of view of her colleague.

"What a good idea," I say.

"This one is only a couple of quid," she continues as she pulls a colouring book from a shelf, and scribbles her number on the inside cover in bright pink crayon. She slaps the book against my chest and glares at me.

"I'll take it," I say.

"Good!" replies Kate with decisive nod. "Glad I could help." She goes to move around me but I step sideways into her path.

"She is a bit of a loner though," I say. "I worry about that. Sometimes."

"Really."

"She used to have a couple of older friends," I continue, "who she saw once or twice a week. They seemed to get along really well. I was thinking of inviting them all over. On Thursday. A bit like a reunion."

"I'm sure she'd like that very much," says Kate.

"Yes. I thought so. I suppose I just need to give them a call. Their parents I mean. If I can find the numbers." Kate rolls her eyes again.

"Can't you just pop round their house!?"

"That's a good idea," I say, nodding, "although, I'm not entirely sure where ..." Kate's expression could crack glass. She snatches back the pad, scribbles something else in the back of the book and then holds it out for me to take.

"Was there anything else I could help you with?" she asks with a sardonic smile.

"Well?" asks Zlata as I get back in the car. "It was right shop?"

"Yes," I reply.

Zlata's smugness fills up the interior as she goes through her usual ritual of torturing the starter motor and revving the engine.

"That was an odd experience," I muse.

"You are actor. She is actor. Of course it is odd."

"No, I mean ... I think she might be in trouble."

"What sort of trouble?"

"I'm not sure."

Zlata puts both hands on the steering wheel, and turns to face me.

"Did she tell you about other two?" she asks. I open the colouring book.

"We appear to have a work address for DJ, and I think this is the name of Ray's nightclub." Zlata glances at the book.

"I know it," she says, and with that the car leaps forward and joins the traffic.

The offices of *Jacobs & Son Car & Van Rental* are moderately impressive compared to those of your usual, independent vehicle hire company. Where one might usually expect to find a prefab porta-cabin there's a small brick building. Where another company might surround their parking lot with a wire fence, there's a proper wall. And where most 'reception areas' would be nothing more than half a dozen ancient plastic chairs in front of your basic painted woodchip counter – all set amongst an explosion of paperwork and charts and notices and clipboards – there are two very nice sofas, a coffee table, a variety of magazines, paintings on the wall, several exotic potted plants (all leafy, green and cared for) – and an impressive beach wood desk. Behind which is DJ.

And he's letting the side down.

He stares at a computer screen, his brow furrowed, his bottom lip curled like a six year old who's been grounded for the rest of his life. Occasionally he tugs at his sweater, which appears to be several sizes too small, but has the company name embroidered on it. On his right breast he wears a metal badge with his name. His real name: Derek Jacobs. I smile.

I stand in the doorway for a second or two more, just to see if DJ will notice me, then I walk into reception and take the seat opposite. He drags his eyes from the computer screen to look at me, and when his brain finally registers who's sitting in front of him, his eyes widen such that it's a wonder his eyeballs don't pop out of their sockets.

"Bro!" says DJ. "What you doin' here?"

"Looking for you, DJ," I say.

"Sssh! Keep yo' voice down bro. The boss doesn't know about the DJ thing. I like to keep all my moonlighting on the down low, you get me?" I glance at his badge.

"Derek?" I ask.

"What? No! That's not my name, yeah!" says DJ with a tut and a toss of his head. "It's like my especially dull 'car-hire persona', yeah?"

"'Car hire persona'?"

"Yeah, well, you can't be like, interesting or nuttin' in this business. You gotta be like ... *bland*, yeah? Customer's expect it."

"Ah," I say with a nod. "You're talking about 'bland awareness'!"

"Exactly bro! Bland awareness. That's it exactly!"

"Derek?" comes a female voice from the room behind DJ. "Are you talking to yourself again?" DJ's eyes widen again.

"Just dealing with a customer. Everything's cool. No need to interfere. Leave it with me." DJ leans forward and lowers his voice to a hiss. "Bro, why didn't you just like call me, yeah? The boss don't like it when my friends come round."

"Derek?" comes the voice again.

"Er, why don't we step outside and see what we've got available, Mr Customer, Sir," says DJ standing up, and making a move for the door, both arms flailing in desperate, silent, beckoning gestures. I slowly ease myself out of the chair and stroll after him.

"Derek!?" The voice is becoming irritated.

"Back in a minute, er, boss," says DJ putting a hand on my shoulder and all but pushing me outside. "Just showing the customer some wheels." We step into the lot.

"I thought you worked for your dad?" I say once we are out of earshot.

"What?" says DJ. "Who told you that?"

"Kate," I answer, with a shrug.

"Right. Yeah well, I do. Sorta. This was his business."

"Was?"

DJ shuffles on the spot and looks at his shoes.

"He kinda left. When I was little."

"Oh. I'm sorry to hear that," I say. And suddenly a small part of DJ makes more sense.

"No worries," says DJ, accompanied by more shuffling.

"So, that was...your mum?" I ask. DJ raises his head to look at me, but something over my shoulder catches his attention, and those eyes widen again.

"Whoa! Who's that bro?" I turn to follow DJ's gaze and am genuinely surprised when I realise he's referring to Zlata, who is still sitting on the bonnet of her mini just outside the entrance to the lot. She raises a hand and waves. "Is that like yo' woman?" asks DJ.

"Er, no," I say with a shake of my head.

"But she's fine looking bro!"

"I'll tell her you said that."

"Maybe you could introduce me, yeah?"

"Maybe."

"Wait, wait," says DJ, grabbing my arms and moving me slightly to one side so that he's hidden from Zlata's line of sight. "Not right this minute bro! Not when I'm like this. I mean, you know, I want her to see me as, I, er, as I normally am. You get me?" I raise an eyebrow.

"I get you," I say. Then a thought occurs to me. "Tell you what, DJ, I'll bring her along to class tomorrow night."

"Wait – so the class is back on again?"

"It is."

"That's excellent news bro."

"I'm very glad you think so."

"So wait – what should I wear?"

I frown. "Wear?"

"Yeah, like – you know – is there anything she particularly likes?" asks DJ. I roll my eyes.

"Just be yourself," I say with a sigh.

"Er, right," says DJ, as if I've asked him to do the hardest thing imaginable. "Okay. Yeah. Meself. I can do that."

"Derek!" The female voice rings out across the lot and behind DJ, in the entrance to the office, with her hands on her hips, is a large black woman in a bright purple trouser suit.

"Oh shit, you better go bro," says Derek, his arms losing the will to do anything other than hang from his shoulders. "Catch ya laters, yeah?" But it's too late, she's stomping in our direction.

"Derek! What have I told you about leaving the reception unmanned?" DJ goes back to shuffling.

"Sorry, er, boss."

"And don't call me that. Now get back inside whilst I help this gentleman." She turns to face me, and in an instant switches on a Sunday School smile.

"That's okay," I say. "I was just leaving."

"Nothing here that caught your interest?" she says, the smile never faltering. "We have three cars coming back later today..."

"I actually just needed a quick word with ... Derek. I hope that was okay?" Suddenly the smile is gone.

"He's not in any trouble or anything?" she asks.

"No! No, of course not. I was merely telling him that class is back on tomorrow night."

"Class?" she says. Out of the corner of my eye I can see DJ staring upwards, presumably in the hopes that something heavy might drop out of the sky and end his misery.

"Er, yes."

"You mean this acting class thing he's been attending?"

"The very one."

The woman takes a deep breath and puffs out her already sizeable chest.

"An' would you be the teacher?" she asks, as though the 'wrong' answer could result in instant death.

"I am indeed," I say.

"So you're the one who's been filling my Derek with these ... crazy ideas!"

"Which particular ideas are we talking about?"

"About working in movies? Being a director? South London's answer to Steven Spielberg?!"

"Steven Spielberg!" I repeat, my eyebrows climbing high on my forehead. "I see. You're right, those ideas really are quite insane."

"Well, that's what I said! Nothing more than pipe dreams!" I steal a glance at DJ. A small fatherless boy trapped inside the body of a gangly young man, trying desperately to become, at the very least, the sum of his parts. And in a fraction of a second I realise that even if we don't appear to have much in common, I've been where he is; yearning for a life where I'd be better suited, where I could be myself, where I could be accepted.

"I can see why you'd think that," I say, turning my attention back to DJ's mum. "But actually, I like to think that what we study at class is a little more ... *fundamental.*"

"Fundamental?" she says, crossing her arms. "Uh huh?"

"Sure, I teach acting skills – but I think that what we *learn* are *life* skills." DJ's mum raises an eyebrow. "When you become an actor," I continue, "you're forced to develop your poise, your confidence. You become more aware of yourself and your environment. Acting hones your ability to improvise and think on your feet, to deal with difficult situations, to communicate more effectively. And of course, that just leads to better relationships – better interpersonal skills." I move closer to DJ and put an arm around his shoulder. "What I'm helping Derek to discover will give him not just the potential to go after those 'crazy' dreams, but also the less crazy dreams. Whatever ambitions he has, I'm hoping that I can help Derek become a better person, a more effective salesman, a dependable office manager, and a more attentive son." I give DJ a squeeze, and a chummy punch in the arm. He looks at me as though I've completely lost it, but I smile back, and then turn the smile on his mother.

"Really?" she says. "Acting can do all that?"

"Absolutely."

"I never knew that," she says.

"Not many people do."

She starts to chuckle. "Well I like the sound of that, I must say!"

"What mother wouldn't?" I ask, my smile getting ever broader. "Or employer, come to that?" DJ's mum chuckles some more.

"Derek," says DJ's mum poking him in the chest with a stubby ringed finger, "why didn't you tell me that your teacher was such a nice man?"

"I ..." says DJ, before running out of words.

"I'm just telling it how it is, Mrs Jacobs," I says.

"When's the next class?" she asks.

"Tomorrow evening. Seven pm."

"I'll make sure he's there on time!" she replies.

"I'd appreciate that. It really is a pleasure to have him in my class. We'd miss him if he wasn't there."

"Well, it's been lovely to meet you, Mr…"

"Lewis," I say, extending my hand and shaking hers warmly, "William Lewis, but please, call me Will, all my friends do."

"Well okay," she says. "But only if you call me Claudette!"

"Claudette. Lovely to meet you."

"You too," she says, and walks back inside. I wait until she's out of earshot and then look at DJ.

"Bro," he says, "I *really* need to know how to do that."

"Is it me or does Ray look like he's being bullied?" I ask Zlata, whose attention is elsewhere. She tears her eyes away from the dessert trolley and looks out of the window, and across the road.

"Which one is Ray?" she asks eventually.

"The big guy."

"They are both the *big* guys," she says with slightly too much emphasis on the word 'big'.

"The one that's roughly the same size and shape as your car," I reply. Zlata frowns. "If you stood it on one end!" Her mouth moves from one side to the other. "The one who looks like he might scream and jump on the nearest chair if you dropped a toy mouse at his feet! The one who keeps getting told off by the other fella!"

"Ah," said Zlata. "Yes. He is…what is word? Timid." We watch as Ray sheepishly takes a piece of card from a woman in an extremely short dress, juggles it for a second or two, before dropping it on the ground in front of her. Then, whilst he tries to bend over without ripping a hole in his trousers, his colleague comes over, slaps Ray around the back of the head, retrieves the card, slaps Ray again, and then points at a corner where he wants Ray to stand. I sigh, and sit back in my chair.

"He's more than just timid," I say. "I mean honestly, he could take on a locomotive and win, and yet by the way he's moving, the way he holds himself you'd think he was scared of his own shadow."

"He is like lion," declares Zlata. I look at her.

"He is *not* even remotely like a lion!"

"Yes!" says Zlata. "Like in old movie. With metal man, and man of straw, and small dog, and flying house, and evil monkeys."

"You mean *The Wizard of Oz*!" I say, the penny dropping. Zlata rolls her eyes.

"I know what I mean," she says, and goes back to eyeing up the dessert trolley.

"You're right!" I say.

"Of course I am right."

"He *is* like the lion." And suddenly I understand why Ray came to the class in the first place. "*Everybody wants something*," I say, "*even if it's just a glass of water.*"

"Wise words," said Zlata.

"Right," I say, getting out of my chair and dropping some money on the table. "Come on."

"What about cake?" asks Zlata.

"No time for cake."

"You go," says Zlata. "I stay and have cake."

"No," I continue. "I need your help."

"Of course! Always you need help. But why this time?"

"I need you to distract Ray's colleague," I say. "Whilst I persuade Ray to come back to the class."

"And you do this how?" asks Zlata as I put my jacket back on.

"I'm going to offer our lion the one thing he wants most of all."

Three disgruntled faces stare back at me from across the room. "So. Nice to see you all again," I say, but get no response. I try smiling, but that doesn't work either. "Sorry about cancelling Tuesday," I continue. The three disgruntled faces morph into one disgruntled face sandwiched between two less-disgruntled-but-still-somewhat-bemused faces – but in general arms are still folded, legs are still crossed, and lips are most definitely pursed.

"You didn't cancel Tuesday," says Kate. "You cancelled the whole class. Forever."

"Well, actually, I postponed it until further –"

"None of us believed that," says Kate. Zlata, who's sitting next to me, shuffles in her seat by way of a comment.

"Right. Well. I'm sorry about that. You see I had some ... was having some ..."

"You cancelled the previous Tuesday too!" adds DJ.

"Yes, yes I know. I realise I haven't been ... I mean I know I haven't –"

"It's okay," says Kate. "We get that there's stuff going on in your life." I blink.

"You do?"

"Sure. That's what life's like isn't it."

"Right. Yeah. That's what life's like," echoes DJ.

"But maybe you should just *talk* to us?" continues Kate, "rather than cancelling the class and deleting all our numbers from your phone!" I can feel the weight of Zlata's stare against the side of my face. I take a deep breath and let it out slowly.

"Right. Yes. Okay. You're right. I apologise."

"Apology accepted," says Kate.

"Anyway – we're back!" I say with some half hearted jazz hands, but the mood in the room doesn't change. I run a hand through my hair.

I can't say I blame them for being annoyed. How long have we been meeting? Two and a half weeks? Something like that. And in that time I have indeed cut one lesson short, cancelled another, and postponed the class indefinitely. Plus, I've been generally unpleasant to be around due to the belly full of resentments slowly eating away at the lining of my stomach. But those resentments are gone now, replaced instead with a burning desire to get Rachel back.

And I can't do that without their help.

Not that any of them know this, of course. And after the way I've been behaving I can't think of a single reason why any of them would be willing to step forward in my hour of need.

I'm hoping they might do it 'for the challenge'.

Or perhaps money.

"I have a proposal," I say. "For the three of you. Some work," I add. "Paid work. Actual *paid* acting work. If you're interested." Three very different people simultaneously raise their eyebrows in a mixture of curiosity and suspicion, combined with some exchanged sideways glances.

"We're listening bro," says DJ.

"First I'd like to introduce Zlata, my, er, agent –"

"Hello," says Zlata. "Please to meet you."

"Zlata has been approached by a client with a somewhat unusual request."

"Very, very unusual," says Zlata, her smile never faltering. I turn to look at my agent.

"Would you mind if I did this bit? It's just..."

"No, no. Please. Go ahead."

"Thank you," I say with a nod, and return to addressing the class. "So, the client in question is a wealthy gentleman, probably in his mid to late fifties – that's about right isn't it?"

"Very old," says Zlata. My eyes narrow.

"Fifty isn't really that old."

She shrugs.

"Anyway, evidentially he works in corporate finance, which I'm guessing must be quite dull –"

"Oh! It is! The dullest of all jobs. Worse even than cleaner."

"Right, yes – so, anyway, Mr Corporate Finance has asked Zlata if she knows of anyone who can create a kind of immersive, interactive, theatrical experience –"

"Something exciting!"

"In which he can live out his fantasies as a –"

"Bastard!"

"I was going to use the word 'villain'."

"That also is good word."

"Yo' kidding man!" says DJ, becoming more animated than he's been since he arrived. "You mean like a play? But in real life!?"

"Er, yes. That's exactly what we mean."

"That's wicked bad man! Like so cool! It's like that film with that famous actor dude. You know it? The dude that married the fit Welsh one?"

"You mean Michael Douglas?"

"That's 'im. Except, well, that the film was kinda lame. But still, it was a well-excellent concept."

"'Well-excellent'? Interesting phrase ..."

"I'm telling you bro – if I was some rich dude with a well-boring financial job, I'd definitely be paying for immersive interactive theatrical experiences – like all the time yeah? But in mine though, I'd be like a super wealthy drug lord! And there'd be some well-fit hunnies just lyin' around my swimming pool, completely nekkid yeah? And I'd be –"

"Okay, thanks for sharing DJ."

"No, but there's a twist, you see –"

"Derek," says Kate, and DJ stops talking.

"So, as I was saying; this would be a paid job."

"How much?" asks Kate.

"Does it matter?"

"I'm just interested," she says.

"Will the fee affect your likelihood of taking on the challenge?" I ask.

"No," admits Kate.

"Then let's talk about that later," I say. "In the meantime I've promised Zlata that I will audition the three of you –"

"Wait, wait!" said DJ. "Audition?!"

"Of course," I reply. "This is theatre, and Zlata needs to see you in action." The three exchange looks again. "But before that," I say, "we are going to need one or two props. Does anyone know where we can borrow a van?"

One phone call later and DJ had arranged to borrow a suitable vehicle from his mother, albeit on the strict understanding that no-one other than DJ was to drive it – which suited me just fine. The hard part had been persuading DJ that I simply wanted him to play the part of a parcel delivery courier. Not an *evil* parcel delivery courier. Not a drugs mule. Not even an undercover spy or an FBI agent – just a regular parcel delivery guy, armed with nothing more than a clipboard and pen.

However, by the following afternoon, once we were sitting in the van – me in the back on a pile of cushions, and Kate in the passenger seat – DJ had warmed to the role considerably, though it probably helped that I told him that Kate would be playing, amongst other things, the part of his 'girlfriend who'd come along for the ride'.

"Right here's fine," I say, as we pull up outside the address Zlata had given me in Seymour Street, just round the corner from Marble Arch.

"We can't park here bro – it's 'permit holders only'."

"You're going to be ten minutes DJ, max." I hand him the two parcels that have been in the back with me. "Make sure she signs for it. Nobody else. Check the signature."

"Yeah, yeah, whatever bro," says DJ, taking the clipboard from Kate, "you told me like a million times!"

We watch as DJ crosses the road and walks up to a particularly austere black door. He checks the names written on the intercom beside it, presses a button, leans forward to say something, and moments later is giving the door a shove, and going inside. It closes behind him and there is nothing more to do now but wait. Kate breaks the silence.

"This is a very strange audition," she says.

"Well, it's not your everyday acting job," I counter.

"So who lives here again?" she asks.

"A friend of mine," I say. "And Zlata's," I add.

"And she knows she's part of the audition?" asks Kate.

"Well, of course she does."

"I see," she says. But something in the tone of her voice suggests that she doesn't believe me. I dig out my phone from my pocket and hold it out for her to take.

"There's a man in a car on the other side of the street who seems very interested in us," she says.

I glance across the street and sure enough there is Archie sitting in his clapped out BMW, looking in our direction. I tug my baseball cap down over my eyes a little more, and slide down amongst the cushions, my hand with the phone still out-stretched.

"It's the same car that's sometimes parked outside the pub we meet in," continues Kate.

"Probably just looks the same," I say. "Do you want to take this?" I wave the phone about a little.

"No, it's definitely the same car. I know because I remember thinking that registration plate ends in everyone's initials but Derek's: KWR."

"I reckon she'll be ringing any moment now," I say, failing miserably to keep the tension out of my voice. Kate turns, takes the phone from me and cradles it in her hands. "You okay?" I ask as I hunch behind the front seats.

"I don't like being lied to, Will," says Kate. "My dad used to tell me he loved me. I always knew when it wasn't true."

"Right," I say, guilt washing over me. I have no idea what to say to that. And besides, any moment –

The phone rings. Kate presses the answer button and holds it to her ear.

"Mrs Richmond?" she asks in a voice so polished it wouldn't sound out of place at a garden party. "My name is Kate. I work for Monsieur Stephan LeBlanc with whom I believe you are acquainted?" There's a pause while Kate listens to the other side of the conversation. I reposition myself so I can see as much of Kate as possible, but her face is expressionless. "I understand that, Mrs Richmond," she continues, "but Monsieur LeBlanc is quite anxious to meet you on a matter of some importance. He suggests this evening at 7pm?" I bite my lip nervously. Kate shoots me a look. "He's aware of that, Mrs Richmond – but he's asked me to assure you that the venue he has in mind won't be allowed to permit anyone who isn't on the guest list. There should be a printed invitation in the box with this phone – do you have it?"

While Kate listens to whatever is being said, I peer over the front seat and watch as DJ comes out of the building, still holding one parcel and his clipboard. He looks up and down the road, then wanders off down the street, checking door numbers as he goes – just as we'd rehearsed.

"Monsieur LeBlanc suggests you take a taxi to the venue, and please make yourself known to the larger of the two gentlemen on the door when you arrive," continues Kate. "Now – I have just one last favour to ask you; if you could place this phone, and all the packaging, in the bin liner provided, and place it outside your front door – just behind the potted plant? We would be extremely grateful. Yes – thank you, Mrs Richmond. No, I do understand. Thank you again. Goodbye." She hangs up, and hands the phone back to me.

"Very good," I say, my heart beating like a rabbit, though slightly slower than before. "I'm very impressed."

"She didn't sound like she was acting, Will," says Kate.

"Well, that's the point of acting."

"No, Will. She sounded genuinely distressed. She asked if you were here. By name. She called you Will."

"Oh, er – she must have slipped out of character for a moment. Happens to the best of us."

"I don't believe you," says Kate. "This isn't an audition, is it?"

"What do you mean?"

"I mean there isn't any interactive immersive theatrical thing, is there?" I pause for a moment – but there isn't any point in lying, she'll see straight through it, and besides, I can't think of a single reason why she deserves anything less than the truth.

"This *is* an audition," I say. "Of sorts. But you're right – there isn't any interactive, immersive ... doo-dah."

"Something else is going on?"

"Yes."

"Can you tell me what it is?" she asked.

"Not right this second."

Kate thinks about this for a moment. "Okay," she says.

"We're helping a friend," I say.

"The lady I just spoke to?"

"And others," I say with a nod.

"Is she in trouble? She sounded like she could be."

"Kind of," I say. "She's sort of trapped. But with our help she won't be for long."

"Okay," says Kate, then something through the window catches her eye. "Someone's coming to the door now. She's putting the rubbish bag behind the potted plant. She's glancing over." I want to look so badly. "She's gone back inside. And now DJ is returning."

"Hand me the walkie talkie," I say. Kate reaches into the foot-well to retrieve something, then hands me a bright pink two-way radio with Disney characters on it. I switch it on and hold down the big green button. "Zlata," I say. "You're on." The radio crackles. "Zlata?" Still nothing. "Zlata – where are you?!"

"This is Secret Agent Zlata, waiting for the instructions. Overs."

"Finally! Where were you?!"

"I had too many clothes on. I had to remove some. Overs." I roll my eyes.

"The bag's there. See you back at base." The radio crackles again. "Zlata?"

"You did not say 'overs'," says Zlata. And then a moment later: "Overs."

"Quit messing about and get the rubbish bag!" I switch the radio off just as DJ gets back in the van, still holding the extra parcel. He looks over the seat at me, positively beaming with excitement.

"Did you see me bruv!? Did ya? I was de best! She was like totally convinced! I was de best parcel guy!" I slide down further until I'm virtually lying on the floor of the van. "I was all like, 'are you Mrs Richmond?' and she was like –"

"Yes yes, that's all brilliant DJ, I'm sure you were very authentic, but can I just remind you that right now you're *still* a parcel guy! So stop talking to me and check your clipboard for 'your next delivery'!"

"Right, yeah! Sorry bruv."

"Kate?"

"Zlata's just coming up the road."

"And our friend in the BMW?"

"Seems less interested." I pull myself up to peek over DJ's shoulder, and am just in time to see an eccentric looking bag lady, of indeterminate age, wearing many many layers, stop and examine the contents of Rachel's rubbish bag before putting the whole lot in a beaten up old shopping trolley.

"DJ," I say. "Get us out of here."

I'm sitting in the window seat of a particularly shabby Chinese restaurant. Across the pedestrianized street I have a clear view of the entrance to *The Saffron Lounge*, outside of which are standing two large, tuxedo-wearing gentlemen. The smaller of the two is going about his usual bouncer business, but the larger gentleman keeps glancing nervously in my direction.

"Stop looking at me, Ray," I say under my breath, "just do your job."

"He cannot hear you," says Zlata, shovelling a forkful of Singapore rice noodles into her mouth. I can't eat anything. My stomach is in knots.

"Maybe we should have given him one of those curly ear pieces," I say – though more to myself than to Zlata.

"Why?" asks Zlata through a mouthful of food. "So you can make him even more nervous?"

"I don't understand why he's nervous at all! He does this every night of the week!"

"Yes, but not with you watching. And not –" but before she can finish her sentence my knotted stomach leaps into my mouth.

"Here she comes," I hiss. "Here she comes!" Zlata cranes her head round to look down the street. "Zlata! Eyes front! We don't want her to see us!"

"Really? I was going to give the big wave, and maybe blow some of the kisses."

I ignore Zlata's sarcasm, and watch as Rachel walks up to Ray and hands him a piece of card. He takes it, reads it, then escorts her into the club. I wipe my mouth with the napkin, gather up my belongings and start to get out of my seat, but Zlata grabs my arm.

"I think maybe you should wait some more. Just for the few moments."

"Why?" She gives a sideways nod, and when I look out of the window, there is Archibald Boot, and he's attempting to bribe Ray's colleague to let him into the club.

"How much do you think he is paying?" asks Zlata.

"Hopefully not as much as we've paid to keep him out." And sure enough, after a moment or two of fruitless negotiation, Ray's colleague takes Archie by the arm, and manhandles him into the street before suggesting a direction he might like to walk, and in a manner that suggests he might regret any other course of action.

I dig around in my pocket for some money, and hand Zlata a twenty pound note.

"For the bill," I say, getting up.

"There is not enough here."

"Of course there is."

"Not if I order cake."

"You're not ordering cake, you're leaving and getting your car! As planned!"

"Always with you the big plan," says Zlata. "But where is the plan for cake?"

"Zlata!"

"Okay, okay..."

I leave the restaurant, cross the road briskly, and disappear down the side street next to the club. Moments later Ray opens a side door, and I slip inside. He closes the door behind me, and then walks me down a corridor. When we arrive at 'dressing room one' he stands outside, looking expectant.

"Good work, Ray," I say, slapping him on the arm and summoning a smile from somewhere. "Good work." Relief washes over Ray's face. "I'll take it from here if you like." Ray gives me a sharp nod, and then walks back up the corridor. I watch for a moment, take a deep breath, and go inside.

Rachel stops her pacing, and turns to face me. She says nothing, just steps closer, takes my hands in hers, looks up into my eyes – and then slaps me around the face!

"Ow!" I say, clutching a hand to my cheek. "What the hell was that for!?"

"For being an idiot!" she says.

"An idiot?"

"What was all that theatrics with the phone earlier?"

"We needed to contact you."

"We?"

"I."

"Why didn't you just call me like a normal person!?"

"Your phone is bugged!"

Rachel looks startled. "Oh come off it!" She says. "How could you possibly know that?"

"Well, I don't – but our friend Mr Boot tracked you down when you left Michael, was sitting outside your house all day, and followed you here – do you really think a little phone bugging is beyond him?"

"So call my mobile! Send me a text message!"

"It's all logged. Michael's watching you like a hawk."

"Outgoing – not incoming!"

"Couldn't risk it."

"Well, why get some woman to talk to me!? Why not just talk to me yourself!?"

"If I'd spoken to you we'd have had the conversation we're having now, followed by a big debate about how it was 'over' and why you couldn't leave the house. This was the only way I could think of to guarantee you'd meet me."

"Really?" says Rachel, shifting her weight onto one leg and putting her hands on her hips. "Well, for your information Will, I only told your floozy that I'd meet you because that's what she wanted to hear and I was worried what idiotic stunt you might pull if I didn't play along! Hardly a guarantee! I almost changed my mind!"

"But you didn't."

"No I didn't, but believe me it's not too late! Good evening to you, Monsieur LeBlanc! I'd like to say it's been lovely seeing you again but I don't think it has!" She turns, grabs her jacket from the back of the chair, and takes a step towards the door.

"Okay! Okay!" I say stepping into her path. "I'm sorry. Maybe it was a tad over-dramatic."

"You think?!" says Rachel.

"But, the truth is..." I took a step forwards, "the truth is, it needed to be; I needed to see if DJ, Ray and Kate could pull it off." Rachel takes a step back.

"Your... drama students?"

"The delivery man was DJ."

"The delivery man... that wasn't an *actual* delivery man?"

"No. And DJ will be delighted you said that." From the expression on her face I can tell she's replaying the day's events in her mind.

"So the woman on the phone was ... Kate?"

"Yes."

"I thought you said she was only seventeen?"

"She is." Rachel's mouth drops open.

"But she sounded so ... mature!"

"She's got quite a talent."

"And ... Ray?"

"The bouncer on the door." Rachel's jaw drops a little more.

"Wow! He was very convincing!"

"Er, yes, well, that's not actually that surprising, really. He *is* a bouncer. In real life. This is where he works."

"Ah," said Rachel with a nod and the barest hint of a smile. "So, a bit of type-casting then."

"Yes."

"Why?"

"Why what?"

"Why did you need to see if they could 'pull it off'? Why all this cloak and dagger nonsense? Did you really think you'd get to see me without consequences? When my husband gets home and discovers that I'm not there – not to mention that I gave his private eye the slip with an invitation to a night club that I somehow managed to acquire – alarm bells will sound. There's going to be a lot of explaining to do when I get in. So," she says, stepping forwards and jabbing me in the ribs with a slim finger, "you'd better make this worth my while!"

"There's been a development," I say, echoing Nathia's words. Rachel looks up into my eyes.

"What sort of development?" she asks. I go to draw her closer, but as I take hold of her arms she flinches.

"What's wrong with your arm?" I ask.

"Nothing," she says, "just a bruise." I gently lift the sleeve of her top with a finger. "I bumped it," says Rachel, as she tries to cover it up again.

"Bumped it my arse! Are those ... are those finger marks? Did Michael do this?" For a moment I can tell she's considering whether to deny it, but then her eyes start to water.

"Yes," she says eventually.

This changes everything. Raises the stakes tenfold. If Rachel's life is in danger, then the bonkers plan I'm still formulating might not play out quickly enough to ensure her safety – and if it actually goes wrong ... No. We can't risk it. *I* can't risk it.

"That does it," I say. "We're going to the police."

"No! Will," she says. "There's no point."

"There's every point!"

"They won't do anything."

"Of course they will!"

"It'll make no difference," she says. "Not in the long term. Except maybe make my life even more difficult. He's untouchable Will, how many times do I have to tell you?"

"But –"

"No," she says calmly. "No police. Now calm down. And tell me what's going on in that head of yours. Do you have a plan?"

"Yes," I say reluctantly.

"What is it?"

"Before I tell you that, I need to know if you have access to Michael's passport?" Rachel blinks.

"Yes," she says. "He keeps it in the top drawer of the dresser, along with mine."

"Good – that's what I was hoping you'd say."

"Why?" I take a deep breath.

"Because I want you to pack a bag ... and leave him for good."

SCENE TWO

Last night – during our secret rendezvous in the back of a seedy Soho nightclub – I told Rachel of my plan to free her from the evil clutches of her husband. A plan that involves Zlata and a trio of misfits. She was understandably dubious, but I assuaged her concerns with a supreme confidence and an unshakeable belief in the potential of my students. They had, after all, helped me to secure our meeting in the first place.

However, by eleven o'clock, as I sit in the upstairs room of the pub and watch the three of them rehearse, I am, I confess, beginning to have some very serious doubts.

"Who are you girl, and what are you doin' in my building?" says DJ in a voice that has somehow managed to find common ground between Sir John Gielgud and Mr T.

"Good day to you, Mr Richmond. My name is Kate. I work for Monsieur LeBlanc."

"Oh yeah? I hear ya. But girl – you don't wanna be working for that guy. He's bad news, yeah? Ain't no way he's ever going to give you the respect you deserve. Yo' so fine, you should be working for me. An' girl, when I say working – you don't really have to do nuttin'. You can be like one of my office babes, yeah? Cos I think you'd look damn fine in a bikini or sumfin –"

"Derek!" says Kate stamping her foot on the floor. DJ's eyes widen, until his irises are like tiny little lilies floating in miniature pools of cream.

"Ain't no Derek here, doll face. Just little ol' me, here in my swanky offices, surrounded by my bitches..."

"Derek, he's not going to say any of those things!" roars Kate with more foot stamping.

"Kate, what are you doing?" I ask. She gives me a look like I've just slapped her round the face.

"What am *I* doing?!"

"Yes."

"I'm *trying* to act – but Derek's putting me off with his... endless bullshit!"

"Maybe so, but it was *you* who dropped out of character."

"Me?! Derek's the one who's not in character!"

"Actually," I say, "even though I have no idea who DJ's supposed to be, and I will probably beat him to within an inch of his life if he doesn't quit clowning around –"

"I'd like to see you try, bro," says DJ with a tut and a head toss.

"– he did at least stay in the character he's sort of created. You, on the other hand, didn't."

"That's not fair!" says Kate, crossing her arms tightly across her chest like a five year old.

"Well good," I say with a sigh. "Life's not fair! As well you know! And it's real life that we're trying to mimic here. You have absolutely no idea what the client is going to say, Kate – none whatsoever. He might indeed come out with some bullshit about you working in a bikini – though to be honest I seriously doubt it – but one thing is for certain; if you can handle DJ and his endless crap, then you'll be able to handle the client. Continue." The room is silent for a moment, then Kate unfolds her arms, takes a long deep breath, and turns to face DJ.

"I'm here, *Mr Richmond,*" says Kate, glowering at DJ, "to take you to see Monsieur LeBlanc. I have a car outside, waiting."

"Sure thing, doll face," says DJ with considerably less enthusiasm than before. "Lead the way." I put my face in my palms and stifle a scream.

"DJ – what are you doing?"

"I'm being this Richmond dude!" whines DJ.

"I see. But a moment ago you were trying to persuade Kate to become 'one of yo' bitches' – and now you're just doing whatever she says." DJ shifts his weight onto one leg.

"Yeah, cos you told Kate that I was clowning around, and that it was all crap, and that you'd beat me up if I continued. So I ain't clowning no more. I'm doin' what you want."

"What I want, DJ," I say getting to my feet, "is for you to think about who you're supposed to be, and how they might react to the situation you're in. So, in your honest opinion, would Michael Richmond just get into Kate's car without question?"

"I dunno," says DJ, as if I've asked him to predict next week's Lotto numbers.

"Well let's think about it," I continue. "He's expecting to have a meeting with Stephan LeBlanc, and instead, this young woman, who he's never met before, turns up in his lobby…"

"Okay bro," says DJ with a huff. "I gettit! But unless this Richmond guy is completely *gay* of course he's going to get in the car with Kate!"

"Not all men think like you do, Derek!" says Kate. "Ray?"

"Yo' got a lot to learn about men, sweet cheeks," says DJ, making an obvious show of looking at Kate's posterior.

"Don't call me that!" she says, at which point the door flies open and Zlata comes in, backwards, laden with bags and boxes.

"Hello everyones!" she says. "I am bringing the costumes!"

"Thank god!" I say as she dumps her items on the trestle table that was playing the part of a reception desk.

"So then, for the beautiful lady," says Zlata, beginning to rummage amongst her purchases. "I have this." From inside a stripy paper bag she carefully slides out a silk blouse, a dark grey skirt, and a packet of black hold up stockings. "Very simples," she says, handing the items to Kate, and then placing a shoe box on top. "But also elegant. Have a look and see." Kate glances at me, and after I've given her a nod wanders off in the direction of the toilets. Zlata continues to root through the bags. "And for my big strong man," she says, "we have these trousers, and also this shirt, which will be tight but I think that is good thing. Also we have this jacket. You will look like super spy. Try them on." She hands the items to Ray. "No need to go to changing room," she adds with a wink, "you can stay right here. No one will mind." Ray blushes, but before I can say anything she's off again. "And for the handsome DJ," continues Zlata, "we have the very smart suit." DJ screws up his face, like the gum he's been chewing has, for no apparent reason, swapped places with a Brussels sprout.

"A suit?" he says. "Seriously? I'm not really the suit wearing type though; I'm more of yo' laid back dude. You know what I mean?"

I sigh. "Which is why we call it a costume, DJ. It's not for you. It's for your character. Put it on."

"Yeah but bruv – I don't really see my character as the suit wearing type either!"

"Then clearly you're not seeing your character correctly, and we have much more work to do. Put the suit on."

"It is very nice suit," said Zlata. "Very stylish. And you will look even more the sexy man." She puts her hand on his chest and slowly lets it run down his front. "You should try it," she coos.

"Well, okay," says DJ, "but just for you, yeah? 'Cos Will's been like busting my chops all morning and I'm well sick of it!" He picks up the suit, glares at me, then turns and walks off in the direction of the toilet, very nearly knocking Kate off her stockinged feet as he opens the door. He glares at her too, and then pushes past.

"Zlata," says Kate, holding a pair of heels in one hand. "These shoes..." Zlata turns to face her, and then claps her hands together in delight.

"You like them, yes?" she asks. "I got them in sale. Very cheap. But also very sexy. You are so lucky to have the small feet – so many lovely shoes to pick from. For me, I have the big feet. No shoes for Zlata."

"But Zlata... they're so..." she looks at them whilst she considered how best to describe her feelings. "High!" she says eventually.

"Not really," says Zlata with a shake of her head. "Maybe, thirteen of the centimetres."

"You don't understand," whines Kate. "I've never worn heels before!"

"It's okay," says Zlata. "You will learn. Go, try them – with the outfit," says Zlata. Kate glances at me, and then disappears again, leaving me, Ray in his underpants, and Zlata standing watching him. After a moment or two I cough to get her attention. It doesn't work.

"Zlata? Zlata!"

"What!" says Zlata, her eyes never leaving the semi-naked man.

"Nothing," I say. "I just thought maybe Ray might like to get changed without an audience."

"He does not mind," says Zlata with a smile.

"Did you happen to get a costume for yourself?" I ask.

"It is all taking care of."

"Taken," I say. "You mean taken."

"I know what I mean," says Zlata.

"So, when you say 'it's all taken care of'... "

"I have a plan," says Zlata. "A costume plan."

"And the plan is ..." I prompt.

"The plan is to have a plan."

"So you haven't done anything then?" I ask.

"No," admits Zlata.

"Okay," I say. "How about this; how about you ask Kate to help you?" Zlata looks back at me, her face like thunder.

"I don't need the help!" she says. "I was very good cleaning lady. And also the bag lady. I can manage this."

"Yes, but Zlata – it needs to be just right. Everything hinges on you being utterly convincing."

"It's okay! Trust me." But I can tell from the twitch in her eye that she is as nervous as me. At which point Kate totters back into the room, grabbing hold of anything she can to keep herself upright. Gone are her trademark Doc Martens, replaced instead with the heels Zlata gave her, though they might as well be roller skates from the way she's walking. Gingerly she crosses the room – arms outstretched, as though she's walking a tight rope. And she almost gets as far as Ray before she finally loses her balance and falls flat on her face. Zlata and I exchange looks.

"Maybe you can help each other," I say.

Jim is in his office and up to his arms in plaster of Paris as I entered the workshop.

"Will!" he says. "I wasn't expecting to see you. What day is it?"

"Saturday," I say, forcing a smile.

"Saturday? Already. I thought it was still Friday."

"Nope. Pretty sure it's Saturday."

"Saturday... Damn." This isn't what I wanted to hear.

"What you making?" I ask, hoping for all the world that it isn't police badges.

"Police badges," says Jim. "Always police badges." I swallow hard.

"Is one of those mine?" I ask. I can't afford to go home, and come back tomorrow. We need all the rehearsal time we can get.

"Yours?"

"My, er, badge."

Jim looks at me blankly.

"Oh, right," he says. "Wondered what you were talking about then. No, these are for some new police drama. Because that's what TV needs right now. Another bloody cop show."

"So, my badge, is already...?" I ask.

"No," says Jim. "Didn't make you one."

"You didn't..."

"Nah," he says, with a sigh and a shake of his head. "I looked it up online. They don't carry badges. Not in the police sense."

"They... don't?" I can feel my world crumbling. Without this prop...

"Apparently it's nowhere near as glamorous an organisation as it appears in the movies, or on telly. There's a shock, eh? Another industry that's one big let down in real life."

"Right," I say, my bottom finding a chair just as my legs give way. "So you didn't make me the badge I asked for. Okay." I don't know what else to say. Jim frowns.

"Well, obviously I made you something else instead," he says.

I look up.

He shakes his head in bewilderment. "Take a look in that cabinet over there," he says, nodding in the direction of a slim grey pre-war filing cabinet, the sort with shallow drawers intended for papers and documents. I open the top drawer. "Not that one," says Jim "Next one down. See it?" I take out a beaten up piece of plastic roughly the same size as a credit card. On the front is a fairly ancient photo of myself, as well as my name, job title, department, and the organisation I apparently work for. On the back, nothing but an embedded brown magnetic strip. It looks as if it's spent many years in a sweaty back pocket, being swiped through card entry door security systems, handed to grubby people by way of identification, dropped on numerous floors, wedged under the occasional wonky table leg, scraped across icy car windows, and to top it all, tossed about inside the odd washing machine. It is perfect in its imperfection.

"Wow," I say eventually.

"It's okay?" asks Jim.

"It's so much better than okay," I say, turning it over in my hands. "I hardly know where to begin. Where did you get that photo?"

"Found it amongst some old college stuff. Well, not that exact photo obviously, but once I'd scanned it in and played with it a bit..."

"I'm blown away," I say again.

"That carrier bag on the floor has everything else you asked for." I pick it up and look inside; everything appears to be in order.

"How much do I owe you?"

Jim waves away my comment. "No need, mate. You've already paid."

"I have?"

"Yep. Memories of better times. It's given me a much needed kick up the arse." He nods in the direction of the desk, and on it I spy a copy of *The Stage*. "I know you said it's pretty hopeless out there, but you've gotta try ain't ya. Ain't never gonna get that dream otherwise."

I think about that as I sit on the tube and rattle back to the Elephant and Castle – about dreams and ambitions, hopes and desires, and the subtle differences between them. For instance, when does 'that thing you've always wanted' go from being 'just a dream' – something that, as the label suggests, is as unobtainable and out of reach as the stars we might wish upon – to a tangible possibility. If you actually *need* that dream in your life, does the very act of needing it so badly, make it more or less likely to happen?

I've always dreamt of a life in theatre – spent my whole life working towards, and waiting for, the day when I would finally be satisfied with my lot. And along the way countless well-meaning folks have told me time and time again that the chances of me ever managing to forge a career in such a competitive environment were ridiculously slight. It is a dream, they said. Just a dream.

But things had changed and right now I couldn't imagine ever being truly happy unless I were with Rachel again – so is that too just a dream? Am I wasting my time pursuing *her*, as I had done a life in theatre?

And what about my fellow actors?

DJ seems to want nothing more than to be respected. Treated like a man – rather than a son or an employee or a bad joke. That doesn't seem a lot to ask really. You could argue it's a basic human right. But without a role model in his life – someone to show him how it's done – he'll never manage to achieve it. And Ray; a lifetime spent failing to live up to the imposing physique that destiny has bestowed on him. Whilst DJ is all but invisible to everyone around him, Ray is too visible but not equipped to deal with it. Is it a dream for either man to expect or want anything different?

And then there's Kate.

But I have no idea what she wants.

None whatsoever.

They are packing up when I finally get back to the pub. Ray passes me on the stairs, and gives me a world-weary nod.

"Hey!" I say as I open the door to the room, "where are you lot going? Ray? Get back here!"

"I tell them we finish for today," says Zlata as she and Kate stack chairs against the wall.

"But..." I say coming into the room. "It's barely nine o'clock!"

"And they work very hard. Twelve hours."

"Yes, but the last time I saw them in action they still had a lot more work to do!" DJ shuffles past me and out of the door. "DJ?" I say.

"Laters bro," he replies.

"DJ!"

"Laters."

"We start again in morning, with the fresh faces," says Zlata, grabbing her bag. "New energy. But now we need rest. We can leave costumes here, yes?"

"Er, well, I suppose so."

"Okay, good. See you in morning."

"Right."

"Bye Will," says Kate.

"Kate! Kate – wait a sec." She stops, but I wait thirty seconds or so for Zlata to get out of the door. "Kate," I ask, "what do you want – in life?"

Kate frowns. "I don't know what you mean," she says.

"Have you any ambitions? Dreams?"

"Aren't they a pointless waste of time?" she says. "That's what you told Ray."

I blinked. "I did?"

"When you cancelled the class."

"Oh ... right," I say, tugging on an earlobe. "Yes, well ... that was before."

"Have you changed your mind?" asks Kate.

"I don't know," I reply after a moment's thought. "Maybe."

"Right," says Kate. "Is that because of your meeting with Mrs Richmond?"

"Yes," I say. "Partly."

"So are you going to tell me the truth now? About why we're doing this?"

"I will if you answer me one question," I say.

"Okay."

"Why did you join this class?"

Kate frowns. "Isn't it obvious?"

"Not to me."

"To get out of that Toy Shop," she says. It isn't the answer I'm expecting. "You've seen it," she continues. "That place is a hell hole."

"Well, it is a little ... rough."

"That's not what I mean," says Kate, her frown deepening.

I cross my arms.

"So explain it to me," I say.

"I live in a room at the back," says Kate. "It used to be a store room I think. But now there's a shower, and a mattress, and an old TV. *He* – the man who owns the shop, the man you saw – lives upstairs. And he's always trying to get me to move up there with him. Into his spare room. He says it'll be more comfortable, but I don't trust him. So I stay downstairs, even though I'm sure he's got a camera hidden in my room."

"A... camera?" I ask. "How... how do you know?"

"He knows stuff," she says, looking at the floor. "Stuff he shouldn't know." I feel myself flush with anger, but also at the embarrassment and shame she must be feeling. "It's okay," says Kate softly. "I sleep in my clothes, and I shower at the local swimming baths. And I go out whenever I can. But when you cancelled the class, Will, I was gutted. That was two nights a week when I didn't have to be afraid of what might happen to me."

"Jesus," I say eventually, though I've long since stopped breathing so all I can manage is the barest of whispers.

"You wanted to know," says Kate. And suddenly I do know. I know exactly what this girl wants, even if she hasn't quite figured it out for herself, even if she hasn't had the courage to turn it into a dream yet, or dare to imagine if it is even a possibility.

"Kate," I say. "Do you trust me?"

"Of course," she says, making eye contact again.

"Then how would you feel... about... moving in with me? Into my spare room. Just temporarily. Just until we've sorted something else out?"

"I'm not going into care," she says stiffly. "If that's what 'sorting something else out' means. I've been there before and I don't want to go back."

"No!" I say. "No, okay, I understand that. But I... I don't think you're safe where you are. And I don't feel happy about letting you go back there. Tonight. Or ever again. I mean, maybe we can send Ray round to get your stuff?" Kate raises an eyebrow. "After we've, you know, worked on him a bit. Made him more scary."

"Okay," she says.

"Okay?" I ask.

"Yes. I'd like that. Thank you."

"Right!" I say, relief washing through me. "Great. Good. Well then ... let's ... go home!" Kate stays exactly where she is.

"So are you going to tell me about Mrs Richmond?" she asks. "And what we're really doing?" I smile, and let out a long sigh.

"Of course," I say. "Everything you want to know."

Zlata had been right: though Kate and I arrive at the pub a little after eight thirty, everybody else – Zlata, Ray, DJ – is already caffeinated and ready to rehearse. Sunday morning has indeed brought with it bucketloads of energy and enthusiasm. And as we go through the regular battery of warm up exercises – but without the moans and complaints that usually accompany them – it's clear to me that overnight my students have emerged from their pupae, and are ready to spread their wings. DJ seems more focused. Ray more confident. And Kate ... well, it's never easy to figure out what's going on inside that young head, but if I had to pick a word, just one word to describe her current mood compared with the one she had only twelve hours ago, I'd have to go with 'happy'.

"And ... relax. Excellent. Just excellent." I glance at my watch. We've done the entire warm up in under ten minutes. Unheard of. "Really, really excellent."

"So, are we moving onto the next scene today bruv?" asks DJ.

"Er, yes. Yes we are. In a moment, but for now everyone just take a seat," I say. "Except you, Ray." The big guy stops moving, and suddenly looks very worried. "I need you to come over here, and stand in front of me." Ray exchanges looks with the others, and then does as he's been told whilst the rest of the class line up chairs, and prepare to watch the spectacle. "Don't worry about the audience, Ray," I say. "At least not for the moment – just look at me. Stand up straight. Let those arms hang comfortably from your shoulders. Tummy in. Chest out. Good. Feeling okay?" I ask. Ray gives a short, nervous nod. "Right then," I continue. "Then let's begin. We're going to find your inner lion…"

"Kate tells me she is living with you," hisses Zlata. I drop tea bags into mugs and sniff the milk tentatively to see whether it's still useable.

"That's right," I say. Zlata stands upright and crosses her arms tightly across her chest whilst her lips thin so much they all but disappear.

"This is not wise," she says. I sigh.

"And why isn't it wise?"

"She is young woman!" says Zlata, uncrossing her arms and waving them around. "Attractive woman!"

"And?"

"Rachel will not like! It is…" she hunts around inside her head for some English words that are close enough to the several thousand Croatian phrases I imagine are competing for her attention, "…most stupid idea you ever have," she says eventually. I sigh again.

"Listen," I say, turning to face her. "You remember I said I thought Kate was in trouble?"

"I remember."

"Well she is. Or was."

"How? How is she in the trouble?" I glance across the room to see what the others are doing. They seem to be engrossed in their own conversations whilst they tuck into sandwiches.

"I'm not going into the details, Zlata, but there was no way I could let her go back to that toy shop, so now she's living with me."

"And what about Rachel?" asks Zlata, her arms folded again.

"If we manage to pull this hare-brained scheme off and Rachel moves back in with me, well, I'm sure she'll understand."

"You are sure?" scoffs Zlata.

"Yes! Especially when I happen to point out that Kate is just as crucial to the success of this plan as you, or any of the others. From that perspective,we owe her." I hand Zlata a mug, she puts it straight back on the table.

"How long?" she whispers.

"How long what?"

"How long is Kate living with you?"

"For god's sake... I don't know."

"But she has friends? Family? Why she not stay with them?"

I take a second to glance over at Kate.

"*We* are her friends." I say. "Come to that... we're her family too. Just us. And as far as I can tell there isn't anyone else in her life." Zlata frowns. I pick up her mug again and hand it to her, before arranging four others so I can carry two in each hand. "And now I've said more than I should. Go and have a chat with her, Zlata. Get to know her. If you *still* think letting her move in is a bad idea, then maybe you can tell me what you think I should have done."

Slowly the three of them walk around DJ, each watching for any sign of movement, or any affectations that are particularly DJ-like. Suddenly, and without warning, Zlata lunges forward, striking DJ just below the ribs with her broom handle.

"Ow!" says DJ "What was that for?!"

"You did the twitching!" says Zlata.

"I'm allowed to twitch!" protests DJ. "Bro! Tell her!" I ignore him and try not to smile too much. "Ow!" says DJ again, as Kate pokes him in the bottom with a fork.

"You're not allowed to say 'bro'," says Kate.

"Look yo' –"

"DJ," I say. "Concentrate."

"But –"

"DJ!" He curls his lip, and as he does so Ray taps him lightly with a feather duster. "A little harder next time Ray," I say. "DJ, stop curling your lip." Kate and Zlata move closer, their faces inches from his, their weapons poised. "Girls," I say, "keep moving. DJ – begin when you're ready."

"The rain," says DJ with a sigh, "OW!"

"Not with the sigh!" barks Zlata.

"The rain," continues DJ.

"Slower," I say, "and calmer."

"The rain," he says, "in Spain,"

"Good. Stand taller."

"Stays mainly, in de plain. Ow!"

"*The* plain, DJ. Really pronounce those Ts." I can see DJ itching to sigh, or huff, or roll his eyes, or anything else – I raise an eyebrow – but DJ does nothing of the sort. Instead he straightens his back, takes a deep, slow breath, and fixes me with an icy cold stare.

"The rain," he says, with a precision and eloquence that I've never heard those lips utter, "in Spain stays mainly on the plain."

"Hello," says Zlata, looking up from the non-existent monitor in front of her, "can I help you?" Though her spectacles are just as imaginary as her computer, she still manages to peer over them.

"I have an appointment with Mr Richmond," says the smart young woman in front of her, "I'm afraid," she says. "I am a little early." Zlata looks back at her screen, a frown forming on her face.

"And you are?" she asks.

"I work for Monsieur LeBlanc. Unfortunately Monsieur LeBlanc has been unavoidably detained – but rather than cancel the meeting, he wonders whether Mr Richmond would care to join him? I have a car waiting outside."

"This is very unusual," says Zlata, creating a telephone handset with the thumb and little finger of her right hand. "I will need to do the checking."

"Of course," says Kate with a slow, respectful nod. "I quite understand."

"Please," says Zlata, punching buttons that aren't there. "Take one of the seats." Kate gives another nod, and then slowly walks further into the lobby, her heels clicking on the marble floor, her head held high as she takes in the impressive building. My heart could literally burst with pride.

Which makes it all the more annoying when my mobile suddenly bursts into life and ruins the moment. In my haste to get the phone out of my pocket it jumps from one hand to the other before clattering to the floor.

"Keep going," I say to my actors as I flip it open. "Hello?"

"It's all arranged," says Nathia. "Monday. Five thirty."

"Excellent," I say. "Thank you." I hang up. Nobody in the room is acting any longer. They are all fixed on me. But that's okay. "We're on," I say.

Scene Three

There's a thump thump thump at the back door. I give Jarad the nod and after some nervous fumbling with the lock, he opens it. He has every reason to be nervous. I know my hands are shaking without even looking at them. Seconds later Zlata walks in, her arms stretched out in front of her, her eyes squeezed closed, whilst Ray, his great huge hands on her shoulders, steers her through the kitchen like a forklift truck to where I'm standing.

"I am blind! I am blind!" says Zlata.

"You're not blind, Zlata – you just can't see."

"Is same thing," she says. At which point she opens her eyes, glances at the chair opposite me, sits on it, crosses her legs and proceeds to examine her nails. I sigh.

"What are you doing?"

"This is where I am supposed to be sitting."

"Yes, but not until Ray puts you there! You can't *see* anything, remember!"

"I know this already! Ray knows this also!" I glance at Ray, who nods.

"Okay," I say with a shake of my head. "So what are you two doing standing there – and why is the back door still open?" DJ and Kate exchange glances before Kate walks briskly past me and into the main part of the restaurant, leaving DJ to struggle with the door. She returns a moment or two later with a video camera on a tripod, and sets it up just behind my left shoulder.

"That needs to be there already," I say.

"I didn't want it to get knocked over – there might be a struggle."

"There won't be a struggle," I say. "Preventing struggles is Ray's department. DJ, where are you?"

"Right here, bro," says DJ, who has finished wrestling with the back door and is now leaning against it.

"What I mean is, *where are you supposed to be*?"

"Oh, right," says DJ, and for a moment he actually looks sheepish. He takes his place to the right of me, legs slightly apart, hands clasped in front of him, his gaze off into the distance, his expression cold and impenetrable – getting this right was an afternoon's work in itself.

"And now," says Zlata, a huge smile plastered all over her face, "Ray pulls off my top!" I sigh.

"It's not a top, it's –"

"I know what I mean," says Zlata.

"Okay, but that's not going to happen until I give Ray the signal –" Ray nods, "– and I'm not going to do that until Kate gives me the thumbs up." I look over my shoulder at Kate standing behind the video camera. She gives me a thumbs up in such a way that I'm certain she would have preferred to use a different finger.

"It's crystal, bro," says DJ again. "We've all been through this like a thousand times!"

"Okay, okay," I say, and sigh. Again. "But from the moment this starts, regardless of whether or not the client can see you, whether you're in the car or the restaurant, whether you're on camera or not, whether it plays out like it did in rehearsals – or not – *everyone* stays in character. Got that?" Nobody says anything. "Zlata?"

"I got it."

"Kate?"

"Yes."

"DJ?"

"Yeah yeah - cool bruv. No worries."

"Ray?"

Ray nods.

"What about Jarad, bro?" asks DJ. Everyone looks over at Jarad standing in the corner. He gives a terrified, rapid nod.

"He'll be fine," I say. Though more to myself than anyone else. I take a deep breath, and look around the kitchen at my fellow actors, some of whom I didn't even know just three weeks ago, but now – well, we're a family of sorts. Acting can do that to a group of strangers. And in the next few hours we're going to find out just how good at acting we actually are.

I check my watch. We're cutting this awfully tight, and then, as if my thoughts are being monitored, I hear the tinkle of the bell as someone enters the restaurant. Thirty seconds later Rachel walks into the kitchen, a dull green suitcase trailing behind her.

"I'm here," she says. "Are we *really* going to do this?"

"Everybody," I say, "this is Rachel. She'll be joining us for part of this evening's performance. Rachel, I believe you've met everyone with the exception of Kate." Rachel turns to the young woman beside me.

"Hello," says Rachel with a smile. "We spoke on the phone. Well done. You were very calm." Kate says nothing. Just gives a short shy nod.

"I assume our weasel-like friend followed you here?" I ask.

"Absolutely," she says. "He's outside. Lurking."

"Right," I say. "Why don't you invite him in?"

"Really?" asks Rachel.

"Absolutely," I say, and then turn to address the rest of the room. "As for everyone else – no more rehearsals. It's time to get into costume and take your places. This, is it. Remember we're a team. Stay in character. Think about what you're doing – why you're doing it. And break a leg." You could have heard a pin drop at that moment. There is an exchange of nervous glances and then slowly, one by one, they all file out through the back door. "Er Ray," I say before he manages to leave, "Jarad and I need to borrow you."

Archibald Boot is standing in the middle of the restaurant when Ray and I come through. Rachel is standing by the front door, arms crossed, like she fully intends to wrestle Archie to the ground should he try to make a run for it. Not that he's showing any signs of wanting to escape. But that'll change in a moment or two.

"Mr *Clarkson*," says Archie, stressing my surname again and grinning that big stupid grin of his. "I really didn't expect to see you again so soon! And in the company of *Mrs* Richmond no less. I believe this represents quite a significant breach of our agreement."

"Indeed it does, Mr Boot," I say with a nod. "Though to be fair, your *client* has hardly kept his side of the bargain: Jarad has been on the phone to Greenwich Council on a daily basis, and yet," I say opening my arms in a gesture that is probably more dramatic than it needs to be, "the closure order remains in force."

"The wheels of local government bureaucracy turn very slowly, Mr Clarkson," says Archie, wringing his hands whilst his grin gets ever broader. "You can't expect things to change overnight."

"Actually that's exactly what I'm expecting," I say, "but first I'd like to introduce you to this man." I step to one side and give Ray a slight nod. He moves forward until he's towering over Archie's weasel-like physique. "This is Ray. Ray doesn't say very much. But I happen to know that he'd like to borrow your inhaler."

"My...inhaler?" asks Archie, the smile faltering just slightly.

"That's right." Without prompting Ray stretches out a hand.

"I'd give it to him if I were you," I say. "It's either that or Ray breaks all your fingers."

"Mr Clarkson! Is that a threat?" asks Archie, puffing out his chest in stoic defiance.

"It's a warning," I say, any hint of politeness evaporating from my voice. "Your inhaler, Archie. Now." Again, without prompting, Ray slaps his other hand on Archie's shoulder, and I swear I can see those little legs shaking as Archie hunts around in his pockets. "Many thanks," I say as Archie hands the inhaler to Ray. "Now, as a token of our gratitude, we'd like to offer you a complimentary tour of our wine cellar!" I walk over to the corner of the room, and just as I've seen Jarad do many times before, lift the trap door in the floor to reveal the entrance to the cellar. I glance at Ray, who in turn nudges Archie, until all three of us are looking into the darkness below. I take the torch from the shelf behind me and shine it down the steps. "It's a little damp," I say, "there might be some mould. But nothing compared to the dust."

"You can't be serious?" splutters Archie.

"I am deadly and serious," I say. Archie peers down into the gloom.

"Mr Clarkson, if I go down there..."

"What's wrong Archie? Feeling a little ... *breathless?*"

"Mr Clarkson! I don't think you realise just how –"

"Of course I bloody realise!" I say, grabbing hold of Archie's tie with both hands, and with one rough action tightening it around his throat. "Why d'you think I asked for your inhaler? Now get down those steps before I get Ray here to make you!"

"Mr Clarkson!" gasped Archie. "Please! I implore you –"

"Ray –" I say with a nod to my enormous colleague, though Ray isn't looking quite so sure of himself any more.

"No," splutters Archie, his watering eyes flicking from me to Ray and back again, "no, please –" Though I still have hold of Archie's tie, I hold my palm out as if to tell Ray to stay where he is – not that I thought for a moment that he had any intention of moving.

"There is an alternative," I say to Archie.

"Please," gasps Archie, "anything. That would be ... most kind."

"Have you got your phone on you?"

"Yes, yes," says Archie, fumbling in his pockets once again. "Here! Have it!" I shake my head.

"Not yet, Archie," I say letting go of his tie. "First you need to call your contact at the council, and tell him to do whatever needs to be done to get this restaurant open again – tomorrow!"

"My ... contact?" asks Archie.

"Whoever you're bribing in environmental health. Do it!"

"I don't know what you mean," says Archie, that stupid wide smile trying its damnedest to reassert itself.

"Fine." I say. "Down to the cellar it is!" I grab his tie.

"No!" screams Archie, "You're right, you're right! I remember now! I was just ... I momentarily ... it just slipped my ..."

"Archie!" I say, yanking the tie again.

"Yes, yes, I understand," says Archie, fumbling with his phone, "although I don't think you appreciate, Mr Clarkson, just how late in the day it is; I seriously doubt..." I shake my head.

"Ray, put him in the –"

"No! No! Wait! It seems I have a *mobile number*! My, er, contact's *personal*, mobile number. I should be able to reach him on that. How fortunate."

"Indeed," I say, letting go of the tie again. Whilst Archie clutches his phone to his ear, and has a brief, urgent conversation with someone at the other end, I look over his shoulder at Rachel who is looking decidedly nervous. Then I glance over at Jarad, and for once he is the calmest person in the room. He jerks his head in the direction of the cellar and gives me a thumbs up, as if granting me permission to let Archie gasp his last amongst the bottles of Chardonnay and Sauvignon Blanc. I turn my face so that Archie won't see my smile, and at that moment the call comes to an end.

"My er, associate," says Archie, "would be delighted to re-inspect this, er, charming premises, tomorrow morning. If that would be convenient." I look over at Jarad, who rolls his eyes and nods reluctantly.

"Good," I say. "I'll take that phone now."

"Really?" asks Archie. "Is that strictly necessary, Mr Clarkson? After all, I've done exactly as you –"

"Let's cut the crap, Archie," I say grabbing the tie once more. "We both know that there is no *Mr Clarkson*. But what you've failed to uncover, in all your 'detecting', is exactly *who* you're dealing with and the level of shit you're now in. The phone, Archie," I say holding out my hand. "Now!" Reluctantly he hands over the mobile. I look down at the icons on the small screen in dismay. It isn't anything like mine. "Goddam it – how do you use this thing?"

"Here, let me," says Rachel, coming over and taking the phone out of my hands. "What do you need?"

"To see who Archie actually called."

"I assure you, I haven't –"

"Shut it!" I snap.

"It says 'Martin Broadbent'," says Rachel, but Jarad becomes more animated.

"Broadbent!" he says. "I speak with him every day! He is man from council!"

"Good," I say. "Keep hold of that phone. We might need it as proof if Mr Broadbent fails to keep his appointment. What's wrong?"

"The call before that was to my husband," says Rachel. "About fifteen minutes ago. Will, that means Michael knows I'm here!"

"Excellent," I say. "He should be frothing at the mouth by now. Archie, take a seat. Jarad, if he says another word put him in the cellar. Ray, you're with me." I take Rachel gently by the shoulders. "I'll be back in a little while," I say, "and then all of this will be over." She gives me a short nervous nod.

As Ray and I walk out of the restaurant, through the kitchen and into the back yard, I catch Ray looking at me, his eyes full of concern, pleading with me for an explanation.

"Relax!" I say as I open the back gate. "Everything's fine! I wasn't really going to put him in the cellar! We were acting! I just needed to help Jarad iron out a misunderstanding between that weasel in there and the corrupt local authority." But Ray isn't moving any longer. "Look, okay – there's a little more going on here than I mentioned earlier. Let's just go, get into costume, and I'll tell you everything on the way."

He digs into his pockets then holds out the inhaler like it's a piece of Archie's soul. I take it from him, and look the big guy in the eyes. "Okay, okay," I say, "I'll give it back to him a little later on. Happy?" Ray gives a nod. "Good." I slap him on the arm, stuff the inhaler in my pocket, and not for the first time marvel at the compassion of this gentle giant.

I'm in full 'Edwin' costume as I enter the offices of *Steele & Richmond* an hour or so later: Edwin glasses. Edwin jacket. Edwin shirt. The blue one. Caroline is busy talking to a slender woman, with sleek jet black hair, and extremely high heels – I move quickly through reception (ignoring Caroline's protests), round the corner, and take the stairs two at a time to the top floor – to its one and only office. Michael is standing behind his desk, phone in hand, as I enter.

"Tell her I'll be down in a moment," he growls into the receiver, then slams the phone back into its cradle. "Edwin!" he roars. "You've got a fucking cheek! Just who the fuck do you think you are!?"

"I know exactly who I am, Michael. The question is though, do you?" Michael raises an eyebrow.

"You're the fucker who's *trying* to steal my wife away." He says.

"Steal?" I say. "You've got it all wrong, Michael. I haven't stolen Rachel. She left you. Plain and simple. Had enough. Walked out on a sham of a marriage that she no longer wanted to be a part of. I was in this room when it happened, remember?"

"Really?" scoffs Michael. "Because from my perspective it looked very much like she was running into the arms of a pretty boy who'd filled her head full of nonsense about how she could manage a chain of fucking ghastly restaurants.

She always was a fucking dreamer, Edwin. But I stamped that out of her once, and I can fucking do it again."

"You'd take someone's dreams away? How very noble of you."

"There's no place for dreamers in business, Edwin! I told you that once before."

"It wasn't business, Michael. It was your marriage."

"Believe me you useless fuck, marriage is just business under a different name! And when I tell her that the idiot she seems to admire so much is far more of a – what was the word you used? – *sham*, I believe you'll lose your appeal." I say nothing for a moment. Now we're getting somewhere.

"Rachel already knows everything there is to know about me, Michael. There's nothing you can say that will change the way she feels."

"And why on earth would I believe that, *Mr Clarkson*? If that is indeed your name. There is no Edwin Clarkson currently working at Amnesty International. Nor is there anyone of that name associated with your address on either the electoral roll or the land registry."

"Mr Boot has been very thorough," I say.

"That's what I pay him to be."

"Well, he wasn't thorough enough. Give me five minutes and I'll tell you everything. The truth."

"The truth?"

"The truth."

"Okay," says Michael. "I'll play your stupid game. You have *three* minutes," he says, "and not a fucking second longer."

"You might want to ask Nathia to join us," I say, pushing my luck. Michael's eyes narrow, then he presses a button on his desk phone.

"Nathia darling – would you mind getting your bony arse into my office for a moment. We have a visitor." Beneath my hairline I feel the familiar prickle of a bead of sweat forming. I push my glasses up the bridge of my nose and wander briefly round the office, stopping to look at the large oil painting hanging on the wall; a corn field. Poppies in the foreground. A medieval town in the distance, with a distinctive church at its centre.

"That's a lovely painting," I say. "Where is that exactly? Croatia?"

"Three minutes Edwin," says Michael. "The clock is ticking." I remove my Edwin glasses, and place them in my inside jacket pocket.

"My name is William Lewis," I say. "I'm an actor."

"A fucking actor?" says Michael, folding his arms.

"*Failed* actor actually. I graduated from the London Academy of Music and Dramatic Art a little under seven years ago. But other than the occasional audition, I've never managed to set foot on a stage, or secure any traditional acting role."

"What's going on here?" says Nathia, coming into the room.

"Your ex-fucking-boyfriend is about to tell me who he actually is," says Michael, his eyes not leaving me for a moment, "and why he's not a trespassing, wife stealing, charlatan."

"Ah. Funny thing about the boyfriend part," I continue. "Four years ago Nathia employed me to play the part of her boyfriend in an effort to conceal from you her true sexuality."

"Will!" says Nathia.

"I'm sorry Nathia," I say, turning to face her. "Truly I am. But it's better this way."

"Better for whom?!" she asks, her eyes becoming all sparkly as tears began to form.

"Everyone," I say. "Trust me." But even as those words roll off my tongue I can see that I've wounded her deeply, and to earn back her trust I'll have to pull off a miracle of gargantuan proportions.

"Go on," says Michael, as Nathia turns her face away to compose herself. I take a breath, let it out slowly and look Michael square in the eye.

"After Nathia terminated my employment," I continue, "I genuinely never thought I would see you again, Michael, or have any kind of dealings with either you or your wife. But then I ran into Rachel."

"How fucking convenient," says Michael.

"It's the truth," I say with a sigh. "She met my agent and then, when she realised who and what I really am, employed me to play the part of Stephan LeBlanc." Gone is Michael's smug incredulity, replaced instead by genuine surprise.

"What?" he says.

"You heard me," I say. He holds my gaze for a few seconds longer, and then looks at Nathia, who by now is as pale as a sheet. Her legs buckle from under her, and she collapses onto the sofa by the door. Michael glances at the phone. And I know what he's thinking: who, then, is the woman in reception?

"Fucking nonsense," he says, though barely loud enough to be convincing.

"It's true. Rachel doesn't work for a French entrepreneur. She *is* the entrepreneur. That restaurant that you took such a dislike to belongs to Rachel and her cousin. They brought me in to help negotiate a deal with Abdul and Sadat Tahan. Your clients."

"You really fucking expect me to believe this shit?" scoffs Michael.

"I'm quite certain you'll choose to believe whatever suits you best," I say.

"So you're telling me that there is no *Stephan LeBlanc.*"

"Never was."

Michael's eyes narrow again. "Then why – *Mr Clarkson* – is there a woman in my reception, waiting to take me to a meeting with a gentleman you claim doesn't fucking exist?"

"She's an actor," I say.

"Another actor!?"

"I paid her to be here."

"You arranged this?"

"Yes."

"And why, the fucking fuck, would you do that!?"

"To prove to you that it can be done? That as unlikely as it sounds, you've been manipulated all along. By Nathia. And Rachel. All in an effort to protect themselves. From you."

"Will," pleads Nathia from the couch.

"Think of it as a choice, Michael. Face the truth – that your wife doesn't love you, and wants to build a life without you; that your friends and colleagues have been lying to you all these years to preserve the life they want without your interference – or continue believing that everything is as it seems, and that you're still in control." Through Michael's eyes I can see his mind turning over all that he's heard. And yet, there is still that flicker of doubt, the merest suspicion that once again he's being lied to. "You don't have to take my word for it, Michael. Go ahead. Get the lady in reception up here. Confront her." Michael nods slowly, straightens his back, takes a deep breath and then presses a button on his phone. He speaks with all the authority I've come to expect from this man, this charming, evil man.

"Caroline," he says. "Please send security to my office. There are two people here who need to be escorted from the building."

"Two!?" spits Nathia.

"Miss Brockenhurst – fuck you and your disgusting dyke sluts – you're fired," says Michael, gathering up papers from his desk and putting them into a briefcase. Nathia is on her feet.

"What? On what grounds? That I'm gay? That I had a pretend boyfriend? You can't do that!"

"I'll think of something," says Michael, snapping closed his case and heading for the door. "I always do. Your personal effects will be forwarded to you. Maybe."

"Don't do this, Michael," I say, calling after him.

"You know, Edwin," says Michael returning to stand directly in front of me. "I'm not entirely sure what ridiculous fucking stunt you're trying to pull here. You can call it 'acting' if you like, most people would probably call it deception – I however, see it for what it is: business. And you're not very good at it." He prods me with a finger. "What did you think I was going to do? Listen to your ridiculous fucking story, and then graciously let you take my wife from me for the second time – whilst the two of you strike deals with the fucking Frenchie? I do what I fucking want, Edwin. No one manipulates me. You should know that by now." He takes another step towards the door.

"This is your last chance, Michael. Stay here. Now. Face the truth."

"Goodbye Edwin," says Michael. "We shan't be seeing each other again." And as Michael walks to the stairs two burly security men came into the office.

"What have you done?" hisses Nathia.

We're man-handled and prodded out of Michael's office; down the stairs, through reception, into the lift to the ground floor, and finally out onto the concourse outside the building. Just in time to see Michael being escorted to a black limousine by a fresh faced, beautiful young woman in extremely high heels. A handsome young black man in a sharp suit opens the door for the two of them, before getting into the driver's seat and pulling away.

"What the hell was all that about!" demands Nathia.

"He was expecting a meeting with Stephan," I say. "Not a car, or a representative – I had to make sure he went through with it."

"Went through with what!?" asks Nathia. "Who was that? Where the hell are they taking him?"

"*Jarad's*," I say, as I watch the car pull out of sight. "And the less you know the better."

"William! You told him everything! Everything! We are well and truly screwed!"

"Not quite everything," I say. "And anyway, he doesn't believe me. You were right, Nathia. He didn't recognise the truth even when it was right in front of him. Instead he chose a more palatable lie." At that moment a beaten up Mini Cooper screeches to a halt beside me. Zlata winds the window down.

"Hurry ups!" she says.

"Go back to your office, Nathia," I say as I walk round to the passenger side of Zlata's mini. "Do whatever you need to do, then call the Fraud Squad." I remove my Edwin jacket, and pick up the dirty beige rain coat lying on the seat. "This'll all be over in an hour or so," I say, as I put it on. I get into the car and brace myself for lift off as Zlata plays her usual tune with the gears.

"And now," says Zlata as the car lurches into motion, "the big finale!"

Scene Four

There's a thump thump thump at the back door. Jarad glances over and then after the usual nervous fumbling he opens the door, before disappearing into the main part of the restaurant.

Kate's first through the door. She says nothing, barely even makes eye contact, and instead walks past me to her spot behind the tripod, the sound of her heels clicking against the tiled floor, the slight swish as she smooths down her skirt and bends forward to switch on the camera.

DJ's next, though you'd barely recognise him in his suit. The person who had once been a gangly, occasionally awkward 'youf' in a crumpled shell suit, is suddenly a tall, lean, breathtakingly handsome black man, in a suit so sharp you could cut yourself, the expression on his face cold and impenetrable.

And finally, Ray. Always the same, and yet this time somehow different. Gone is his nervousness, replaced instead by the menacing confidence I always knew was there. He steers our 'guest' through the kitchen with the merest of prods, and roughly pushes him into the chair in front of me.

'Guest.'

The word suggests we invited this man into our lives. And though some of us may have done, in one way or another, 'guests' generally leave. Even the ones who outstay their welcome move on *eventually* – leaving you with a godawful mess to clear up. But leaving isn't something this man is accustomed to doing. This man stays, makes himself at home, and takes possession of anything he likes. Anything at all. And he doesn't leave. Not ever.

But that's about to change.

I straighten my coat – the smelly old rain coat that I stole from a charity shop in Blackheath – and I make a mental note to re-donate it when all this is over. Then I glance around the kitchen; DJ has already adopted his pose. I hand him a folded piece of paper and something that looks like it should belong on the key fob of a posh car. Then I glance at Kate, who gives me the thumbs up. I give Ray the nod, he grasps the sack hood, pulls it off roughly – and finally our eyes meet.

"Edwin!" roars Michael, as he starts to get out of his seat. "What the fuck... have you completely lost your fucking mind?" I give Ray a look, and he slaps a giant hand on Michael's shoulder so hard I swear I hear bones crack. Michael sits back in the chair and looks up at Ray, who curls a lip unpleasantly. A nice touch. We worked on that for quite a while.

"Before we go any further, Michael," I say wearily, "I would like to remind you that I gave you a choice. You could be on your way home right now – an empty home, but a home none the less. Instead, you forced my hand."

"More fucking acting, Edwin?" growls Michael, his eyes still flashing with rage. I shake my head, partly because this is the correct reaction – good acting is all about *reacting* – but also in genuine amazement that this man can continue to be so stubborn.

"Not this time, Michael," I say. "Allow me to introduce my colleagues. This is Agent Thomson." I turn and look at

DJ who continues to stare forwards. "The lady behind the video camera is Agent Richards. And the gentleman who put the bag over your head and escorted you from the car is Agent Harris." Michael's eyes narrow.

"*Tom, Dick and Harry*?" says Michael with a huff. "Seriously? Is that the best you could come up with!?"

"Those might not be their real names," I admit.

"And who are *you* supposed to be," asks Michael. "Fabian of the fucking yard!?" I reach inside my jacket and hand over an ID card. He blinks in astonishment. "Interpol?"

"Not just Interpol," I say. "The 'International Fraud Prevention & Money Laundering Intelligence Bureau'... to be precise. I keep hoping someone will come up with a catchy acronym, but most of my colleagues lack a sense of humour."

"William Lewis? The same name you gave me earlier?"

"Who I am is pretty irrelevant, Michael – in the bigger scheme of things." I take back the ID. "I'm really just a cog in a much larger machine, a machine whose remit is to keep tabs on people like you."

"Bullshit," says Michael.

"It's true," I say. "You're the biggest case of my career, Michael. Four long years of undercover investigation following your impressive lifelong career as an international con-man. Not just a con-man, either – you're *the con-man's con-man.* A magnet for every crooked entrepreneur in Europe." Michael's mouth opens and closes a couple of times.

"Bullshit," he says again, though with considerably less conviction.

"You want proof? I have a list somewhere," I say, and root around my coat pockets. After a moment DJ reaches inside his suit and produces a folded piece of paper. He holds it out for me to take. "Thank you, Agent

Thompson," I say, and unfold the list. The same list that I took from Nathia's dining room table just ten days ago. "*Kipps Olivier Limited*; *Carole, Knight & Carpenter*; *Grimmer & Grimmer*," I say, picking out names at random. "*J Guthrie & Co.*; *Harris, Harris and Harris*; *Tindall and Partners*; our old friends *The Tahan Brothers*; *Sebastian Enterprises*... it just goes on and on. Even *Mr Archibald Boot* is getting in on the action. It's like a who's who of London's greediest people. And where there's greed, there's inevitably corruption. You wouldn't believe how many man hours – literally thousands – has gone into following the stench of impropriety through the hundreds of companies and people you've had dealings with." I put the list back in my pocket. "Mind you," I say, "none of them can hold a candle to you, Michael. The number of times I went to my superiors and told them we should involve The Met, let them stop you in your tracks – tear your little empire to the ground, and lock you away – but then you'd strike *another* deal, with *another* shady company or individual, and suddenly my superiors' eyes would light up, and we'd have more work to do, more paperwork to follow. Isn't that right, Agent Thompson?"

"It's all about statistics to them, Sir," says DJ, his voice clear and crisp. I sniff, and nod to myself.

"Yes," I muse. "I suppose it is. You see, you're the golden goose that lays one rotten egg after another, Michael. I honestly believe I could spend the rest of my career just investigating the shit you dredge up."

Michael says nothing.

"I'll give you a moment," I say. "Just to take it all in." Slowly Michael's race reddens.

"*You're fucking my wife*!" he rages, spraying me with spittle. I glance at Ray, who pushes Michael back into his seat.

"Really?" I say, wiping my face with a handkerchief. "That's what you want to focus on? After everything I've just said?"

"Well, aren't you?"

"Yes. I am in a relationship with your wife. It was, however, an accident. An unexpected consequence of discovering her secret dealings with Monsieur LeBlanc, and seeing just how involved they are with your illegal financial activities."

"So the Frenchie is fucking real again, is he!?"

"Of course," I say. "And you can't imagine how delighted I was to discover that neither he, nor your wife, were aware of what a crook you are. Though your wife didn't take the news too well. After all nobody likes to discover they've been married to a thief and a liar, even if on some level they always knew it to be true. Inevitably, I guess, she needed someone to ... well ... to comfort her."

"You fucking bastard!"

"Name calling? That's all you have?"

"This is fucking bullshit!"

"Yes, I can see why you'd say that. You've had quite an afternoon. It must be difficult to know what to believe."

"And where does Nathia fit into all of this?"

"Miss Brockenhurst? She's been working with us this whole time. Edwin Clarkson and our 'relationship' was my primary cover. Though she only signed up for six months. After four years we really felt we'd asked enough of her."

"So she's not a fucking..." He can barely bring himself to say the word.

"Lesbian?" I ask. "I have no idea." Michael's mouth opens again, but this time there's a pause, and I can see he's finally buying it. Of all the 'truths' on offer him today – this one is beginning to seem the most plausible,

"So what was all that fucking... *nonsense*... earlier?" he asks, with as much venom as he can, but genuine curiosity is getting in the way.

"Our last ditch attempt to get you back on track, Michael, doing what you do best; finding the scum of the universe for me and my colleagues to follow – *whilst at the same time* giving you a legitimate reason to drop this frankly annoying fixation you have with me, Monsieur LeBlanc, and your estranged wife. It was a long shot, but my superiors consider you something of an asset."

"He was never going to go for it, Sir," says Kate from behind her camera. "With respect." I look in her direction, and then nod sagely.

"Yes," I say. "You're right Agent Richards. *You're too bloody greedy, Michael*! You can't bear to let anything go – even when it shouldn't have any real value to you!" Michael's eyes are like saucers. "But you know what the irony of it is? You're instincts were right on the money. Your wife actually *is* the most valuable of all your assets. She's the only reason you're not going to prison."

"Prison?" he asks.

"I want to throw you to the wolves, Michael. Have you pay for all the lives that you've ruined over the years – directly and indirectly – but if I do that there will be a long, messy and expensive court case, one which your wife will inevitably be caught up in – and I don't want to see that. She doesn't deserve it. It would be far better for her if you simply *disappeared*." I get out of my seat, walk past Kate, and grab the case that Rachel left in the doorway earlier this afternoon. I can see from Michael's face that he recognises it. Then I root around in my pockets and this time produce a passport.

"So, here's what's going to happen," I say. "I'm going to give you a few minutes to, in your own words, give Agent

Richards and her camera a short confession of your activities over the past few weeks. Then, when that's all done and dusted, you're going to leave the country. This evening. I have here your passport, and a suitcase of your clothes. And right now, waiting for you in the restaurant," I nod in the general direction, "there's a gentleman who I suspect will be very willing to drive you to the airport. Especially when Mr Boot realises that he too might have to skip the country." I place Michael's passport back in my coat pocket; I can't risk handing it to him just yet.

"And why the fuck would I do any of that?" asks Michael.

"Because Michael, even as we speak Ms Brockenhurst is on the phone to the fraud squad, and by tomorrow morning your home, your offices, they'll be heaving with the boys in blue. And there'll be nothing left for you here in England other than a long, nasty investigation, followed by an even longer prison stretch at the end of it. And believe me, Michael – we have a lot of resources at our disposal. We can give the authorities *plenty* of muck to throw at you. You will never see the light of day again."

"So let me see if I've understood this correctly," says Michael, a look of disgust creeping across his face so intense I wonder if he's about to vomit on my shoes. "You're offering me a chance to flee the authorities, in order to spare my fucking cheating wife the *inconvenience*, and *embarrassment*, of a court case?"

"Yes. Aside from the derogatory remarks, that's it in a nutshell."

"You know Edwin – you're still playing at business. And you're still not very good at it!" Michael leans forward as far as Ray will let him. "Business isn't about accumulating possessions, or assets, or trophies – it's about *depriving* the other man of what they have. That's how the game is played. *That's how you win.* And I will *never* let you keep Rachel, even if I have to destroy the fucking bitch in the process." And for perhaps the first time, I finally see Michael for what he really is, and realise that, in a sense, Zlata was right all along. He really is the devil. Or at the very least a monstrous demon feeding on the faults and fears and insecurities of everyone around him, until there's nothing left but pain, and misery, and loss.

"So, that's what I am to you, is it?" says Rachel, stepping into the kitchen from the corridor that leads back to the main part of the restaurant. "A 'bitch'."

"Precious," says Michael, a nasty, humourless grin flickering across his face. "There you are. I was wondering when you were going to make an appearance. Well, isn't this fucking cosy. Your boyfriend here was telling me how he expects me to leave the fucking country. If I don't, apparently there might be a 'court case'." He indicates the quotation marks with his fingers. Then throws me a sneer.

"I know," said Rachel. "I was listening."

"But of course you were, my love. And you can imagine, I'm sure, how fucking terrified I am at the prospect."

"Enough to consider destroying me apparently," says Rachel. Michael gives her a long cold stare.

"That's up to you, precious," he says. "You of all people know what I'm capable of. Whereas your boyfriend here – for all his probing and duplicity and big words – *hasn't a fucking clue.* Four years of following me around, Edwin, and you still don't know who you're fucking dealing with. So bring on your fucking court case, and let me show you how much I enjoy a good scrap."

"If that's what you want," I say.

"Do you even have the fucking authority to arrest me?"

"No," I say with a shake of my head. "We're just an intelligence agency. Law enforcement is someone else's remit."

"That's what I thought," says Michael, getting out of his chair. Ray glances at me and I shake my head. "Well then," continues Michael, "I'll see you in court." He walks over to Rachel, traces of a swagger in his stride, and with one hand takes hold of Rachel's face. I go to intervene but she's fought free before I've even taken a third step, and a second later there's a sharp smack as the flat of her hand connects with Michael's cheek. But he barely moves. Just laughs. The deep, joyless hollow laugh of a man so corrupt, so twisted, so broken, that were you to open him up I truly believe you'd find a gaping chasm that leads to hell itself. He takes one last look at the people in the room, and then walks through to the restaurant leaving everyone in the kitchen holding their breath. And it feels like an age before we hear the sound we've all been expecting.

There's a very masculine yelp of pain, the crash of furniture being turned over, followed by the smash of plates, glassware and cutlery hitting the floor. Our cue that tonight's performance has moved into the other room.

I move quickly through to the restaurant, followed by everyone else, and when I enter Michael is lying on his back, next to a broken table and chair, surrounded by shards of glass and crockery – and standing over him, with one foot on his chest and brandishing a broom like a weapon, is Zlata.

She's dressed predominantly in black. Black coat. Black dress. Black leggings. Enormous Doc Martens boots – black. Even her makeup is dark and gothic. The fingerless gloves are a particularly nice touch.

"Before you go, Michael," I say, taking my place next to her, "there is 'just one more thing'." Zlata and I exchange looks.

"Get this fucking bitch away from me!" shouts Michael, but as he tries to get up Zlata jabs him in the shoulder with her broom and he squeals in pain.

"In a minute, Michael," I say. "First... I believe you're acquainted with Ms Ivanović?"

"Hello Michael," says Zlata. "You remember me?" Michael stops struggling. He looks up into Zlata's face I see his eye twitch slightly. Now we really have his attention.

"I believe the last time you met," I continue, "other than your unfortunate run in with a cleaning lady a month ago, you were enquiring as to whether Miss Ivanović could lend you a bar of soap?" Michael's eye twitches again. "That's when you weren't making deals with her father of course; Dragan Ivanović."

"How did you ..." starts Michael. I crouch down to answer him.

"We're Interpol, Michael; *international* is part of the job. The clue's in the name, if you think about it. But even I have to admit that we got really lucky when we found Zlata." I glance up at Zlata, and then back at Michael. "I realise it was a while ago, Michael, but what you probably didn't realise at the time was that her father, Dragan, had some fairly nasty business associates. Men to whom he eventually owed a substantial amount of money. Money that evidently, *he gave to you.*"

"Those men have the good memories," says Zlata. "They would like very much to meet you, Michael. And I would like to make for them, the introduction."

"So let's go over this one more time." I say, producing Michael's passport. "You're going to leave the county. Where you go and what you do when you get there is entirely up to you but, fail to make a flight this evening and *I promise* you'll be behind bars by the weekend, and on Monday I *will* start the necessary paperwork to deport you and hand you over to my Croatian colleagues. What they'll discover is that you were *far more* involved with Dragan's illegal business practices than perhaps even you remember.

"On the other hand, leave the country tonight and none of that needs to happen. Though should you continue to involve yourself in Rachel's life in any way whatsoever and Zlata here will give her 'Uncles' a call, just to let them know where you are."

"You are between the rock, and the very hard place," says Zlata.

I hold out the passport for Michael to take, but he doesn't move, just looks at it, then at me, then at Zlata, and then back to me.

"Fucking blackmail?" says Michael. "That's the best you've got?"

"You can call it blackmail, Michael, I prefer to think of it... as business."

Michael snatches the passport out of my hand, shoves it inside his jacket pocket and then slowly we both get to our feet, Michael brushing dust and bits of broken glass from his expensive suit as he does so. He straightens his tie and takes his time to look at everyone in the room. When he gets to Archie – who's been sitting in the corner by the fish tank the whole time – I try not to smile as Archie raises a hand and gives Michael a half-hearted wave.

"You know, Edwin," says Michael, turning back to me. "If you're the best Interpol's got to offer then I've been far too fucking cautious for far too long! Nobody is going to believe your fucking cock and bull stories Edwin, *nobody*!" Instinctively I take a step backwards. "This woman's father was a *weak, pathetic imbecile*!"

"He was smart businessman!" returns Zlata with a stamp of her foot, but Michael doesn't take his eyes off me.

"He wasn't part of the Croatian Mafia! He simply made a modest income ripping off tourists who were even more fucking stupid and gullible than himself!"

"He worked hard!" says Zlata, her voice cracking, the pitch rising. "And you took it all!"

"I didn't *take* fucking anything!" says Michael moving towards Zlata and grabbing the broom before she has a chance to use it again. "I strung him along with some bullshit tale about working in tourism and watched in utter astonishment as your dear old Pops handed over his life savings to a complete and utter stranger. *He was a fucking idiot*!" hisses Michael, his face barely inches from Zlata's. "Is it any wonder that his teenage daughter opened her legs like a *cheap fucking whore*!"

This has gone far enough. I open my mouth to speak but before I can think of something – anything – to say to bring the situation back under our control, Zlata steps back, reaches inside her coat, and pulls out her gun.

"Zlata!" I say. "No! What are you doing?"

"It's no good, William," she says, her voice shrill and shaky, the gun trembling in both hands. "I told you – he is devil! He is monster! He does not deserve life!"

"But this isn't the way, Zlata!" I say edging towards her, as Michael backs away.

"But you hear him!" she screams, through a series of sobs. "We will never be safe from this devil – not now, not never! He must die!" I shoot a glance at Michael and for the first time *ever* I see genuine fear in his face.

"You don't mean that," I say, reaching out to touch her shoulder.

"I know what I mean!" she replies, shrugging me off. "Move out of way!"

"Ray – a little help here!" I say, and then I lunge for the gun.

Zlata's kicking and flailing and hitting me with her free arm as we struggle, piling into more furniture and narrowly missing the fish tank, but eventually I get hold of her hand, and bend back her thumb until she releases her grasp on the pistol and it clatters to the floor. At more or less the same time, Ray finally manages to get Zlata's arms behind her and pull her off me.

For a moment time really does seem to slow to a halt. Just long enough for me to notice that the three of us – Michael, myself, and Zlata – are now points of a triangle, at the centre of which is the gun. And it's this frozen moment that sticks in my head when I think back to that night, because everything that happened afterwards was really just a blur.

One second Ray has hold of Zlata, the next she is free.

One second Zlata and Michael are exchanging looks, the next the three of us are going for the gun, but it's Michael who gets there first.

I barrel into him, the two of us moving across the restaurant like clumsy ballroom dancers, my hands trying to prise his fingers from the pistol.

There's an ear splitting crack.

My chest is on fire.

And as I stagger back from Michael I noticed a spray of red against his shirt, and large red dollops on his hand. The hand that still has hold of the gun.

I look down at my own hands. The palms are dripping in blood. My chest is a pool of deep red syrupy liquid. I can feel it oozing out of my mouth.

"Rachel," I manage to splutter.

But the room is beginning to swim.

I see faces, hear the muffled sounds of people calling my name...

"*Will*..." they say.

Because that's what my friends call me...

But then...

Nothing.

Scene Five

"Wakey wakey, Mr Actor." I tentatively open one eye, then both, and look around at the faces surrounding me – all of them a varying mixture of concern, happiness, relief, and confusion.

"Has he gone?" I ask, propping myself up onto my elbows. "Did it work?" Rachel smiles.

"He grabbed his case and was out of the door before anybody had a chance to say or do anything," she says.

"And the weasel man," says Zlata, "was in the hot pursuit! We have done it! Woo hoo!"

A frown forms on Rachel's face. "Were you ... asleep?"

"No!" I reply. "Well ... maybe. Just for a bit." I start to get up, but my chest is really painful.

"Unbelievable!" says Rachel.

"Cut me some slack," I say, struggling to my feet, "it's been one hell of a week!"

"Why are you pulling that face?" she asks.

"That damn squib!" I say. "Jim was right. Stings like a son of a bitch." Without asking, Rachel starts to unbutton my sticky red shirt, and I notice Zlata raise an eyebrow and attempt, unsuccessfully, to hide a smirk. But the expression on her face soon changes when Rachel starts to remove the remains of the exploded packet still taped between my ribs.

"Ouch!" I say. Rachel sucks in air through her teeth then bites her lip.

"That," she says, "looks really painful!" She grabs a chair. "Sit back down again," she commands. "Jarad, do we have anything for burns?"

"I'll go and see," says Kate.

"It looked convincing though, didn't it?" I ask. "I mean, from where Michael was standing?"

"Bro, it was like, amazing!" says DJ.

"Thank god," I reply. "Excellent timing with the squib control, DJ."

"Thanks bruv," says DJ, beaming from ear to ear. "How did you get the blood to come out of your mouth though?" I dig my hands in my pockets.

"Blood capsules," I say, handing them to DJ, "They taste foul!"

"Here you are," says Kate, returning from the kitchen with a bag of frozen peas, a tea towel and an antiseptic spray.

"Thank you," says Rachel.

"Thing is bro, I'm still like, getting my head around everything. I mean – who was that weasel looking guy? And why was he in the restaurant? And all those things the Richmond guy said? Did he like actually know Zlata from before? How much of what went down was actually made up? I'm confused, you know?"

"He was quite the actor," I say, and then wince as Rachel presses the freezing cold bag of peas, wrapped in the tea towel, against my bare skin.

"Oh shush," she says. "Hold this here a moment. I'm going to get a bowl of water to clean you up."

"Yeah but," continues DJ, "everything... it seemed so ... *real*, you know?" DJ's eyes are pleading with me.

"That's what acting is all about, DJ," I say.

"Yeah, yeah – I suppose."

"Come on Derek," says Kate. "You, me and Ray should go to the pub."

"Oh, okay," says DJ. "But what about Will? And Zlata? And Rachel?" Zlata, who had stopped paying me any attention a while back to flirt with Ray, turns round at the sound of her name.

"I will come to the pub in ten minutes," she says. "Maybe the half hours. And I will buy my three favourite actors a bottle of the finest wine – one with the sparkles! And then we will discuss business. And I hopes you will all come and work for Zlata!" I blink and look up at her in utter disbelief.

"You're signing them?" I ask. "Putting them on your books?"

"Of course! They are all very fine actors. Because they have very fine teacher. Now go," she says to my students. "And I will join you soon as." Then she sits down next to me and we watch as they leave the restaurant: DJ still looks confused, though there's a confidence in his stride that wasn't there a day or two ago. Ray gives me a knowing look, and a nod to go with it. I'm not entirely sure what he means by that. Maybe he's telling me that he'll fill in the blanks for DJ. Or maybe he's telling me he won't. Or maybe he's just saying *see you on Thursday*, or *thank you*, or something else. It doesn't matter really.

And Kate? Well, Kate just smiles.

"See you later," she says. Though more to Zlata than me, and once the bell over the door has tinkled their departure I turn to my friend.

"Thank you," I say.

"What fors?"

"Taking Kate under your wing."

Zlata shrugs.

"She is nice girl. We will have the good times together."

I nod, and then look down at my blood-stained hands.

"Zlata," I say. "Where's my watch?" She smiles.

"I have for you new watch," she says, and hands me Michael's Rolex.

"Zlata," I say, "I wouldn't be seen dead wearing this watch!"

"You mean *pretend* dead!" says Zlata. I look at her for a moment, then reach behind me and drop the Rolex in the fish tank.

"I know what I mean," I say.

For a Monday evening the South Bank is positively heaving with people. But we don't care. We stroll, arm in arm, through the crowds, past the food stands, past the cafés, past the living sculptures and street entertainers. And we hardly say a word. We're revelling in the hubbub. Allowing the noise and the nonsense to fill our minds with something other than the worry and stress of the past few days and weeks.

Eventually we see an empty bench, one facing the river, and without even conferring we sit, and cuddle into each other. We look across the river at 'the City', home to countless financial institutions. Boy, have they got a shock waiting for them in the morning.

"Do you think he did it?" asks Rachel after a while. It takes me a moment to figure out what she's referring to.

"Michael? Get on a plane?" I ask. She nods. "He's probably somewhere over France by now," I say.

"But do you think he is? Maybe he never went to the airport!"

"He'd have been an idiot not to."

"But how can you be so sure?"

"It's what I would have done," I say, "– if I were Michael."

Rachel shudders. "You're nothing like him!" she says. "You couldn't be like Michael if you tried!"

"I'm an actor," I say. "Being *like* people is what I do. And *if* I were ever to play the part of a middle-aged, arrogant –"

"Evil!"

"– investment tycoon –"

"Con-man!"

"– one who was wanted by the police for fraud –"

"Twenty years of fraud!"

"– having accidentally shot my wife's lover in the chest –"

"Ex-wife!"

"– I'd definitely be making use of my passport and the conveniently packed suitcase of clothes. Trust me. He's on a plane. But either way, he's gone for good."

"But what if he's not," says Rachel. "What if he finds out you're *not* actually dead? This is Michael we're talking about! He's incredibly resourceful. It's just a matter of time! What do we do when he returns?"

"Listen," I say, taking her by the arms, "he's *just a man.* Except now he's a man on the run – wanted for fraud, and – so far as he knows – murder! He has no home, no office, no staff, no assistant, and from what you've always told me, no friends! I doubt even Archie will want to help him now! He can't use his bank accounts or credit cards because they're probably being scrutinized by the Old Bill, so basically, he has *nothing* but the clothes on his back, the cash in his wallet, a suitcase, a passport, his cunning, and a price on his head! Just surviving should keep him occupied for a long, long time. If he wasn't Michael I could almost feel sorry for him!"

"Don't you dare!"

"I said *almost.* Look I can't promise we're rid of him forever Rachel, but for now, and possibly a while – I believe we're beyond his reach."

"Okay," says Rachel as I let go of her. "Thank you," she adds. Then she grabs hold of my arm and leans her head against my shoulder.

"Everything can go back to normal now," I say.

"I'm not sure I even know what normal is any more," she replies.

"Well, you and Jarad can reopen the restaurant," I say.

"We can."

"And I'll go back to running flirting courses and teaching drama."

Rachel smiles. "Maybe Zlata will find you some work. Proper work."

"Maybe," I say with a sigh. It seems unlikely. "Did you know Kate has moved in with Zlata?"

"She has?" asks Rachel.

"This morning," I say.

"That's excellent news."

"Yes. It is. So I suppose things aren't getting back to normal, are they? They're better than normal." There's a pause. Like amongst all the people and the hubbub, there's a giant question mark floating in front of us, waiting for us to address it.

"And what about us, Will?" asks Rachel.

"What about us?" I counter.

"What happens now?" And I realise in that moment that I've made some huge assumptions about what I thought would happen next, whereas Rachel has assumed nothing at all.

"Well," I say, "how about this." I take her face in my hands, and then I kiss her. A long lingering kiss that feels like it's been waiting in the wings since the end of Act II – and even before I let go of her, from the way she's kissing me back I already know what she's going to say next. I stop kissing and look at her, and she smiles back without opening her eyes. That shy smile I've come to love so much.

"Can we go home now?" she asks.

Act IV

Scene One

I wait a day or two before I contact Nathia and invite myself over. She isn't smiling when she opens the door.

"William," she says. "I thought we'd agreed that I was never going to see you again?"

"This will be the last time," I say. "Promise."

"Hmmm. You've made that promise before." She stands there for a moment like she's considering what to do next. "Would you like to come in?" she asks eventually.

"Thank you," I say, and follow her through to the kitchen.

"I'm assuming you've seen the news?" she asks.

"Hard not to," I reply. "It seems to be everywhere."

"Yes, it does," she says, and I can hear the melancholy tone in her voice. And it may just be my imagination but the kitchen seems utterly spotless, as if she's just moved in. Or is preparing to move out.

"I'm sorry, Nathia," I say. "For everything." But it isn't enough. It probably never will be.

"Have the police been in contact with Rachel?" asks Nathia as she leans against a worktop.

"Of course, but it seems they're satisfied that she had nothing to do with Michael's illegal dealings. Her solicitor reckons that she might lose the house though. And potentially her flats. Those apparently fall under the umbrella of Michael's assets."

"Yes. They would," says Nathia.

"What about you?" I ask.

"Me?" asks Nathia. "I've spent the last week 'assisting the police with their enquiries'."

"They don't think you're anything to do with *Vanadium Global*, do they?"

"No," she says with a shake of her head. "Other than not knowing the whereabouts, contact information, or indeed anything, about the elusive Stephan LeBlanc, I am free of suspicion."

"That's good."

"I'm also out of work."

"I know," I say, and let another wave of guilt wash over me. "Can't you go into business for yourself?" I ask.

"Doing what, William?" she retorts, that Nathia iciness more prominent than ever.

"What you do!" I say, frustration getting the better of me. "Striking business deals! Finding businesses that need investors, and then finding investors..."

"It's not quite as simple as that, William," says Nathia with a world weary sigh. "This is an industry that works largely on reputation. And what reputation I had is now forever linked with the City's most recent, and possibly most notorious, fraudster. Finding clients might be a challenge!"

"Would it?" I ask. "Rachel and Jarad still want to expand. There's your first client right there." She rolls her eyes and shakes her head.

"William, finding clients in need of money is easy. Finding clients with money to invest is another thing entirely. And *nobody* is going to let me invest their money for them unless I can point to another client who I've already brokered a deal for. Preferably, one who *isn't* behind bars, or being investigated by the law!"

"Right," I say when the dust has settled. "That's annoying."

"Isn't it!"

And then an idea occurs to me.

"So let me see if I've understood this correctly," I say, a smile creeping across my face. "In the absence of an actual client, what you *really* need is someone to play the part of a satisfied client..."

"William!" says Nathia, her voice raising an octave. "You'd better not be suggesting what I think you're suggesting!"

"It sounds to me Nathia, *darling*, like you might be in need of my services after all..."

THE END
(for now)

Acknowledgements

Good heavens. Here I am again. Writing an acknowledgements section. If there were any justice in the world this would be a much longer section of many many pages – ones that, at the *very least*, describe how so many people in my life came along and helped me get from a fleeting idea I had for a bonkers story, to the book you now hold in your hands. Maybe one day I'll get the chance to tell you more, but for now, trust me when I say that this should be *far more* than a simple list of people 'I ought to thank' – without these people, you wouldn't be reading these words at all.

In no particular order, heartfelt appreciation goes out to:

Peta Nightingale, from LAW, for your continued patience, support & belief.

The folks at Amazon UK for choosing to back this book.

My long suffering assistant Jules, for making sure all the crucial stuff in my life happens and for being generally spectacular.

Wendy Steele for reminding me – when I needed it most – to trust my instincts.

Della Galton for her insightful wisdom and being my very own literary paramedic.

My first readers: Valerie Mugridge, Muge Dixon, Janet Guthrie, Gerald Hornsby, and Angela Johnson for their extremely valuable feedback.

Me ol' pals Patrick Rutland & Robert Grant for their support and 'interesting' plot suggestions (in the end the alien thing just didn't seem right, and *nobody* else wanted me to kill off Zlata).

Lenka Gordonova of WITBI Accountancy for her innate Czech-ness, and invaluable corporate finance knowledge.

Slaven Krznaric for his translation skills and all things Croatian.

Sally Lawrence of Outloud Productions for her theatrical insights.

Katherine Stephen for her much needed grammatical advice & proof reading

All my Facebook pals for their continuing support and for letting me fill up their newsfeed.

And to *you*, whoever *you* are, for taking a chance on this book and for reading past 'the end'. Drop me a line if you get a chance. I'd like that.

Thank you all.

You Might Also Enjoy ...

The debut novel from Peter Jones

The Good Guy's Guide To Getting The Girl

"Apparently Cinderella needs her Prince Charming, so I spent the evening dressed in bright yellow three-quarter-length trousers, and a coat with far too many buttons.

I'd finally had it with Ball Gown women."

Jason Smith, 29, self-confessed 'good guy', is single. Finally.

But now that he is, all the girls he'd happily give up one side of his bed for – like, for instance, his old school crush Melanie Jackson – are long gone. Or married. Or crazy. Or inexplicably obsessed with the office heart-throb, Gary.

Or are they? Has Jason stumbled on a fool-proof way to meet the kind of exciting, fun woman he's always dreamed about – or is he about to gamble his career, his friendships, and any hope of future romance, on a schoolboy fantasy?

From best-selling author Peter Jones comes this quirky comedy romance, about guys, girls, and finding love at the turn of the millennium.

Visit amazon to buy the book
and find out more Peter Jones at
PeterJonesAuthor.com